THE BONE SHROUD

THE BONE SHROUD

JEAN RABE

BOONE STREET PRESS
ILLINOIS

© 2018 by Jean Rabe
Cover design by Juan Villa Padron
Interior design by Susan H. Roddey
Editing by Linda Allen

Boone Street Press

First Edition: March 2018

Name: Rabe, Jean, author
Title: The Bone Shroud / Jean Rabe
Description: First Edition. Boone Street Press
Identifiers: ISBN 13: 978-1-7320036-0-6 / 10: 1-7320036-0-2
Library of Congress Control Number: 2018933868
Printed in the United States of America

For Steven Paul Leiva
and his twelve dogs
who search for Ray Bradbury
by the sea

ONE
OCTOBER 4

IREM MADIGAN'S MISTAKE was stopping in front of a window display.

The little gift shop not far from the Termini Station flaunted bars of starfish-shaped soap and arrangements of tiny silk roses. She peered through a beveled glass pane. The labels were in Italian and English. Inviting.

A trace of vanilla slipped out the open door, adding to the allure, and she swore she could taste cinnamon. Perhaps she'd browse the aisles and find a trinket for her mother. But this was her first day in Rome, and she would have plenty of opportunities for shopping.

Irem's fingers danced across the smooth window grilles, indecisive a moment too long. Someone yanked her clutch away, and she whirled to see him racing down the brick sidewalk.

"*Ladro!*" Irem took off after him. "*Ladro!*" Irem was not well-versed in Italian, but she'd studied a guidebook, and "thief" was one of the words that had stuck. "*Ladro! Ladro!*"

The sidewalk was choked with people in the early afternoon, chattering in Italian, French, English; many of them with maps and cell phones in hand. It was typically warm for October, in the mid-seventies, and after the morning's downpour the sun had come out, and with it a gaggle of tourists.

"*Ladro!*" she shouted.

"Get him!" A man encouraged, raising his fist.

"*Cours vite!*" That sounded French. "*Attrape le!*"

"Cosa succede?"

"Shit and back again," Irem cursed.

There was money in that clutch, a new iPhone, her Field Museum ID, credit cards, and the wedding invitation that had tugged her here. She was angry at the thief, and at herself. She'd read up on Italy. It wasn't supposed to be dangerous to walk alone around Termini Station and south by the Piazza Vittorio Emanuele. Rome was safe in general. Tourists rarely reported problems… other than pickpockets. A big city girl, she should have been more alert.

It was difficult to see through the press of bodies, but the thief was tall and gangly, with a short black ponytail that bobbed above the heads of the passersby. Four blocks, five blocks. She focused on the ponytail and ran, gaining despite weaving among people so oblivious they didn't bother to get out of her way.

A shrill whistle speared through the clamor of conversations and the scattered blats of car horns. Another whistle, then a siren. Maybe someone had called the police.

Irem's shoes had low pompadour heels, uncomfortable to run in, but she managed. Thank God she hadn't packed stilettos for the museum soiree. She felt the right leg of her nylons run with an annoying tickle.

"Shit," she grumbled again, somehow sprinting even faster, slipping between two middle-aged ladies with enormous shopping bags and barely dodging a stand of party dresses being wheeled onto the sidewalk.

Six blocks, seven blocks.

Everything was a blur of color—the clothes of the pedestrians, the vibrant awnings on the old buildings, the painted brick fronts of businesses. Irem felt buffeted by scents, too: warring perfumes and car exhaust. Her senses were overloaded, but she stayed focused on the ponytail.

The tall thief darted between two buildings, and—more furious than worried—she didn't hesitate to follow. The alley was filled with trash bins and crates piled high, the clutter making it too narrow for a car to pass through.

"Stop!" she screamed. "You son of a bitch!"

He glanced over his shoulder, and in that instant he tripped. He managed to keep himself upright, but he lost seconds. Irem closed.

"I said stop, asshole!"

Irem leaped, raising her leg, twisting, and kicking him. He staggered and she followed with a second kick that dropped him to his knees. Her clutch and a man's thick wallet fell out of his hands, and she slipped around to stand in front of him.

"Don't move."

He snarled and reached to his waist, and the thought flickered that he might have a weapon. She delivered an elbow strike to the side of his head, and a palm heel blow to his sternum that put him on his back and had him gasping.

"I... said... don't... move, you son of a bitch," she growled.

There was no risk of that any longer: she'd knocked him to the edge of consciousness, and his head lolled to the side. It looked like she might have broken his jaw.

The sirens grew louder, then quit. She heard the slap-slap-slap of shoes against the brickwork. Irem did not look up.

"You son of a bitch," she repeated to the thief, then attempted an Italian translation: "*Tu bastardo.*" She'd learned those words, too. Profanity came easy to Irem. She stopped herself from kicking him again — although she really wanted to for that satisfying sense of "good measure." She bent and picked up her clutch.

The slap-slap-slapping stopped with the arrival of a police officer.

"*Ladro,*" she said, pointing at the downed man, who moaned softly. "And looks like he *ladroed* from someone else, too." She gestured at the thick billfold. *And made me ruin my hair and nylons and probably my night at the Conservatori.*

"English?" The officer had a rich-sounding voice. "Are you—"

"Yeah, and I'm hoping you speak enough—"

"Certainly. Are you British or—"

"American. Chicago."

9

"Ah! Toddling town. I have been to Chicago. I should have recognized the accent. The Cubs, White Sox, and the Sears Tower." He raised a hand and waved to someone behind him.

"It's called the Willis Tower now." Irem looked back the way she'd come. A police car had pulled up on the sidewalk, blocking the end of the alley, a blue and white Fiat Stilo with POLIZIA on the side, bubble lights on top flashing. Another police officer jogged toward them. They dressed similarly to the cops in Chicago. The second had a quick, staccato voice, too fast for her to pick out anything other than "*ladro*."

"*Ladro*," she repeated, knowing that word would be forever engraved into her brain. Speaking to the first policeman: "This is my purse. I didn't do anything—"

"*Giorno di Natale!* You knocked him into Christmas," the English-speaking officer said. "Are you a police officer there? In Chicago?"

"No. I work in a museum."

"You can take care of yourself."

"Yeah, well, I used to study hapkido."

"You were a hard-working student."

"Listen, I didn't hurt him all that bad. I can't be in trouble for this. He's the one who—"

"You are fine," the officer returned. "*Ambulanza*," he said to his partner, pointing to the thief on the ground.

Fine? Irem didn't feel fine. She felt four dozen shades of angry, her blood pressure soaring. Her feet ached from running in the heels.

"I was window shopping. He swiped my purse and took off and—"

"I see that," he said. "That he swiped your purse."

"—and I chased him."

"I see that also."

"He shouldn't have done that, swiped my purse."

"He knows that, I think." He grinned at her. The officer was striking, had a strong face and a long nose, dark eyes that flashed and held hers for a moment.

"So... do I gotta go down to your station? Do I need—"

"If you want to —" She noted that he looked at her hands, and no doubt saw that she wasn't wearing a wedding ring. "We can go to the station if you want Miss —"

"Irem Madigan."

"Miss Irem Madigan of Chicago who works in a museum."

"I'm an archivist at the Field."

"I have been to the Field Museum, the Shedd Aquarium, and the Museum of Science and Industry."

"That's nice."

"I can take the information here, Miss Madigan, at the car, a simple pickpocket report. *Borseggiatore.* Or we can go to the station if you would prefer and —"

"*Borseggiatore.* What's that?"

"Pickpocket."

A special kind of *ladro*. Irem inhaled deeply, and the fusty scents of the alley made her cough. She opened her clutch and pawed through it to make sure nothing was missing — although she didn't see how it could have been; the thief had had no time to rifle through her things during the mad dash.

"Here would be great. I'm supposed to go to this reception and —"

"I understand, Miss Madigan. This will not take long."

"*Ho chiamato un ambulanza,*" the other officer said to his partner. Irem had heard him place a call on his radio. "*Guarda lui.*"

"*Buono, Valentino.*" To Irem: "The ambulance is coming for this miscreant, Miss Madigan. Our city, it is safe for tourists like you ... mostly. But there are —"

"Pickpockets. *Borseggiatore.* Yeah, I discovered that."

He reached into his pocket, took out a business card, and passed it to her. Printed in Italian, it read: *Polizia di Stato*, Gregario Ricci, *Agente Sceito*, and an address and phone number she assumed referenced the police department.

"Thanks, *Agente Sceito* Ricci."

"It means senior officer. Seven years on the force."

Senior officer? He didn't look all that old to her, maybe thirty. And handsome. His eyes held hers again. She broke the gaze and slipped the card into her clutch.

"Thanks. That form?"

"This way. And you call me if you have any more troubles here, yes? Or if you need someone to show you our beautiful city or share an evening meal at one of our many fine restaurants. I would be happy to do that. I would most enjoy hearing stories of Chicago."

"That might be nice." *Did he just halfway ask me out on a date? And did I just halfway accept?*

"*Buona giornata!* I hope the rest of your stay in Rome will be less stressful."

"I'm sure it will be," she said. "I can't imagine it getting any worse."

The thief groaned and rose up on his elbows.

"*Tu bastardo, Borseggiatore,*" Irem said to him. Then she followed Gregario to the car.

TWO

SOMETIME DURING THE CHASE, Irem had ripped the side seam in her ochre gabardine dress, one the fanciest garments she'd packed. She remembered passing a boutique that had a rack of dresses on the sidewalk. She stopped there, replaced her shredded nylons, and found an A-line princess dress that hit her at mid-calf and worked with her shoes and clutch. Fog gray, made of pique and shantung with a beaded top and spaghetti straps, she had to admit it was lovely and better than what she'd been wearing — which she dropped at a dry cleaners that advertised mending.

Last stop before the museum: a salon where one of the beauticians spoke a smattering of English and quickly swept her mussed hair to the side for a look so unique and attractive she couldn't help but take a selfie. She'd run by this place, too.

She walked toward the Palazzo dei Conservatori, holding her clutch tighter than before. Because of the pickpocket, she was fashionably late. Irem's first impression of the museum: *I could spend my entire two weeks of vacation right here.*

The Palazzo dei Conservatori was an impressive collection of buildings with roots stretching back nearly six hundred years to when Pope Sixtus IV gifted bronze statues to the people of Rome. She glanced at the various pieces of statuary and framed art along her route, holding deep inside the dueling scents of floor polish and history.

Irem's brother had supplied the invitation here, to a reception honoring his fiancé's archaeological discoveries.

Without his repeated prodding, coupled with a request that she serve as his "best man," Irem wouldn't have considered stepping out of Illinois. With all her being, she feared flying. The final nudge came when Irem's significant other broke things off a handful of weeks ago. She plunged into an abyssal depression, got an expedited passport, and bought a plane ticket and a box of Dramamine.

She'd read up on the Conservatori, learned that paintings in the Capitoline Picture Gallery were touted to be the oldest public collection of its kind, featuring masterpieces by Rubens, Titian, and Caravaggio. Irem intended to come back and leisurely appreciate them.

"Where have you been?" A young man rushed at her, wrapped his arms tightly around her, and spun her like a child. "I checked with the airline, they said your flight landed last night. I was so worried. You didn't call. I wanted to meet you at the airport—"

Irem had refused that; she didn't want her brother to see what she looked like after nervous hours in the air.

"I was fine, Lev—"

"I tried to call you. The hotel, your cell. Over and over and—"

She kissed his cheek. "So good to see you, Lev." Irem extricated herself and stared up at his olive-brown face. Her younger brother, Levent, was gorgeous—intense dark eyes, perfect nose, angular jaw, a short beard, and shallow dimples that gave him a mischievous aspect. The long mop of coffee-colored curls, however, didn't fit with his black tuxedo. When he'd lived in Printers' Row south of the Loop, his hair was practically shaved to his scalp, and she thought that had suited him better. In Chicago, he'd had nothing but jeans and paint-spattered T-shirts in his closet. She thought those suited him better, too. She had to concentrate not to cry; she'd missed him terribly.

"I ended up with a connecting flight in Washington, and it was late. I turned my phone off, crashed at the hotel, and then—" She decided not to go into the pickpocket incident. "In fact, I haven't turned my phone back on yet. I really *should* have called you. It was inconsiderate. I'm so sorry."

"I'll get over it." He shrugged. "You are so beautiful. The dress, your hair. Wow. Makeup even. Jewelry. Fingernail polish—shade of magenta three-eighty! You look—"

"Thanks, Lev, I—"

"Amazing. You look amazing. We have so much catching up to do," he said. "Four years since—"

"—you left Chicago," she finished.

"Left for good. I love Italy. I will never leave here. Never ever. And you will love it, too." He gently squeezed her arms and grinned wide. "I am so happy you are here. Come, the reception is in the gallery."

He waved his arm, indicating a wide doorway at the end of the hall through which she saw a throng of exquisitely dressed people. He continued to chatter about Rome and all the things he would show her in his city. Then Levent's words got tangled in the conversations of the other guests, everything a confusing susurrus. There was music, too, underlying the voices, Vivaldi. Irem was not a fan of classical music, but she recognized that one of the *Four Seasons* played.

It seemed that all the guests wore too much cologne, and the scents clashed and delivered a headache. Irem decided not to stay long, between her feet and now her throbbing temples she felt besieged. She realized this was not the place for a reunion. Tomorrow, she and Levent would find a quiet setting.

A server glided past, and Levent grabbed two glasses, pressing one into her hand.

"It is a Frascati white, a mix of Malvasia Candia grapes with—"

"When the hell did you learn about wine, Lev? It was all beer and—"

He leaned close so she could better hear him. "The financial backer of my fiancé's dig owns a vineyard outside the city. This wine is catered from there. Hungry?"

Irem saw a passing tray of toppings mounded on thin slices of dark bread.

"White truffle ravioli and grilled lamb," he said. "And over there is—"

"Not hungry," she lied. "I couldn't eat a bite." *When had Levent's beer and pretzel passion turned to white wine and grilled lamb?* She recalled seeing a convenience store on her walk here and hoped it would still be open so she could grab a cheese sandwich and a bag of potato chips. "Not hungry at all. But thanks. Now... about this fiancé —"

He nudged her toward a tight circle of people that graciously parted to reveal a tall man.

"Benito, this is my sister, Irem. And Irem, this is my heart, my fiancé, Benito Abruzi."

"*Meraviglioso!*" The man embraced Irem in a bear hug. His cologne was musky and sweet. "*Ci incontriamo! Finalmente!*"

"English, Benito," Levent urged.

"Ah, *Certo*. English. *Scusa*." Benito released her. "Your brother has told me so much about you. That you are beautiful and curious and smart. So wonderful to finally meet."

"And he's told me so much about you," she returned. *Except for the fact that you're old enough to be our father. No wonder he never emailed me a single picture.*

Benito Abruzi was charismatic, although Irem couldn't call him handsome. Broad-shouldered, and with a narrow waist, his silhouette reminded her of a dirk balanced on its tip. He was dressed in a silvery-gray tuxedo that showed off his tanned, weathered face. His hair — what amounted to a tonsure ring — was salt and pepper, his face clean shaven, and his eyes so brilliant a blue she wondered if he wore colored contacts. Benito's hands were calloused and strong, no doubt earned from his work in the field, and his fingers devoid of jewelry.

"We have so much to talk about," Benito continued. "Too noisy here. Too many people, and I must be attentive to them. So tomorrow, *per favore*. Tomorrow you must join me at my dig. We will get to know each other properly, you and me. Levent says you have a degree in ancient civilizations. Something in common, very old things."

"Yeah, very old things."

"Irem graduated from Purdue with a degree in museum studies." This from an obviously proud Levent.

"A Boilermaker!" Benito beamed and mimicked bouncing a basketball. "So you will join me and my small crew, yes? And you and I will learn more about each other. We will spend all day under the city in the dirt."

The wedding was on the eighth, and Irem had intended to spend one or two of the in-between days with her brother, sightseeing. The Forum, Trevi Fountain, the Spanish Steps, and Castel Sant' Angelo were on her list. She hoped to do more sightseeing on her own after the ceremony, probably back here, to the Conservatori. Yet the thought of an archaeology dig was intriguing, especially so she could check out the old fart that Levent was so enamored of.

"Well, I—"

"Of course, she will," Levent cut in.

"*Meravigliosa*! In the morning then," Benito said. To Levent: "Go, show her my pieces." He spun back to the circle of people.

Irem drained her wine and set the empty glass on a tray. Then she let her brother lead her from the gallery and down the hall. She was thankful to be away from the press of people with their myriad scents and wagging tongues, conversations in Italian that she couldn't understand beyond a scattered word or two.

"Where did you meet him, Lev? You never told me—"

"A retro bar, not far from here, and—"

"Do you realize—"

"—that we still interrupt each other's conversations?" He grinned wickedly. "God, I've missed you."

"Benito... he's—"

"Last I heard, you like older men, too. That karate instructor—"

"Hapkido, not karate."

"That *hapkido* instructor, Reggie—"

"Ronnie."

"I never cared for him."

"You never met him, Lev."

"Don't need to. Don't want to. I read your emails. He's not good enough. What do you see in a sweaty muscle man who teaches people how to hit each other? Karate, really?"

"It was *hapkido*. And it's over."

"Good."

"And he was only seven years older than me, not—"

"Twenty-five. That's what you want to know, right? Benito is twenty-five years older than me. He just celebrated his forty-ninth birthday. *Just*." Levent put his hands on her shoulders and turned her to face him. "Irem—"

"Lev, do you *really* love—"

"Yes. We had wine on our first meeting. I watched him roll his glass between his hands and he peered over the edge of it as if teasing himself what it would taste like. I drank my own wine, too fast maybe, it tingled against my lips like there was electricity in it, and I held the last of it in my mouth, savoring it, and he still hadn't taken a sip. Wine hadn't tasted so good as it did in that moment, and then I realized the electricity came from his eyes and our connection." He shrugged. "Maybe there was nothing to the wine at all. Maybe the moment just made everything wonderful."

Irem trembled from his description and envied him. She had a knack for remembering conversations. This one would stay with her.

"I love him, Irem. Really. Finally. For the first time. I am in love. And with an archaeologist of all things. Not a painter. Not a sculptor. A man who digs and tunnels and comes home to me filthy. A man who favors wine over beer. Who the hell cares how old he is? If I'm happy, that's all that matters. If he's happy—*fantastico*. Nobody knows how long they will spin around the sun on this polluted rock. Why not spin merrily?"

Irem hugged him. *He's too old for you, Lev.* But she kept the words inside. *It won't last, dear brother. Marrying him is a mistake.* "I'm glad you're happy." A pause: "Archaeology, eh? So you're taking me on this dig with you and Ben—"

"Oh no. I love the beautiful things he brings up from the earth, but I've no inclination to go digging for them. I'll drop you off. I've got an advanced oils class and—"

"So you haven't graduated. You said you were done with—"

"My bachelor's yes. In sculpture. But I've enrolled in a graduate program in oils and portraiture."

The eternal student, Irem thought. Levent had graduated at sixteen from the Chicago High School for the Arts, and then spent the next four years meandering through various curricula in the School of the Art Institute of Chicago before being accepted into RUFA — The Rome University of Fine Arts. At least he'd finally gotten a bachelor's degree.

"So you and Reggie —"

"*Ronnie,*" Irem corrected again.

"Are truly done, eh? After what? Two years?"

"Three." *More like three and a half.*

"I thought you were going to get married and —"

I thought so, too. "You gonna show me Benito's finds?" She didn't want to get into a discussion with him about her ex-fiancé. She'd rather clash with him about the age of his significant other... but not tonight. "My feet are sore, and the rest of me is tired. Besides, if I'm going to the site in the morning —"

"Okay. These rooms —" He gestured along the hall, "are filled with Benito's treasures. Benito found all of this, but everything belongs to Rome. Priceless, these things are. A fortune he has given to the city. It opens to the public tomorrow."

Irem loved all things ancient, and the theater masks and bronze images of Romulus and Remus were stunning. She reflexively took her phone out, turned it on — noting the messages Lev had left, and snapped pictures.

The most singular object was a large tapestry framed under glass. From one angle it looked like a bleached Art Deco couch throw, from another just an elaborate pattern of threads, an eclectic stretch of fabric she might find at the Needle Shop on Lincoln in Chicago, the design not quite paisley or vintage hippie. But it was definitely old. She turned her head and thought she saw the image of a wolf or a dog, perhaps some mythological beast, and the suggestion of a rearing horse. Little skulls dotted some of the sections. It was at the same time gorgeous and disturbing. Four people stood admiring it, a thickset bald gentleman, a slight woman, and two middle-aged men so similar in appearance and build they must be twins; she caught them all in the frame as she took more pictures. The slight woman turned and smiled at her, not seeming to mind being photographed.

"Benito says that piece was a funeral wrap, like the Shroud of Turin. He uncovered it months and months and months ago, but it took a while in preservation and restoration. Longer than it should have because of the restorer's death."

Irem's curiosity tugged her toward it and she snapped a few more photos. "Death?"

"It is oddly beautiful, don't you think?"

"Death?" she repeated.

"The restorer died of a heart attack a few days after starting work on it. Lovely woman, seventy or seventy-one, I believe, said she never wanted to retire. In a sad way she got her wish. Her husband died driving home from her funeral, a car accident. Benito wonders if it was suicide, as the husband was so inconsolable at the services. Some of the museum staff say it is cursed, the shroud." He looked to the doorway as a trio of women came in. "The museum had to bring in a new expert to finish the restoration."

"And that new restorer—"

"He's still breathing," Levent returned. Then he brightened: "My Benito, he is remarkable, isn't he? *Davvero bravo!* These finds? That tapestry, the sculptures? And he cooks. He's making a special cake for our wedding reception, a small one just for the wedding party. The wine—"

"—is being catered by me." The bald man who'd been studying the tapestry turned and extended a hand to Levent. "*Buona sera*, Mr. Kartal-Madigan. Good to see you again. Have you tried the vintage tonight?"

Irem winced. *Kartal-Madigan?* Their last name was Madigan. Their mother's maiden name was Kartal. She supposed Kartal-Madigan sounded exotic, something an artist would embrace.

"*Magnifico*, Mr. Shamoon, as always." Levent shook the man's hand. "Irem, this is Benito's chief patron, Mr.

Hamadi Shamoon. Mr. Shamoon, this is my sister, Irem, from Chicago."

"It is always a pleasure to make the acquaintance of a beautiful woman, *Signorina* Kartal-Madigan." The man's voice was silk. The name, the color of his skin, and his features, she guessed he was Egyptian, and she put him in his mid-fifties. He took Irem's hand, raised it to his lips, and kissed it. "You are here for the wedding?"

"Yes."

He had a working man's hands, the fingertips rough. He took a polite step back. The slight woman who'd been gazing at the cloth smiled wider. Young, plain-looking, no makeup, her only jewelry a simple cross on a long silver chain. Maybe his daughter.

"Irem. That is Turkish, correct? It means 'garden in heaven,' I believe," Hamadi said.

She nodded, surprised. "My mother is Turkish, my father Irish. My mother loves flowers—"

"And hence, your beautiful name."

"The wine is just as my brother says, Mr. Shamoon. Exquisite," Irem said.

"Then you must come to my winery and sample more. I will personally give you a tour. My vineyard is God's gift to Italy." Hamadi looked over his shoulder, one more glance at the ornate cloth. "I must leave now for an appointment."

Irem took another picture of the quartet as they retreated.

Irem glided closer to the cloth. "I've seen burial shrouds before, Lev."

"All the mummies at the Field and—"

"The mummies didn't have burial shrouds. Never seen a shroud quite like this. Where did Benito—"

"—find it? Underground somewhere."

Irem took Levent's picture next to the shroud.

"Underground, wrapped around a body," Irem softly mused. "Who might have been buried in something so interesting?"

THREE

THE SHOVEL MADE A DISTINCTIVE *thunk* as Hamadi drove the blade into hard earth. The wooden shaft creaked as he levered it back and forth, loosening dirt that hadn't been disturbed in a very long time.

Sophia shivered watching him, although it wasn't cold this early October night. She crossed herself as he grunted under the heaviness of the clod that he freed, lifted, and placed to the side. Then he forced the blade in again.

Two more men started digging — twins who worked in unison. Sophia took up her shovel and joined them.

The sounds of their efforts drifted across a cemetery devoid of headstones. For the setting's lack of color — everything shades of gray — Sophia thought they could have been actors in an old black and white movie. The few trees appeared as charcoal smudges, leafless branches dangling down like twisted arthritic fingers that clacked a scolding at her when the wind gusted.

Sophia swallowed and swore she could taste the grave soil.

The full moon and one hooded lantern provided the only light; anything more might be spotted from the road that stretched along one side of the property. They had planned well, coming here after their appearance at the Conservatori. Just shy of midnight, the locals were all sensibly in bed. Not a single car had passed by. Still, they worked swiftly — just in case.

The prize was down more than the customary six feet.

"*Finalmente*," one of the twins announced, signaling they'd reached their goal. "*Velocemente!*"

Sophia climbed down; the lantern lowered while she brushed at the dirt and freed the rotted planks of the coffin lid. The cloth wrapping inside fell apart when she touched it. Sophia crossed herself again and brushed the tatters aside, holding her breath not just because of the odors of death and fuzzy, moldy earth, but because eyeless sockets stared at her.

Hands shaking, she removed only one thing, passed it up, and replaced the tatters and wood planks. The twins let down a rope, and she climbed out.

The grave was filled in again, the scant sod returned, and the diggers walked over it. Hamadi thumped with a flat-back shovel to level it, and with a nod he pronounced it done. Not perfect, but the plot was well back on the grounds and likely rarely visited.

Sophia used a bow rake to even the surface all around, eliminating their tracks. She was the last to leave, dragging the rake behind in a sweeping pattern as they retraced their steps, words to the Lord's Prayer tumbling from her lips:

"*Padre nostro, che sei nei cieli, sia santificato il tuo nome –*" The rake nearly slipped, her hands had become wet from nervous sweat. "*Rimetti a noi i nostri debiti. Rimetti –*" she repeated until she reached the SUV. Never before had her trespasses been on actual holy ground.

The weather report called for storms tomorrow, and the rain spatter would further mask their intrusion. Already clouds were scudding across the sky.

Was that the face of God scowling? Sophia cast her eyes down. God would forgive, and might one day reward her.

Hamadi leaned on his shovel like it was a crutch. "*Suora, non preoccuparti. Nessuno noterà,*" he said. "Sister, no one will notice. Do not worry."

He squeezed behind the steering wheel. Shovels and rake stowed in the trunk, headlights off, passengers settled, and prize secured, Hamadi edged the SUV onto the road and cruised away.

Sophia closed her eyes, touched the rosary in her pocket, and smiled. "*Nessuno noterà,*" she agreed. *I am not worried.*

FOUR
OCTOBER 5

HUNDREDS OF EYELESS SOCKETS FIXED Irem in place.

"Incredible," she said with a shiver.

Skulls covered a large section of wall in the underground chamber, stacked floor to ceiling and packed tight. Femurs formed an arch above them, and finger bones were scattered along the base like straw edging. Two complete skeletons, skulls tipped down as if in prayer, were clad in brown robes rotting from age.

The air felt ancient.

It was so incongruous to what stretched directly above them, a vibrant, sprawling city filled with life: women in the latest fashions clicking their heels against sidewalks, tourists rushing to the next attraction and snapping pictures of everything in their path, taxis honking, pigeons fluttering down to grab the crumbs dropped by those eating breakfast at outdoor cafés.

This was lifeless and solemn and appealed to Irem for her love of history.

There were more bones on the opposite wall and along the corridor she and Benito had traveled; all of them used as decoration, including vertebrae chandeliers and skulls and crossbones placed long before pirates had used the symbols.

"These catacombs are a major attraction," Benito said. He pointed to the ceiling where evenly spaced lights provided minimal, but appropriate, illumination. There were guardrails to keep people from disturbing the remains. "A dozen or so tourists at a time—always small groups—

25

are led through every afternoon. Here and nearby, as the many burial catacombs cover miles and miles. Everyone is told to wear comfortable shoes."

Irem wore comfortable shoes this morning, with thick terrycloth socks that were making yesterday's blisters a fading memory. She noted that the stone floor was smooth and shiny from the countless feet that had crossed it.

"All these bones. Remarkable," she said. *Macabre*, she wanted to add. Despite the eeriness, there was something beautiful about it.

"Some of these burial vaults date back to a hundred and fifty years before Constantine made Christianity legal in Italy." He droned on as if giving one of the tours. "Down another tunnel is the world's oldest painted image of the Virgin Mary. This particular vault, with all the skeleton art, is part of the Capucin Crypt. The bones of more than four thousand friars are entombed here. Historians say it was meant to be respectful, never intended to be morbid."

"Dust to dust," Irem whispered.

Benito chuckled. "Dust we will all be, eh?"

And where will my brother be when you are dust, Benito? Twenty-five years between you and him. Was it the age difference that bothered her, or the fact that her brother had found love and was getting married?

Irem was thirty-one and had always dreamed of having a child or two—and thought she'd be starting on that soon with the man she'd been living with. She'd been so in love with him it still physically hurt when she thought about it, her stomach twisting and chest tightening. Ronnie had said on a walk in Grant Park last April: "Let's make it legal, finally," and so they had planned to get married the week before Christmas. The beautiful dress she'd bought was in a box in her closet, the printed invitations—with tiny foil poinsettias for trim—discarded, her mother devastated. At summer's end he'd found someone even younger, another of his hapkido students. When Irem discovered the affair and confronted him, he'd admitted there'd been a few others. He asked for the ring back when she called off the wedding.

Benito had been saying something else, but she'd missed some of it.

"There are words carved at the end of this crypt—we won't be going down that way today, but I can take you some other time if you'd like. It reads: 'What you are now, we once were. What we are now, you will be.' T.S. Eliot said similar: 'In my beginning is my end.' Truth, eh?" He shrugged. "I suspect my assistants have been working a few hours. We usually start before dawn, but I slept in because of the reception last night." He continued down the passage.

"Before dawn?"

"Before the city wakes up. I am on a teaching sabbatical, but I still guest lecture some afternoons. I need all the morning to work down here. Sometimes I come below on weekends. The hours are long, but there is joy in it."

"You can come down here anytime?"

"Yes. We hold the necessary permissions. Anytime."

She knew he had a separate way in from the public entrance; he'd showed her, a key-combination door coded to L E V E N T. Much shorter than the roundabout path he'd taken now to let her see the friars' bones.

"Just the three of us, my assistants and me. I keep my crew small for many reasons. Mostly to keep the discoveries quiet."

The brickwork and plaster had crumbled in places, frescoes faded, but Irem imagined how colorful it all must have been centuries past. She likened her foray into the Roman underground to stepping into a sepia photograph, the bones and everything else shades of cream and brown, the hues seeming to run together like a chalk drawing caught in a damp fog. She sucked in a breath, tasting dust and stone. The air was certainly breathable, but it was increasingly damp the farther they traveled.

"What made you become an archivist, Irem?"

She wondered if he was truly interested or just making conversation.

"Eh? What drew you to study ancient civilizations?"

"I just love history. Obsessed maybe."

"And I am obsessed with your brother. I brought him down here only once. He is claustrophobic. Lev, he said this place felt like a *bara*. Oh, what is the word? Coffin. He said it felt like a coffin."

"Bara." She waited a beat: "He said he met you at a bar."

"Funny, we'd each gone there to meet someone else, but neither of our dates showed. Lev and me, we talked for hours. It fell into place from there."

"Levent is twenty-four." There, she'd broached the subject.

Benito stopped, and she nearly bumped into him.

"Ah, you are concerned about the years."

"Yes."

"I like younger men. He likes older men. It works."

"I'm glad he's happy," Irem lied.

"I am happy, too." He smiled broadly.

She felt the ground tremble, touched the wall and sensed slight vibrations. Probably some large truck passing overhead, the driver likely oblivious to what was beneath his wheels.

"Lev told me same-sex marriage isn't legal here." There, another subject that had been simmering in her brain. She'd been invited to a wedding… but was it a *real* wedding?

Benito gave a clipped laugh. "Rome… Italy… is funny. At the height of the Roman Empire it was almost commonplace. Emperor Hadrian and Antinous, Mark Anthony and Curio, Nero and… well… it seems like Rome was more advanced in ancient times. Christianity came along. One man. One woman."

"I'm not sure God made those rules, Benito." She wished her parents were more open-minded; it might have kept Levent in Chicago.

"I do not think God made those rules either. Our ceremony is in a friendly Methodist church downtown. I am Christian, but I belong to a denomination that has no building. Levent loves this church and attends it occasionally. It is so beautiful, this place, and so we will wed there. Civil unions, at least in some of the cities such as Rome, are legal. Lev and me, we are calling this civil union a wedding. Do you disapprove—"

"Of same-sex weddings? Of course not." *Or do I? I'd like to think I'm open-minded, accept that love is love. But sometimes I am too old-fashioned for my age.*

"It is good Lev's sister supports him so."

Nice Lev has somebody. I don't even have a cat.

The tunnel was so narrow here that the broad-shouldered archaeologist walked sideways and held his pack close to keep it from catching on jagged sections of the walls. This part was not accessible on the tourist route, and she doubted that just any underground traveler could find it — unless he knew where to look.

She almost didn't notice the black iron gate that blocked an even narrower side passage. A metal sign the size of a baseball card read: *Vietato l'accesso. Vietato l'ingresso ecetto.* In smaller print beneath it: No trespassing. Authorized personnel only. It had a battery-powered key code in addition to a big padlock. Benito typed in A B R U Z I and then fumbled in his pocket for a key, opened the padlock, and gestured Irem through. He locked it behind them. Irem thought someone ought to teach Benito about creating secure passwords. At least these were ones she'd be able to remember.

The tunnel beyond was inky dark, and he pulled a long flashlight from his pack; the bright beam was tinged blue and showed that the slope went down sharply and curved out of sight. He squeezed in front of her.

"Watch your step here."

A chill shot through Irem, the sensation coming out of nowhere and intensifying.

This place is already so difficult to find, what's down here that needs passwords, an iron gate, and an impressive-looking lock?

FIVE

"HOW DEEP ARE THE CATACOMBS?"

"Irem, Rome is an onion, and as we peel back the layers we discover more and more of it. Not terribly far from here — above ground — is the Basilica of San Clemente, built in the twelfth century. Beneath that is a basilica built in the fourth century; and under that a first-century Mithraic temple. Maybe the layers of Rome reach to the center of the earth." He grinned like a happy child, and she could see why Levent was attracted to him. "Have you been to the Colosseum?"

"Not yet, but it's on my list."

"Nearby the Colosseum, under it, are layers stretching down eight stories, where the ancients mined for building materials. With special permissions, maybe you could go. It's all Swiss cheese, you understand."

"No," she said. "I don't understand."

Benito made a huffing sound and stopped; she nearly bumped into him. "Picture the Italian underground like a giant block of Swiss cheese. The volcanic rock is easy to cut... so that's what people long ago did, making passages and caverns, tiny rooms, crawlspaces. Some collapsed, some hidden, some will never be discovered — I hope. Some are discovered today. The cheese, we walk through these tunnels, this enormous piece of Swiss cheese. Little mouses we are. Rome sits on top of all of this." He started walking again.

The passage curled and widened and came to a section where the walls and an arch were made of old bricks — to

31

Irem's practiced eye they did not seem any older than the stonework near the skulls.

"How old is this?"

"Fourth century," he replied, confirming her guess. "From about the same time as that basilica beneath San Clemente."

"And you determined this by—"

"By what you will see below. This, here, was solid, bricked," Benito explained. "It took many permissions to be able to take the bricks away and make this opening, replacing some of what came down to create the arch. It was not difficult to bring it down, so old and dried the bricks. It was like they wanted to fall and give up a secret." He ran his fingers along one side to illustrate jagged places where bricks had been.

She'd noted a few other sections of wall a dozen or more yards back that also appeared to be incongruously bricked over, as if something might be behind those places, too. Maybe Benito would eventually break it all down.

The shaft continued, doubled back on itself, and wended always down. Benito's light bounced off the walls, the shadows looking like specters keeping pace. They passed through two large chambers that had already been excavated. Irem speculated that the area had been formed by an underground river centuries past, and was curious who had blocked off this section of the passage... and why. The next excavated chamber held some of Benito's supplies, including cases of bottled water, a sleeping bag, and a Coleman portable flush toilet like a well-to-do camper might own.

He saw her looking at the toilet. "Too far from our dig to conveniently reach the public restrooms. It was not easy to bring that down here. But not *impossibile*. It has wheels." He let out a long breath. "Still, I am not looking forward to taking it back out. But such is the way, eh?"

Just beyond this, the tunnel widened so they could walk shoulder-to-shoulder, and in one broad section they hunched over, backs rounded like turtles and scraping against the low ceiling. When they could stand upright again she noticed pitons driven into a wall near a small excavated room; they might have been for portable lights or tools, as they were a recent addition, not a trace of rust on them. This section of the tunnel had elaborate brickwork, and high near the ceiling she spotted chiseled symbols, helmets with horns and rearing horses. The silence unnerved her, and she nearly engaged Benito in conversation again, as she had dozens more questions dancing in her mind. She stopped herself, fearing she might say something judgmental, letting the broken record play again.

Benito Abruzi is nice, smart, and although not an old man, way the hell too old for Lev. She liked him, and she didn't want to.

One more turn and she heard music, oldies rock, Pink Floyd. A man was singing along. Light came from ahead.

"My assistants," Benito said, as the tunnel opened into a broad chamber with a low ceiling. "Santiago and Lacy Garcia."

The two archaeologists looked up from a patch of floor they'd been poking at. Irem's first impression: Hispanic, college aged, wearing navy sweatpants and long-sleeve T-shirts, his heather gray embellished with a faded Oakland Raiders football logo, hers the rosy color of ripe peaches with a large printed slogan—BEER. LIME. & SUNSHINE. Definitely young. They nodded to Irem. The man's clothes were clean, not a trace of dirt that she noticed. The woman, however, was a sharp contrast. Her shoes were scuffed, her pants—with holes at the knees like a country singer favored—smudged with dust, hair in a ponytail but tangled, face streaked, shirt tucked in at the front, loose in the back, and snagged.

"Good morning, Dr. Abruzi," Lacy said to Benito.

"Hey, Doc." Santiago dipped his chin and went back to work.

Two small laptops were stacked in a corner. Probably belonged to the Garcias. Benito struck her as "old school." A tray next to the computers held batteries, extra flashlights, masks, gloves, and an assortment of archaeological instruments that looked like dental picks and jewelry tools. Two backpacks appeared empty because of their flatness.

"Lacy and Santiago are in a graduate archaeology program at Stanford. They came over early in the summer and are spending the entire fall semester with me. Hopefully they will stay on next spring, too, if I can convince them and their university."

"Convincing us will not be the problem," Santiago said. Softer: "We'll drop out if we have to."

"Nice to meet you," Irem said. Stanford had been on her radar before she settled on Purdue, a public university, which was nevertheless expensive. Stanford, private, and in California, was way the hell out of her price range, considering she hadn't won much of a scholarship and didn't want to take on horrific student loans. "Stanford. Impressive."

"Full academic ride," Lacy said proudly, as she resumed work.

"For her," Santiago cut in without looking up. "Some of us with smaller brains have to sign our future away to a savings and loan."

"Cue the violins," Lacy said.

"Sister and—" Irem started.

"Husband and wife," Lacy said, somehow hearing Irem over Pink Floyd's *Another Brick in the Wall*. "Got married our freshman year."

Santiago added: "Celebrated our fifth anniversary eight days ago. We're in it for the long haul."

"I cooked for their anniversary." This from Benito. "Penne a la Melenzane with mostaccioli, and a squash and artichoke salad. And dessert of course. Mango mousse."

Irem remembered that the cheese sandwich with a Snickers candy bar chaser last night from the convenience store was damn tasty.

"You an archaeologist, too?" Lacy asked.

"I'm an archivist."

"For the prestigious Field Museum," Benito provided.

"Interesting," Santiago said. "Most of this stuff will end up in museums." Then he dipped his head even lower to the floor and picked earnestly at something. "Interesting," he repeated. "But it sounds boring. More fun being out in the field like this."

"Sant!" Lacy scolded.

Irem didn't consider her work boring, but she was a little frustrated. After seven years there'd been no movement in her department; no one above her leaving, no chance for her to advance. She sometimes thought about applying to the Metropolitan Museum in New York, often thought about finishing that doctorate degree.

This is fun, Irem saw Lacy mouth.

Irem focused on the music, punctuated by the sound of the Garcias chiseling, and scrutinized the site. Definitely centuries old, but not *ancient*. More than a thousand years, less than two, she guessed. There were six lights on tripods, cables running to a small generator — all of that would have been onerous to drag through the twisting tunnel. She suspected cell phones wouldn't work this far underground. She pulled hers out to check. No signal. But the camera function worked.

Strings tied to wooden stakes marked grids on the floor where they intended to do more digging. Irem spotted a handheld metal detector against a wall. She'd seen something like it on a History Channel program about Oak Island; they used the detectors to find silver, gold, and other precious metals. It was probably how the Garcias and Benito determined where to excavate for bodies — skeletons buried with jewelry or armor.

"May I take some photos?"

"I prefer no," Benito said. "We are trying hard to keep this quiet and are a long way from publicizing this find. Not even Lacy and Santiago can take pictures."

"Sure. I understand." But the secrecy made her more intrigued. Besides, someone had been filming; there was a palm-sized movie camera next to the metal detector. She really wanted pictures of this to show her friends at the Field.

The room appeared to be a natural cavern, except one wall of it was extensively worked, carved flat and covered with copious engravings. The images were deep and intricate... men and horses, words in strips, nothing she could read, but something she recognized — Latin symbols, a stylized 8 represented H. If she had a book or the right app on her iPhone she could figure it out. It reminded her of a section of the tapestry in the Conservatori. Some of it had color; perhaps it had all been painted long ago and moisture had washed it out.

"Where did you find the tapestry, Benito? The one I saw last night at the Conservatori? I see a few similarities in this wall. The horses and the little piles of skulls. Who was buried in it?"

Lacy reached over and turned off the music. "You mean the bone shroud, right? The one hanging in the museum?"

Irem continued to study the engravings, then the section of floor where the Garcias worked. Part of a human skull was visible; it looked like they were uncovering an entire skeleton. A divided tray nearby had heavy-looking jewelry in it and pieces of rotted cloth and leather.

"That tapestry," Benito started. "I say shroud, as when I found that it was wrapped around a well-preserved body. It was uncovered miles from here at another site. About a year ago."

"Not too far from where Doc found the Romulus and Remus pieces," Santiago said. "Wish we'd been there."

"That cloth led me here," Benito said. "We started on this site four months past. We have done considerable work, cleared the passage, cleared those other chambers. These young people work fast. Perhaps too fast." He crossed his arms and put his shoulders back, and Irem noted he had about two inches to spare between the top of his head and the chamber ceiling. "I will tell you this, Irem, because you and me will soon be family."

"I can keep quiet," Irem said. "I'm perfect with secrets."

"That shroud was a map," Benito said. "To those who could read it. But the people at the Conservatori, the general public... they will never realize how to decipher it. I almost did not turn it over to the museum. But it needed serious restoration and to be protected."

The silence settled heavily, and Irem waited.

"That it's a map... *was* a map... that it led here, and that it will lead to other places," Lacy cut in. "That's our secret."

"*Segreto*," Benito agreed. "Maybe someday a scholar looking at it in a certain light might make some connections. But I do not think so. The restoration inadvertently removed most of the clues, made it unreadable. Tragic and fortunate at the same time, eh? If other archaeologists, anthropologists, careless treasure hunters... diggers... had caught a look at the raw fabric they would be tearing up the sewers and catacombs throughout Italy. They would be pillaging, stealing, and ruining so much. It would be like a race in an Indiana Jones movie."

"On steroids," Lacy put in.

"Yes, so perhaps the restorer's unfortunate repairs were instead fortunate. The restoration made it less of a map."

"What's so special about this dig site?" Irem's curiosity was a ravenous creature.

Lacy stood and worked a kink out of her neck, then glanced at Benito.

"It is okay, Lacy. Irem will be family to me, and there are no secrets with family," Benito said. "Levent knows. Irem can know as well. Irem, I believe this chamber is the resting place of very important people."

Irem's skin tingled. *C'mon. Tell me. Tell me.* She twisted the ball of her foot. "Tell me."

Benito paced and rubbed his chin. "If I have interpreted the bone shroud correctly, this chamber we stand in is the burial vault of Attila the Hun's generals." He waggled his fingers at the skull in the floor. "That is one of those generals, maybe, probably. Someone of stature, certainly, connected to Attila by the artifacts we have uncovered. There should be additional important remains nearby."

"And Attila himself?" Irem hushed.

"We had to carefully pull the earth down to find that tableau." He pointed to the ornately carved wall. "I am confident Attila is behind that. These symbols—" Benito indicated a block that Irem recognized as Latin; some symbols translated directly to the English alphabet. "These say *Flagellum Dei* sleeps forever here."

"*Flagellum Dei*. The Scourge of God," Irem said.

"*Certo*." Benito's eyes were wide with excitement. "Attila was called that. He was the greatest barbarian ruler, and he terrorized the Roman Empire… the Balkans, Greece, Gaul. The Romans called him The Scourge of God."

"Oh my."

"We will excavate the entirety of this chamber first, while we see if there is a way to reach the other side of that wall without harming the carving. Perhaps another tunnel exists. Perhaps we need to approach it from somewhere on the other side, come in from the top, come in through a passage we have not yet discovered. I do not know. But those words: *Flagellum Dei* sleeps forever here. Those words mean I am right, that I interpreted the shroud *corretto*… correctly, and that Attila's remains are very close."

"Oh my. Oh my," Irem repeated. Suddenly all plans for visiting tourist spots above ground were dashed.

"We're going to unearth Attila the Hun," Lacy said, "We're going to be freakin' famous."

Softer, Santiago added: "If we don't all end up dead."

SIX

"GOD CREATED THIS PERFECT VINEYARD," Hamadi pronounced.

Sophia tipped her head back as she meandered with him through the rows of grapevines. She relished the feel of the sun on her face. The air smelled fresher here than in Rome, a mere dozen miles away, and it was filled with birdsong and the musical conversations of the harvesters. She imagined it was close to what heaven must be, and she wished this day... this moment... could go on forever.

"There is no finer vintage than what my grapes yield," he continued. "No more blessed land in the world."

She'd stopped to let the faint breeze wrap around her, and he reached over and tugged on her sleeve to get her moving again.

"*Si,*" she agreed when they reached the end of a row. "*L'Italia è perfetta.*"

"I believe angels kiss the earth in my vineyard, Sister. We tread on sacred soil."

Hamadi used a cane this morning. The ground between rows was uneven, and knobby roots hid in the grass. He'd had his right knee replaced seven months ago and was protective of it. She knew the cane was a precaution, feeling forward with it like a blind man might. Hamadi had several walking sticks, all expensive and decorative. This one was her favorite. The handle was the carved head of a Jack Rabbit, ears laid back for gripping. It had amber eyes, and the shaft had a walnut lacquer and brass ring accents. She was with him when he'd purchased it, following a delightful lunch at a sidewalk café. She still swore she could taste the amarena gelato dessert, the cherries so sweet.

He tapped at a root with the end of his cane, the soft sound pulling her from the delicious memory. He'd refused to take a walking stick to the Conservatori, too proud to look weak in front of all those people. And the other night he'd relied on a shovel to feel his way across the rutted ground of the dark cemetery. It had been clumsy going, and she'd worried for him. She would make it her responsibility to bring a cane for him on their next sojourn.

"*La musica stasera?*" Sophia asked him.

"English, Sister. You will enjoy the musicians tonight." He stopped to inspect a cluster of grapes. "It is a small ensemble that I heard in a club a month ago. The songstress is exceptional."

"*Amo la musica.*" Noting his scowl: "Of course, English. I love music, Uncle."

She knew Hamadi preferred English when they were around his harvesters, who were all women and who all worked overly long hours for modest pay. Female harvesters were sought by vintners because of their thin fingers, able to reach in to pluck the grapes more delicately than men with larger fingers could.

All of Hamadi's harvesters spoke only Italian. Using English in front of them was like talking in secret. Sophia didn't mind the opportunity to practice the complicated language. Hamadi spoke seven languages fluently, and she hoped to one day accomplish the same.

Sophia's parents frowned on Hamadi; she thought it more jealousy because of his wealth than any true animosity. And they disapproved of her, leaving the convent to come to the vineyard. There was little contact with them anymore. They would disapprove even more strongly if they knew everything, would likely stop speaking to her altogether. But Sophia was happier here. She'd been the youngest nun at the convent, joining directly out of high school, believing that was her calling and trying for three years to fit in. The sister closest to her age was almost fifty years older. Nothing

40

in common except God, Sophia grew increasingly listless and discontented... until during one of Uncle Hamadi's visits he offered an alternative.

The vineyard was a relaxing fit, and God was everywhere, even amid the grapes. Easier to worship him on these grounds, she thought, heaven closer here than it was to the austere convent. She touched the rosary in her pocket, smiled, and thought again of the sweet, creamy gelato.

"What brings you joy today, Sister?" Hamadi inspected another cluster.

A *memory,* Sophia almost said, *clear and wonderful and tasty in my mind.* "Being here," she returned. "Learning something new today."

"And what new thing did you learn?" It was a question he often posed.

"That wine was discovered six thousand years ago in the Middle East, and that the art of winemaking was refined by the Egyptians." She paused. "It was in a history book I borrowed from the study."

"*Sapientia vino obumbratur,*" he said. It was Latin for "wisdom is overshadowed by wine." Hamadi patted her arm. "I have other Egyptian history books you might enjoy reading."

"Being a part of something *importante.* And the harvest, Uncle. Those bring me joy today also. I love harvest time."

The grape harvest would continue for another week because Hamadi insisted the work be done by hand. Some vineyards used mechanical harvesters with nylon arms that shook the fruit loose onto conveyors that whisked the grapes into bins. Faster, but often the grapes split open, and that was detrimental to the final taste, she'd learned.

"Only human hands here," Hamadi had told her. "I will not have my plants beaten to surrender their fruit. Cruel to the plants, and bad for the wine."

He'd taught her that finding the ideal balance of sugar, acid, and tannin levels determined harvest time. The weather played a part; this had been a mild fall, extending

41

the growing season. The vineyard's income would be higher than usual.

"We will celebrate our wine tonight," he said. "Maybe I will let James come to the party. At least for a little while."

"He adores music," Sophia said. "Be warned that he might try to sing along with your musicians."

Tours and tastings at the vineyard were booked solid, and there were parties scheduled in the main building the next three nights. Sophia looked forward to this evening's revelry. Grape stomping would be among the activities. She might participate. And maybe tonight she would dance.

"The harvesting we did the other evening at the cemetery," Sophia broached, "I think it is like winemaking."

"Hand-picked," Hamadi said as they turned at the end of a row and started up another. "At the optimal time."

"It will yield no bitter vintage. When is our next *soggiorno*?" Sophia made a face and snapped her fingers, trying to call up the word in English. "Yes. Sojourn. When is our next sojourn, Uncle?"

"*Our* next sojourn is after the harvest festival, in seven or eight days at the earliest. There is no hurry. The gentleman isn't going anywhere."

She'd noticed his emphasis of "our," and that worried her. Would there be an earlier trip without her? "After your archaeologist's wedding?"

Hamadi nodded. "*Our* next one is after the wedding, yes."

Again the emphasis. She frowned.

"Yes," he continued. "You and I will celebrate Dr. Abruzi's civil union first."

"There is something you do not tell me, *Si*?"

"The wedding will be a useful distraction."

Sophia made a face. "But we are going, to the wedding?"

"You and I are going to the wedding, yes." They turned down another row, and Hamadi walked slower, inspecting the grapes more closely.

Sophia decided not to press him on his secret. Still, she couldn't keep all of her questions inside. "Your archaeologist still pursues the Scourge of God, *Si*?"

"Yes, Sister Sophia. He is single-minded about the barbarian's bones. Our friends will make certain that his young associates keep focused on that particular prize, too, and that their eyes do not wander elsewhere." He paused.

Her eyes sparkled. "And while your archaeologist uncovers the Scourge—"

"—we will continue to uncover our own treasures," Hamadi finished. He popped a grape into his mouth. "In the Scourge of God's shadow, you and I will find something to alter the world."

SEVEN

IREM WAS SURPRISED TO SEE car headlights and traffic signals holding off the night. Time had melted in the tunnels.

It had rained recently, adding a thin layer of freshness to the air that was otherwise heavy with the big city smells of car exhaust and too many people. Business lights reflected in wide, shallow puddles, the mirror image of a nearby fluorescent sign looking like wiggling pink and green snakes that extended from her feet.

Her legs ached from the climb, and she resolved to enroll at a gym when she returned to Chicago... pursuing something other than hapkido, which held acrimonious memories. But, for now, she'd exercise her ever-present curiosity.

"Benito, what did Santiago mean 'if we don't all end up dead'? I didn't want to ask him when he'd said it." *But I should have.* It had niggled at her brain for hours. Irem had plenty more questions—those all relating to Attila the Hun and the Roman underground, the bone tapestry and why it couldn't be used as a map any longer, who'd been buried in it. She intended to answer at least some of those on her own later with a thorough Google search on her iPhone. There had to be scads of websites about the famous Hun. "Is Santiago worried the underground is going to cave in? Or is it the tapestry? Does he think it's cursed? Does he think pursuing Attila—"

"*Neinte.*" Benito shook his head.

"Then what is he worried about?"

"The bone shroud is not cursed, Irem. That's the stuff of fantasy fiction. The deaths of the restorer and her husband were unfortunate to be certain, the museum intern to drugs and alcohol. *Sfortunato.* Unfortunate."

Intern? A third death? Levent hadn't mentioned that.

"No curse. I am not superstitious, and neither are the Garcias. If Santiago is worried about the tunnels giving way, he would not be digging with me. He has the fears of a young archaeologist new to the dark parts of this field. That is all."

Benito stopped and stared at the sidewalk, let out a long breath.

"Dark parts." Irem wasn't willing to let the question drop. Her curiosity pushed her to pursue it. "Dark parts? Of archaeology?"

"*Mi scusi,*" a man said, brushing by them and wrapping his long rain slicker in close. "*Sono di fretta.*" He said something else, softer, lost in the giggle of a sequined woman passing by.

"*Non è un problema,*" Benito called after him.

The sequined woman giggled again and blew a kiss to an elderly man leaning against a post, then pointed a finger at Benito and winked. Irem guessed she was a hooker.

"So what did Santiago mean—"

"Archaeology is—" Benito ground the ball of his foot against the pavement. "*Brutale.* Cutthroat, Irem. I had to think of the English word. Cutthroat is a good word. In some circles the competition for finds is not unlike divers racing to discover a sunken ship full of treasure. I think that is an apt analogy." Benito directed her south and around a white-haired woman with a walker, a man with a cane following. "Santiago worries that if someone discovers what we do, who we work to uncover, they will try to steal our find. His concern is not unfounded."

"Because Attila the Hun is a huge deal." She said it softly.

"*Un grande affare.* Yes." He hooked his arm in hers, and they strolled without talking the length of the next block. On the corner a restaurant with a red and green awning had its front door propped open, the scents of seafood and other tempting aromas drifting out. "Shall we?"

"Don't you have to get home to Lev?"

Benito shrugged. "He will have eaten hours ago. And I will have many nights to go home to him. Have had many nights already. For nearly a year we have lived together. I am enjoying your company, and I am hungry. You?"

"Very hungry." She had lived with her significant other for more than three years. Would Lev and Benito last longer?

Benito ordered the Mussels Posillipo, and she settled on the Shrimp Renato. The menu was in Italian and English, and the description of "butterflied and broiled in a wine sauce topped with melted mozzarella cheese and prosciutto" sounded not too fancy... at least not compared to the other items. Irem preferred simple fare; McDonald's and Taco Bell were her favorite places.

"May I select the wine?" Benito asked Irem.

"Sure. Yes, please."

"*Una bottiglia dei* Riesling," he told the waiter. "The Bollo, Veneto." To Irem: "It is a fruit wine, not as fine as what was served last night, but light, with notes of peaches, pears, apricots. It will go well with our food."

"Sounds good," she said, deciding Benito was entirely responsible for her brother's wine education.

Irem looked at the clock on the wall: almost nine p.m. The restaurant was more than half full.

"People in Rome eat at all hours," he said. "Like New York, this city does not sleep." He pulled out his cell phone and worried at the keys. "Telling Lev where we are." A pause: "He says back, *godere*, enjoy. Wait." He stared at his screen. "Lev says also you must turn your phone on, Irem, and that you must meet him for lunch tomorrow."

"Lev doesn't think I have my phone on often enough. Thinks it should be on constantly. I just get tired of seeing people always always always staring at their phones instead of each other. Heads down all the time. It looks like they're praying."

"The off switch is your protest."

"Yeah. An attempt to keep my humanity."

47

"I *really* like you, Irem."

"I'll turn my phone on when we're finished eating," Irem said. "And, yeah, you're right. Lunch with my brother would be nice." Softer: "I've missed him. In Chicago he was a big part of my life." She felt guilty, so caught up in Attila the Hun that her brother had drifted to the back of her mind. But he'd been the one to nudge her to Benito's dig.

Attila the Hun. She still couldn't believe it. One of the most notorious historical figures ever might very well be beneath this city. And she might get a chance to see his moldy bones before the discovery was revealed to the rest of the world. She might be able to truly touch history. *Please, God, let this not be a dream.* She wanted so badly to call her friends in the archive department and tell them all about this. But Benito had sworn her to secrecy, and she would honor that... despite her mind itching with the excitement.

They'd been fortunate to get a table by the window. She stared out at the cars passing and saw a man across the street just standing there. The lights from the business behind him brightened and showed that he was the one who'd bumped into them on the sidewalk a few blocks ago.

Coincidence?

She shook off the eeriness of it and noticed string music playing softly in the background; hushed conversations from other tables accompanied it.

"I'm not sure Chicago sleeps either, Benito. I've an apartment downtown, not far from my parents' bar. Any hour of the night I hear music and sirens. Except for college, I've spent my whole life in the city, so I'm pretty numb to the racket. But being underground today... it was weird, you know. When the Garcias finally turned off the CDs and the noisy generator finished charging the batteries for the other equipment, I could hear every breath, every footstep. I could hear silence. It was, I dunno, almost spooky." She looked up as the waiter brought the wine and had Benito sample it. When she glanced out the window again, the man was gone.

"*Molto bene,*" Benito said of the wine.

The waiter poured two glasses.

"I liked it, though," she said. "Both the noise and the quiet, and everything about today. It was pretty wonderful." Irem liked the wine, too.

"An archivist. I would think that is a quiet *il compito*... uhm... *lavoro*... endeavor. Sorry, I have been fluent in English for nearly twenty years, and I still sometimes search for words. A quiet endeavor, *Si*, locked away in the secret parts of the museum and —"

"Quiet profession? Oh, the Field's only quiet *after* hours. And the people in my department enjoy noise."

"Sometimes noise is beautiful." He laughed. "You must let me cook for you while you are here. Not tomorrow, but the night after. Yes?"

"I'd really hate to impose —"

"Please, Irem."

"I —" She paused, fearing what he might come up with, an unpronounceable dish with ingredients she wouldn't like. "Sure. That would be nice. *Meraviglioso*."

"Great. Wonderful. *Meraviglioso!* I will make for you my famous soup... stracciatella romana, broccoli di rabe on the side, and taglierini al pesto. Nothing difficult, everything delicious. A good meal before the next day's festivities."

"*Meraviglioso*." But the word came out flat this time. *I'd rather have a quarter pounder with cheese.* "Where did an archaeologist get a passion for cooking?"

Benito took a sip of wine, held it, and then swallowed. "They are linked, food and archaeology. Agriculture, eating, is essential to people in all ages. Ancient cultures' celebrations, religion, and communities... it all includes food. Tools of the kitchen and harvest. It has impacted the evolution of men, animals, societies, influenced art and war. Perhaps, Irem, I should instead prepare for you a medieval course from the late thirteenth century: black beet, lampreys in cold sage soup, rissoles, white sauce of —"

"I think the first option sounded fine." She paused: "I wanted to ask you about the bones. Not the ones on display in that exhibit you walked me through, the tourist path, but the ones you've excavated. The Hun bones. They looked remarkably intact."

He lowered his voice, and she strained to listen. "The Roman soil, deep underground, it preserves, Irem. And these skeletons we pick through... the people they once were... they were neither very young nor very old. Everything... it is perfect for us, or as close to perfect conditions as an archaeologist looking for Attila the Hun could wish for. *Perfetto!*"

The meal arrived and they ate, sharing snippets of small talk about their respective cities. When the quartet that had been seated next to them got up to leave, he finally addressed her burning question.

"The danger part, Irem. One's friends and partners will backstab to take sole credit for an amazing discovery. Worse is the possibility relic hunters will sweep in and steal. It is why I have a crew of only two, and I trust the Garcias completely. If word of our dig leaked —" He whistled and raised his hands. "The theft from dig sites in Egypt was staggering. Elsewhere? More than half of the eight hundred sites in the Inner Niger Delta around Mali were plundered. We archaeologists have the threat of grave robbers, looters... selfish and *stupido* souls."

"Okay, I get the fear of looters. But I don't see how anyone else could claim your find." Irem finished the shrimp and decided she would come back to this restaurant and be a little more adventurous with the menu. "You filed paperwork, you've permission to excavate."

His voice dropped to a conspiratorial whisper. "We need to find something substantial, something that definitely proves Attila is buried here, some provenance beyond the skeletons of men we *believe* served under him. Then we gain serious protections. The wall carving is good, but not enough. Not quite. But very close. Very."

"And you know the skeletons were Mongols because —"

"Like bones excavated in Hungary. Elongated skulls. History says some Mongol parents disfigured the skulls of children, wrapping bandages tight to elongate them. It set these people apart, made them look *different*, perhaps frightening."

"You need the big barbarian himself."

"*Certo.*" He talked fast now. "We get behind the wall. I don't want to harm that beautiful wall, and find the Scourge of God, document that, and then the site is protected and publicized, guards are posted. It remains our find, and we can work with less fear of theft until everything is removed to a safe place." He paused and rubbed his chin. "There is excitement in digging, finding, but there is ego as well. Wanting the credit, the pedestal to perch on. The Scourge, if we find him. *When* we find him. Amazing. So few people in the world can touch history. You understand?"

"Yeah, I really do." Irem thought it was too bad she only had twelve days of vacation left after tonight. Those places she wanted to see… the Forum, Trevi Fountain, the Spanish Steps, Castel Sant' Angelo… as she finished the wine she wondered if any of them would get checked off her list. The touristy thing didn't seem as shiny as ancient bones in the dirt.

With Benito's okay, she might spend most of her time crawling through the bowels of the city in pursuit of the Scourge of God, Attila the Hun. Attila-the-freaking-Hun. She folded her napkin.

Her vacation was definitely not going to be long enough.

"There is money in this, yes?" Irem realized the question was rude, but her curiosity was still hungry. "Finding something as important as Attila the Hun?"

Benito frowned, and she worried she'd pissed him off.

"Archaeology is not typically a way to get rich. So important an archaeologist's work, and yet the money is not typically good… for the average archaeologist."

Irem knew Benito wasn't in the average category.

He took a sip of wine, then divided the last of the bottle between their glasses. "Indiana Jones… ah, it makes the public think archaeologists get some big payday from their discoveries."

"Well, don't they?"

"Levent said you are curious."

"Can't help myself." Irem tried to look apologetic.

"It has to be a big find."

"Like Attila."

"*Si*. Like Attila. And we wouldn't get rich from the artifacts. Those belong to Rome."

"The prestige."

"*Si*. I will have more opportunities *because* of this—when we find Attila. A better position at the university, perhaps. Higher fees for my lectures. My patron, no doubt, will give me a bonus. My patron already has paid me well." He leaned back in the chair. "I should do *very* well if Attila is where I believe him to be. But rich? Such is not an archaeologist's lot."

"Archivists neither," Irem said almost glumly. "Especially ones that can't seem to get a promotion or anything beyond a piddly cost of living boost."

Benito leaned forward and raised his glass to hers. "To Attila," he said.

"To Attila," she echoed.

The lightning flashed, and in it she saw the man again. He was right outside the restaurant, his face hidden by shadows.

EIGHT

"WE MUST HAVE A TAXI for you," Benito said as they left the restaurant. He stepped to the curb, but Irem put a hand on his arm.

She glanced right and left, and didn't see the stranger that had sent shivers down her back. Her imagination, she decided. Simply coincidence.

"My hotel's only three or four blocks. Look. Lean that way. You can see the top of it from here." She wasn't carrying a purse and knew to be wary of pickpockets now. The black belt in hapkido gave her confidence. And Rome was safe for tourists — the friendly cop and the Internet had told her so. "I'm not taking a cab for that little bit."

She ignored her protesting calves. "Are you starting before dawn tomorrow?" She figured to go under the city early and scamper up in time for lunch with Lev. Again she scolded herself for putting the dig before her brother.

Attila versus Levent.

Attila versus —

"You truly enjoyed the site today." Benito's wide grin showed his perfect teeth. "I have a meeting with a restorer at the Conservatori in the morning, a scheduled lunch with the archaeology department at the university —"

" — busy busy."

"Yes. Then I will go below in the afternoon. Sometime in the afternoon. Probably two, no later than three. The obligations keep me out before that."

Irem frowned.

"You want to go back, Irem?"

"Well, yeah. Hell, yeah, actually. So, how will I know what time for sure tomorrow afternoon?"

"You give me your cell phone number, yes?"

She did.

"And you turn it on tomorrow, yes?"

"I'll keep it on."

"Good. You go see something beautiful in the morning. St. Peter's Basilica maybe. Trevi Fountain. The Colosseum, though it is not so beautiful. The Basilica, I suggest. Get Lev away from his easel and make him go with you. All he talked about was taking you shopping and to see the sights. I will call when my lunch is finished and meet you at the gate below. Do you think you can find your way to the gate by yourself and—"

"Sure. I don't get lost."

"Maybe I will have a key made for you, to the gate, for you to use for the next several days so you do not need to match my hours. The password to the keypad on the gate is my last name."

I know, Irem almost said.

"I should make it more complicated, my passwords. But this way I never forget the code. Yes, I will get you a key."

Wow. Irem was flattered, especially after his dinner talk about relic theft and protecting archaeological finds.

"You and me, we will be family. I can trust family. And you respect history."

"That's awesome, Benito." Irem was honored.

A car horn sounded like a scream, the driver laying on it hard. Irem saw a pedestrian who was crossing the street in front of her jump back, hollering a string of curses in Italian. Irem picked out "*Tu bastardo.*"

"That was close," Irem said. "Same in Chicago, I guess stop lights are only a suggestion to some drivers."

"I will walk you to your hotel."

"No. Really, I'm fine. Really. Your apartment is that way, right?" They were on Marsala, and she pointed down Vicenza to her left. Too bad he didn't live so near the Attila site like the Garcias had managed.

"I will walk you halfway, then. Lev, he said you are stubborn."

"Okay," she conceded. "Halfway."

Most of the people on the sidewalk were couples, she noted, and it was not as crowded as during the day. They passed a pair who appeared to be teenagers, and it sounded like they were from Boston by their distinctive accents. Maybe they were on their honeymoon; they looked only at each other. Benito had told her he and Lev weren't taking a honeymoon, not right away. He didn't want to lose days from the dig. But sometime after Christmas they would escape to Palermo or Sicily and celebrate then. She thought about her ex- and their planned honeymoon to Turtle Island in Fiji, and felt the shrimp rising. Irem focused on the notion of Attila, and her stomach quieted.

"I'm good here," she said after two blocks. "Thank you, Benito, for a most marvelous day and a delicious dinner."

"Very well. Tomorrow, Irem." He kissed her hand and turned down Marghera, which ran parallel to Vicenza. Only a few people were on the sidewalk there, and the lights were not as bright, making the rain-slick pavement look like oil. A car alarm sounded nearby, more honking, and a blast of music came from the open window of a cruising blue Alpha Romeo.

"Tomorrow." Irem kept her gaze on the beautiful Romeo, spun to head to her hotel, which loomed closer now, and then after taking a step turned back. She thought she'd seen something out of the corner of her eye… something… the man! The one who'd bumped into them, the one watching across the street while they ate. Had he been following them? Another coincidence?

Looking down Marghera, there he was! At least she was pretty sure it was him, several yards behind Benito. Tall, with a long, dark rain slicker and a fedora hat with a stingy brim. But from the back, and with all the shadows from the buildings, she wasn't wholly certain. Was her imagination dancing?

She nearly called out, and then decided Benito likely wouldn't be able to hear her with the traffic noises. Besides, she should make sure it was the same guy. Night-dark, nearly a block away, maybe it was only her mind playing tricks, fueled by the archaeologist's talk about relic theft and secrets.

She took off after them at a fast walk.

"*Proffessore* Abruzi!" She heard the stranger call out to Benito.

Proffessore... Professor, she understood that word. The stranger knew the archaeologist... or knew who he was. Not a coincidence then that he'd bumped into them and watched the restaurant. Maybe he'd waited to find Benito alone. Curious.

"*Proffessore!*" The man hollered louder.

This isn't my business.

"*Che cosa vuoi?*" Benito stopped and turned, and Irem pressed herself tight against a door to a closed store. The building was unlit, and she prayed the shadows were thick enough to hide her. Benito, who'd been so good to her all day, certainly wouldn't invite her back to the site or hand over a key to the gate if he thought she was a busybody, poking her nose where it didn't belong.

"*Stai lavorando oggi ...*" The stranger said to Benito.

Christ on a tricycle! Why did they have to speak Italian? Irem made out the word "work," *lavorando*. Maybe they talked about the dig.

The man spoke loud and fast, and Irem imagined spit flying from his mouth. He gestured, too. "*Attila? Chiudere?*"

Attila, okay, they were definitely talking about the site. Irem's mind churned. Benito had told her his team consisted of the Garcias and himself, small to keep it quiet. Well, she knew and so did Levent, and maybe the vintner who was footing the bills. So who was *this* guy? And why would he know about it?

Not my business, she told herself again. *Not my business.* But she couldn't run along to her hotel right now—not without risking being spotted and her curiosity left unsated.

"*No so,*" Benito answered. "*Chiudere, spero.*"

Irem got the first part: "I do not know."

The stranger threw his hands to his sides, then made a fist with his right and slapped it against his left palm. Was he threatening Benito? The conversation in the restaurant flooded back to her… about artifact looting and find-stealing, the danger and competition. *"Una grande affare,"* Benito had said to her. Finding the tomb of Attila the Hun was a very big deal.

Who the hell was the stranger to Benito? Once more Irem told herself it was not her concern. A tourist, she was here for her brother's wedding, to see the fountain, the Basilica, to buy a knickknack for her mother, to fly back home white-knuckled on a hated airplane and go back to work in the Field Museum, archiving things way the hell less interesting than the bones of a world-famous barbarian.

The stranger spoke again, faster, some of the words sounding angry.

Irem wished she had studied the Italian phrasebook more diligently and taken a second pass through *Italian for Dummies*. She thought the stranger had just told Benito to take his time working on the dig.

Lento. That was slow, right?

Lightning flickered overhead, and the soft rumble of thunder echoed off the building's facade. Irem felt the wooden door frame against her hands tremble. She trembled a little too, from nerves. *What the bloody blue hell am I doing, eavesdropping on my future brother-in-law?*

When Benito turned east again, his back to her now and the conversation apparently concluded, she nearly pushed off and ran in the opposite direction. But she waited, kept watching, and swallowed hard when the stranger loudly said:

"Aspetta mi soldi."

Benito whirled back to face the man.

She comprehended the word *soldi*. It meant money. Irem held her breath, grateful when the lights of a nearby building went out, thickening the darkness. A stoop-shouldered man exited the door to her left, locked it, and nodded politely to Benito and the stranger, then ambled west, right in front of her and apparently not seeing her. Benito and the stranger watched the bent man until he reached the corner and turned north on Marsala.

Again the stranger mentioned Attila and money. She picked out a few other words: *Concentra...* concentrate, focus. *Marito...* husband. *Sicuro...* secure, safe. What the four dozen shades of bloody bright blue hell were they talking about?

Irem dug her fingers into a crack in the wood, felt it tremble again when another rumble of thunder reverberated in the canyon of buildings. Rain started, slow fat drops that pat-a-tat-tatted against the sidewalk. She saw the stranger reach into his coat and retrieve something and thrust it at Benito.

It didn't matter the currency, Irem recognized a folded wad of money. *Sweet Jesus on a skateboard!* She nearly said aloud.

Benito took the money and stuffed it into the front pocket of his jeans.

Their verbal exchange continued.

Something about "only for the Scourge of God," Irem picked out.

The rain came harder, she lost the conversation, and Benito turned up the collar of his jacket and resumed his course to the east, his feet slap-slapping against the sidewalk. Irem had stayed dry because of the building's overhang. But that was about to change, as it was time for her to go. She saw the stranger look in her direction.

Did he see her?

When the lightning lanced directly overhead, she got a glimpse of his face. Square, with a wide thick nose, deep-set eyes. He might have a beard, a short one, but the image was too quick, like something illuminated by a camera flash. Young... she got the sense he was young. Irem held her breath again and heard her heart thrumming in her ears.

"*Chi c'è?*"

Is anyone there? Who is there? Irem knew he'd asked something like that.

Laughter came from the west, three women under umbrellas on the corner. They started down the sidewalk.

One of them waved to the stranger. He turned at the intersection and shuffled away, hunching his shoulders as if that might help keep him from getting soaked.

Irem couldn't see Benito. He must have turned a different corner and was on his way to his apartment on Vincenza... with a wad of euros or whatever currency was in his pocket. She should go back to her hotel and take a warm shower, forget about what she'd just witnessed—as she couldn't truly be sure just what she had seen. Should leave... but that wasn't what she opted to do.

This is none of my business.

When the trio of women passed her—they were middle-aged, all with unbuttoned trench-style raincoats, businesslike dresses underneath, one carrying a briefcase—she waited a beat and fell in behind them. When they got to the intersection of Via Dei Mille, Irem looked right, seeing the man a half block ahead. She paused at the corner streetlight. Irem's hair and clothes were plastered to her, and she was uncomfortably cool.

Truly this is none of my business. What the hell am I doing?

Irem told herself it was because of her brother that she continued to dog the stranger, hugging the buildings and hoping he wouldn't turn and notice her. It was her nature to be inquisitive... and she'd always been protective of Lev, at least until he'd moved away. But it wasn't her brother that kept her following this man. It was Attila the Hun. The stranger had mentioned Attila.

Irem guessed they were parallel to the Termini Station when the man pivoted on the ball of his foot so abruptly she couldn't react.

"*Chi c'è?*" His eyes were daggers sticking her in place. Lights from second floor windows spilled out, and she was sure he could see her. He had one of those beards so short it looked like he'd forgotten to shave. Some found it stylish; Irem thought it made a man look lazy. His nose was crooked, and he had a heavy brow.

"Rowan," she lied. "My name's Rowan." It was the name of another archivist at the Field and the first thing that had floated to her tongue.

His eyes narrowed, and she had the sense he was looking through her.

What was I thinking, following him? My brain's turned to Jell-O.

"Eri Abruzi con Proffessore?"

She shook her head. "No. No I am not." She was pretty sure he'd asked if she was with Dr. Abruzi. "I'm a tourist. *Turista.* Can you point me to the Termini Station? *Indicazioni…* Termini Station. *Lo sonopersi.* Lost." She wasn't lost, but she didn't know what else to say. Her cockiness had vanished when he'd stared her down. And the black belt in hapkido didn't seem so impressive at the moment. There were at least a dozen feet of sidewalk between them.

In one smooth movement he opened his rain slicker and withdrew a gun. She was too far away to try to kick it out of his hand.

"Holy shit!" She spun and ran, zigzagging up the sidewalk, legs pounding. "Shit. Shit. Shit." He wouldn't shoot her, would he? Couldn't shoot her. She was unarmed, no threat to him. A lost tourist looking for the Termini Station.

There was no one else on this street, not in this block or the next that she could see. Probably everyone had retreated inside because of the late hour and the rain that had turned into a deluge.

Was he following her? She wasn't going to risk a peek over her shoulder. Yes, he was following! She heard him shout something and faintly could hear his feet slapping behind her. Then she heard a *crack*. And another.

"Shit!" Irem had watched enough *Law & Order* marathons to know the sound a gun makes.

He was shooting at her on a public street!

She raced around the next corner, back onto Marghera now, feet slamming against the sidewalk, the rain a veritable wall of water. Thunder booming. A car honked, then a second.

Faster!

God, her legs felt on fire, and so heavy. They didn't want to move.

Move!

Then she was back on the corner of Marsala, the street an impressionist painting smudged with gaudy colors amid the dark. Her hotel was a block and a half away. There were people under awnings, standing in the entrances of restaurants.

A line of cars on the street in front of her, headlights and taillights a smear of brightness reflecting off windows and pavement. The rain tat-a-tatting against hoods and awnings, all of it sounding angry. Someone laid on a car horn.

Irem panted and ducked under an awning, where a dozen others crouched, all of them chattering in Italian, the words bees zooming in and out of her ears. More honking. The cars on the street hadn't moved; they must be stalled by an accident. Her hands shaking, she pushed the hair out of her eyes and pulled out her cell phone, turned it on. Did Italy have a 9-1-1? That police officer she'd met—Gregario.

She had his card in her purse, which was in her hotel room. Big fat lot of good his phone number in her purse did her right now. She waited, expecting the man in the stingy-brimmed hat to come around the corner and kill her.

"*Donna, sei tu bene?*" asked a middle-aged gentleman huddling behind her.

"Fine," she said, guessing he asked if she was all right. "*Bene.*"

"*Veramente?*" His woman companion seemed genuinely concerned.

"No," she answered, wondering if they knew English. "I'm not fine, actually. I'm frightened and angry and soaked and plenty of other things. Mostly frightened."

The woman looked at her curiously, clearly not understanding English.

"*Bene,*" Irem said, and the woman smiled.

Rome was supposed to be safe for tourists, right? The Internet and Gregario said so. Pickpockets were the problem. There weren't supposed to be men with guns.

No. I'm not fine at all. Someone just tried to kill me.

NINE
OCTOBER 6

IREM WOKE TO THE SOUND of her cell phone chirping.

Groggily: "Hello."

It was Levent, and it was 11:00 a.m.

"Sis, lunch ... remember?"

"Give me twenty minutes. Ah, better make it thirty." She saw that he'd texted the restaurant's name and address. "Bless you, Lev. Great choice for lunch." Her stomach growled in anticipation.

As soon as she disconnected it chirped again. Maybe Lev decided on a different restaurant.

"Yeah?"

"Miss Irem Madigan of the Field Museum?"

"Uh, yeah."

"You called my desk last night."

"Oh, yes! I did call you, Gregario."

Irem had... as soon as she got back to her hotel room. Gregario had not been there, and so she reported the shooting to another officer.

"Ari. Call me Ari. I was wondering if you had plans for today. We could—"

"I already have plans. I'm meeting my brother for lunch."

"*Meravigliosa*," he said. "I will join you."

Levent always looked great, Irem thought, and today he appeared more like his old self. Maybe it was the comfortable surroundings. He wore jeans and an off-white T-shirt printed with a crisp image of Botticelli's *Birth of Venus*. A navy blue windbreaker was draped over the back of his chair; it was seventy degrees, he didn't need the jacket. But it did look like it might rain again. Irem shuddered at the thought of more rain. She couldn't get last night's rain — and everything it entailed — out of her head.

"Six thirty-five." Levent pointed at her shirt. "Nice."

She raised an eyebrow.

"Terra Rosa Six thirty-five. It's a good shade on you."

When had her brother started referencing colors like he was picking out oil paints? Ah... she remembered him putting a number to her nail polish two days ago.

"Thanks. I got it at Macy's." *From the sale rack in the basement. Quite a few pieces in Terra Rosa Six thirty-five hanging there.*

"One of the few things I miss about Chicago," he said. "Macy's at Christmas, the elaborate window displays." A pause: "And you. I've missed you. And I've —"

"Uh, Lev... see that guy walking in?"

"The policeman? He's headed toward us."

"Yeah, listen, Lev —"

"*Buongiorno*, Miss Irem Madigan!" Gregario was at their table in a few long strides. He grinned and slipped his hat under his arm. "And you are her brother —"

"Levent." Levent stood and shook Gregario's free hand and glanced curiously at Irem before sitting back down.

"Lev, I met Senior Officer Gregar —"

"Ari."

"I met Ari on my way to the Conservatori."

The policeman nodded. "Amazing, your sister is, stopping that pickpocket to retrieve her purse! Broke his jaw with one punch."

Levent's eyebrows rose. "What?"

"Oh, she didn't tell you?" Gregario seemed surprised. "Well, I will tell you as we order, yes? She was most impressive. The entire department is talking about it."

"This I would like to hear," Levent said.

He proceeded to give Levent an abbreviated version of the events as they made their selections and brought everything back to the table.

"Yes, my sister is indeed amazing," Levent said. He selected a seat across from Irem, allowing Gregario to sit next to her.

"And a magnet for misfortune," Gregario continued. "The shooting last night. I read the report a little while ago. Irem must think our city so danger—"

"Shooting?" Levent nearly knocked over his drink.

Irem smiled nervously and held the chunk of the quarter-pounder in her mouth and let the flavor soak into her tongue.

Gregario nodded. "Your sister could have been killed."

"What the hell? Irem—"

Irem wished she was somewhere else. "I should have called you I guess, Lev."

You guess? Levent mouthed, eyes wider than she'd ever seen them.

She quickly told him about walking down the dark street after her late dinner with Benito, about the square-faced man she couldn't see quite clearly enough to pick him out from pictures, the gunshots, running for her life. About the two police who came to interview her after she called.

"It shook me up, the whole thing. I just—"

"It is wrong that Rome treats a visitor this way," Gregario said. "A thief and now a—"

"I'm fine. I turned down the wrong street, that's all. It wasn't lit. Bad neighborhood. I shouldn't have been there. Really. I was walking alone and—"

"You should not have been alone. It would have been my pleasure to share the evening," Gregario said.

Irem had made no mention of the Attila dig to the police who came to the hotel, and scant mention of Benito Abruzi... only that he'd been her dinner companion and that they'd parted company before the incident. "You and me, we will be family. I can trust family," Benito had told her. She wasn't ready to put Benito under law enforcement scrutiny. Not just yet. That might crush Levent and put Attila out of her reach.

Gregario nodded. "I read the report twice. Too dark, the street. Businesses closed, no lights. No security cameras there. And no witnesses. But the officers found spent casings."

"I saw the gun when the lightning flashed. I heard the shots," Irem admitted. "Two shots, I think."

Gregario continued. "Still, my fellows investigate. Truthfully, there is... what is your expression? There is too little to go on."

"What the hell..." Levent hushed. "Benito should have walked you back. That late... what the hell were you thinking? Dark street by yourself?" He looked across to Gregario. "In Chicago she got beat up in the subway. She's a magnet for sure."

"Big city girl, Lev. I went the wrong direction after dinner, that's all. I won't get turned around again. Promise. Let's talk about something else. Like this wonderful lunch." Irem focused on the burger. It tasted like home and heaven and mollified some aching sweet spot in her soul. She chewed it thoughtfully, swallowed, and took a bigger bite.

"Yes. Enough talk of unfortunate and frightening things. A good choice for lunch, Miss Madigan." Gregario's eyes sparkled. "I had not been to a McDonald's in months."

"Irem. Call me Irem."

"A fun place this is. Thank you, Irem, Levent, for allowing me to join you." He dug into his Big Mac, eating quickly. "A pleasure, American food with new American friends. I must come here more often."

"In the summer we would have to stand in a long line to get a table here," Levent said. "Though that's mostly because this place has the only public bathroom near the Pantheon." He glanced down at the fish sandwich, large fries, and cookies on his tray. His fingers were wrapped around a cappuccino. "But October, not too bad, no long lines." He took a sip and let out a satisfied sigh. "One euro for this. Anywhere else in the city, I'd have to pay three times that much."

"So that's why you picked McDonald's? The price of coffee?" She wanted to keep her brother occupied so he wouldn't ask her more questions about last night. Irem noticed Gregario hadn't taken his eyes off her. He really was good looking.

"Coffee? Cappuccino. Good cappuccino." Levent scowled. "One euro cappuccino. And served in a good neighborhood, where you can walk alone."

Irem ate more of the sandwich. *So delicious.* But did it really taste all that good, or was she just so set in her ways she needed this like a fix? An addict? *Maybe I'm a fast-foodaholic.*

Gregario finished his sandwich and pulled a pen and a business card from his pocket, and started scribbling. "This is my personal cell phone, Irem. You can call it anytime."

She took it. "Thanks, but I—"

"I came to lunch just to see you, make sure you were all right, and so I could ask you out properly. Face to face, best invitation, yes? Face to face?"

"I—"

"So I am asking you out properly. Tomorrow night?"

Levent cut in. "My fiancé is fixing dinner for us."

Irem feared he would invite the policeman to join them.

"The next evening then—"

"Is my wedding day," Levent continued, "so I claim that, too. But the nights after, the ninth, tenth, and eleventh. Irem has nothing those evenings. The twelfth, thirteenth—"

Thanks for speaking for me. Irem put the card in her pocket.

"The ninth then, yes?" Gregario said. "And then maybe those other nights, too, if you like my company. Please call me on this number, and we will select a time. A proper meal, at our leisure. I hate to hurry now, but I spent most of my lunch break just getting here. I cannot miss the department meeting." He scooted back from the table. "Please call me. That way I will not be a pest, calling you so often. Please call me, text me, and I will take you to my favorite restaurant, La Pergola at the Cavalieri. It is in a very good neighborhood. No one will snatch your purse or shoot at you."

"Uh, sure," Irem said. "I'd like that. The ninth." *Did I just say 'yes' to a date?*

He smiled wider. His teeth were perfect.

Levent whistled softly after Gregario left. "La Pergola. That will set him back a good part of his paycheck. Sixth floor of the hotel, gorgeous view, three-star cuisine. He wants to impress you. Good that you're going out with a cop. Safer for you. Protection."

"I don't need —"

"Alone, at night. What were you —"

"I'm done talking about last night."

"Fine." Levent glared. "Then spill about the pickpocket."

"*Borseggiatore*," she said.

"What?"

"*Borseggiatore*. It means pickpocket, a specialized *ladro*."

"I know what a *ladro* is. What's this about flattening the *Borseggiatore* in an alley, breaking his jaw? Spill. This lunch break will last as long as the conversation needs to take to get it all out of you. When you're done spilling on the *Borseggiatore* you're going to tell me — again — about almost getting killed last night. And then you're going to tackle the Ronnie issue, the break-up that got you to step on a plane and come to my wedding."

Irem caved and elaborated about the thief and the shooter, but she still didn't mention Benito meeting the square-faced man. She'd talk to Benito first. But would that conversation come before they found Attila's grave? What lengths would she go to for the chance to touch history?

"How much do you really know about Benito Abruzi?" Irem fixed him with a steely gaze. What if he has secrets, Lev, things he keeps from you?"

Levent grinned. "Everyone has secrets, Irem."

TEN

IREM PAUSED AS AN ELDERLY man at a neighboring table talked about his blood thinner medications with his companion, who was surfing something on her phone.

"Spill, Irem. You're not done. The break-up?"

"I got mugged, the brown line, Armitage Station, late one night almost four years ago."

He sat back and locked eyes with her.

"It pissed me off, you know, being a victim. Bruises, money lost, expensive cell phone lost, a nightmare replacing credit cards and everything. Live in the city my whole life and avoid trouble. But that one night—"

"—and what's that got to do with—"

"I took a self-defense course. Ronnie was the teacher. He was engaged at the time, but I... we..."

"You slept with him."

She didn't answer that.

"And he said he loved you, dumped the fiancée for you," Levent continued.

"Yeah."

Levent sipped at his third cappuccino.

"We moved in together pretty fast. It was comfortable. Last spring, three years together, he proposed. Three years. I thought it was gonna be forever." She didn't tell Lev about the wedding gown in a box in her closet and the tossed invitations and the visions of one or two kids and maybe moving to the suburbs. Or of the bridesmaids she uninvited — and who, thank God, were able to return their Chicago Bears blue dresses.

"Three fucking years we lived together. I thought everything was perfect. *Perfetto*. Then he started seeing another one of his students." *Younger.* "I found out by accident. Answered his cell when he was in the shower. Then I scrolled all the texts."

"So that was it then?"

"Yeah."

"No second chance for him?"

"He didn't ask for a second chance. And I wouldn't have given him one." She didn't mention that Ronnie had admitted there'd been more women, that apparently he'd never been exclusive. "Yeah, that was it. So then I found something else... a nice one bedroom on West Lake, thirteen hundred a month, five hundred square feet; it's a good building. I win. I've got my freedom and a black belt in hapkido."

"*Merdoso.*"

"You're being polite," Irem said. "Ronnie's worse than that. *Figlio di troia.*"

"*Stronzo,*" he cut back. "*Testa di cazzo.*"

"Better." Irem had learned the Italian curse words first. "I just thought that he was the one, ya know? I think, maybe, he really did love me in a way. I think he got scared of a commitment. It took three nights out drinking with Rowan to realize I wasn't the problem." Actually, three nights *getting drunk* with Rowan. Irem drained her soda with a noisy sucking sound.

"You'll find someone else."

"Maybe. But I'm fine with my life just the way it is." Not wholly, she thought. It was lonely in her apartment after three-plus years *living with Ronnie*. "*Single fits me just fine.*" I need a cat.

Levent shook his head, curls bouncing. "You need someone, sis. I found Benito, and I wasn't looking. You're beautiful. Smart. Beautiful. Funny. Wear six thirty-five all the time. Beautiful. You look great in it. You'll find someone, too. Hell, you already found someone, a handsome police officer who is going to take you to an expensive restaurant. He is smitten, I think. Maybe you will find love in Italy just like I did."

"I don't need an expensive restaurant. I'm happy with Mickey D's." She fixed him with a frown. "And I'm done with relationships, especially a long-distance one."

"He seems charming. *One* date."

Irem changed the subject. "Honestly, Lev, you don't intend to come back to Chicago... ever? Sure, Italy seems great and all. And you're marrying an Italian." *An Italian with too many years on him and apparently a shady side.* "But Chicago is home. Family, you know. At least come for a visit."

Levent grew serious. "I've lived here four years, and this civil union counts as marriage for citizenship. I've got all the paperwork filled out, and I'm legally changing my last name to Abruzi. I'll send in all the documents after our wedding. I'm going to be a citizen here, sis. It's what I want. Be happy for me. This is home. *Casa mia.*"

"I am," she said, "happy for you." But was she? What was Levent marrying into? Numb, she settled on. *I'm numb with all of this.* Maybe she should have come to Italy when he'd initially asked four years ago. Maybe she could have talked sense into him then about moving back home. Maybe with her nudge fate would have given him a different path and he never would have met the archaeologist.

And she would have never been teased with Attila the Hun.

"There's no test I have to take, and no requirement to speak Italian, although I'm fluent. I just read Michael Connelly's latest Harry Bosch book in Italian. Natural for me now. Are you still reading fantasy and science fiction? Andrea Camilleri, she's good. You'd like her stuff. I've been so into mysteries lately and —"

Irem wiggled her cup. "I'm going for one more refill. Be right back."

When she returned to the table, she also had a double cheeseburger and a small envelope of fries. "Still hungry," she said, noting Levent's raised eyebrows. Who knew when she'd get a good meal like this again? "And, yes, I still read science fiction and fantasy. I have a Mike Resnick paperback in my hotel room."

He tapped the back of her hand. "Tell you what, sis. Benito wants to see Chicago. We'll come for the Blues Festival next June. Can you get us tickets for whoever's playing in the Petrillo Shell? Say... two nights of tickets?"

"Yeah, I can do that. Mom will—"

" —never know that I'm in town. Got it?"

Irem sadly nodded. "Yeah, I got it." Levent "came out" during a family dinner. Dad, displaying bigotry on a level Irem had never seen before, pronounced Lev "a mistake," told him to pack his stuff and get out. Mom just stood there in a mix of grief and shock and said nothing. Irem had her own apartment then, and Levent moved in with her until an efficiency opened a few months later on the floor above.

That coming out night had also thrown a wedge between Irem and her parents, just not as impenetrable a wedge. Things had never been as casual and friendly again, holiday dinners were shorter, and she only stopped by their bar once or twice a month.

"Maybe find out who's at the Crossroads Stage," Levent added. "They still have Soul and R&B Day, right?"

"Oh yeah." Irem loved R&B. "So... Benito likes blues?"

"Well... not yet." Levent folded his sandwich wrapper into a tight square, smoothing the edges. "In our early days he wasn't much into music, but since the Garcias have been working for him—" He chuckled and finished his last fry and folded that paper, too. "It's all oldies rock, and mostly American. Journey, ZZ Top, Led Zeppelin, he listens to. He bought Rush's *Permanent Waves* and Aerosmith's *Toys in the Attic*. Like I said, moldy oldie stuff."

Because he's a moldy oldie? Irem held the words inside.

Neither talked for several minutes, the conversations of the other diners swirling around them. Someone—maybe the restaurant—had music playing; it was soft, sort of like what she'd hear in a Chicago office building elevator. She watched a quartet of middle-aged women pass tourist brochures back and forth. It looked like they were trying to decide what to see next. They were dressed in bold colors, and she wondered if Levent mentally assigned numbers to each shade. They were the only ones who did not have phones out on the table texting and surfing while they chatted.

Irem thought she ought to go see something touristy tomorrow, let Lev show her his city. She should spend as much time with him as possible… that had been her plan before being lured to Benito's dig yesterday. Attila was just so damn intriguing.

"I know your wedding's in two days," she said. "But maybe you can squeeze in a few hours, maybe tomorrow before dinner, to go see something with me? Just a few hours." That would still leave time for Attila.

"Sure. Sure." Levent looked excited. "There is so much to show you. Let's take the whole day. So you and I will see the city tomorrow and the tomorrows after the wedding for as long as you are here." He paused: "Leaving space for all your dinners with the handsome cop."

One date, she mouthed.

"Sis?" Levent poked the back of her hand with his finger. "You're thinking about the dig, aren't you? Take tomorrow and see the amazing things *above* the ground with me. Then go back to digging in the dirt with Benito. I shouldn't have encouraged you to go down there in the first place. My fault. What the hell was I thinking? You would not have been shot at last night if—"

"That'd be nice actually, you and me all day tomorrow and maybe—"

Her phone chirped, and she pulled it out of her pocket.

It was Benito, inviting her underground.

Levent's words from several minutes ago surfaced: "Everyone has secrets."

Irem suspected Benito had a wealth of secrets. Maybe some of them were deadly.

ELEVEN

THIS TIME WHEN IREM TRAVELED the twisting tunnel with Benito it was different. The shadows were darker and they grabbed at her, making it slower going as if she slogged through sludge. She swore the air smelled worse too, dense and not enough oxygen in it, and she feared she might suffocate. Her chest heaved. A panic attack? Because she didn't trust Benito? Because maybe, just maybe, she should have told the cops about him?

Definitely she was having a panic attack; good thing the archaeologist was in front and couldn't watch her unravel. When she'd finally ventured back down to the Chicago subway after the mugging—before taking the hapkido classes—she'd hyperventilated to the point that another passenger called an ambulance, which she stubbornly turned down. She'd come close to hyperventilating on the plane. There were meds for this, right? Paper bags to blow in.

Settle down.

The stone wall vibrated against her hand ever so slightly… something big and heavy was driving past on the street above. She pressed her palm flat against the stone, concentrating only on that sensation and thinking it trembled almost seductively, like a lover's lips on her skin. It put her on the fine edge of anticipation and made the shadows less ominous, the fusty air easier to breathe.

Benito was talking—about Lev and the wedding, the catering at the church and the appetizers planned at the

75

dance bar, the band that would be playing. She didn't join the conversation, as the details of the day weren't interesting to her. Attila was.

This treasure hunt—because that's what she considered it—was a bright flame and she was the moth attracted to it, perhaps dangerously, absolutely addicting.

Then they were going deeper at a sharper angle, and the vibrations no longer reached her, and Benito had stopped talking.

Settle down.

"I had the feeling we were being followed last night," Irem began, thinking conversation might help, the need for noise making her raise the subject. She knew that going underground with the archaeologist had fueled her anxiety. Safer on the surface, right?

But Attila the Hun might be down here. And she'd eagerly accepted the key Benito had pressed into her hand several minutes ago. She'd thrust it deep into her pocket like it was a prize to protect... right next to Gregario's card with his phone numbers on it. Thoughts warred in her head: Attila vs. the thug with the gun; Levent vs. the tonsured archaeologist; discovery of a lifetime vs. safety; common sense vs. this reckless delving.

Pick the delving. Pick Attila the friggin' Hun.

Everything would be simple if she'd instead spent her vacation with Rowan and one or two others in Lake Geneva, Wisconsin, just over the Illinois border. Paddle boat rides, trendy little shops, drinking wine and eating cheese on the screened-in porch at Popeye's down by the lakefront. Staring at the fall colors and listening to the rustling leaves on all the birch trees. It was a tradition of sorts, their little getaway, always after the town's tourist season was done and the cheaper hotel rates kicked in, and this year she'd broken that habit and taken her Turtle Island stash and had come here.

Lake Geneva, Wisconsin, vs. Rome, Italy. Practically nothing beat Wisconsin cheese and that lakeshore. Well, practically nothing until now. Attila trumped just about everything that bumped around in her brain.

Pick the delving.

"You know," Irem continued, "the little goose bumps you get on your neck? Someone watching you. Someone following you. It felt like someone was following us."

"Probably just all my talk about archaeology being dangerous," Benito returned. "I probably spooked you. I would not worry."

"I guess." But his telling her not to worry just made her worry more. *What was he hiding? How many secrets did he have?*

"How was lunch with Lev?"

Was he purposely changing the subject?

"Good," she said. "It was nice. McDonald's. And I always think McDonald's is nice." A pause: "How about your lunch at the university?"

"Boring. With every bite I wanted to get back here. So I hurried them all along."

Settle down.

It felt cooler today in the chamber where the Garcias worked. Irem would wear a jacket on her next foray, should've borrowed Lev's windbreaker. Despite her unease about the square-faced man and Benito, she almost regretted promising tomorrow to her brother. This site was more tempting than a juicy quarter pounder with cheese, and it looked like they were making serious and fast progress. More than half the chamber had been excavated, and strips of plywood covered a section of the floor up against the Scourge of God carved wall.

"We've a surprise for you, Dr. Abruzi," Lacy said softly.

"Wait on it," Santiago told Lacy.

"Surprise?" Benito leaned close to what the pair worked on.

"I dunno," Irem broached as she circled the Garcias to see what they'd found. "Looks like the other skeletons to me." An entire skeleton had been revealed; it looked to be a short man with wide shoulders. On a piece of canvas nearby, hunks of rotting armor and jewelry were laid out. A string-and-peg grid on the far side of the chamber showed where they'd already excavated, and one spot where they intended to.

The stranger last night had wide shoulders like the skeleton.

"I really thought someone was following us, Benito," Irem said. "A big guy with a long slicker and a hat with a stringy brim. The guy who brushed into us on the sidewalk. Him. And then I saw the same guy again watching the restaurant where we ate. He was standing across the street. And I could've sworn he followed you after we split up. It was… creepy. He had this hint of a beard and—"

Benito frowned. "*Che sciocchezze… è tutto frutto della tua immaginazione.*"

"Huh?"

"Oh, sorry. It is all in your imagination, Irem. I don't remember anyone bumping into us last night. And I am enough paranoid I would know if someone followed us."

A shiver raced down her back. *What the hell is he hiding? Something. It feels like something.* He'd talked to the man who'd jostled them, took money from him. *Settle down. Don't push too hard or there'll be no Attila.*

"Doc, we went topside last night a little earlier than you. I saw a big man in a trench coat, hanging around the tourist entrance. He had a small brimmed hat, just like Irem said. He started to follow me and Lacy, then swung around and went the other way. I noticed him 'cause he had a beard like me. Well, not as nice as mine. I didn't like the look of him."

"A hint of a beard," Lacy said. "And I'm with Irem, he looked creepy."

"You are all spooked for no reason," Benito said. "Nothing for concern. Your imagination dances."

"Yeah, I know. No worries." Santiago pointed to the skull. "Definitely another Hun."

Irem noted that the forehead appeared elongated. *What was Benito hiding?*

"Just like the other two skulls." This from Lacy. "So all three skeletons from this room were Huns. Important ones." She nodded toward the canvas and the objects laid out on it. "And the two from the other chamber, Huns, absolutely. No complete bone sets, though close with one of the skeletons. Really close."

Irem pushed the image of the square-faced man to a corner of her mind; she'd revisit the topic with Benito later. Carefully so as not to jeopardize her participation in this. She squatted next to the canvas. The jewelry was stunning.

"Wow. My specialty is documents, but I'd love to archive some of that."

Diadems, bracelets, a horse-head fibula, and coins — which had an image of an elongated bearded face.

"That was battle armor," Santiago told her. "Rotted, the moisture in the ground did a serious number on it. A restorer is going to be busy for a while, and the back side is a total loss. The jewelry's perfect, though. Over there, Doc—" he gestured with a dirt-caked arm. "Take a look. We brought those out this morning. That should be enough provenance, right? To get this protected, dig up Attila."

"Is this my surprise?" Benito asked. "This helmet? It is beautiful."

Irem padded over behind Benito. On the ground behind the thankfully quiet CD player was a helmet in a tray. It was made of metal, and with hammered metal curving horns, a fur strip along the front was horribly deteriorated; the leather flap that extended from the back had partly disintegrated. Despite its sad appearance, it was ornate. Next to it a short, straight sword had an elaborate pommel, and the remnants of a scabbard were underneath it.

"The helmet of someone very important," Benito said. "Of someone close to the Scourge of God."

"Yeah, with the coins — Attila's mug on them. The coins and the helmet and the armor, I'd say we got a lock. The sword... that should seal the deal. One of his generals. Has to be," Santiago said.

"And the skeletons, the skulls," Lacy put in. "Definitely Huns, like I said. Final answer. A hundred and ten percent certain."

"Someone close to Attila," Irem hushed. "Seriously wow."

Lacy laughed. "It wasn't necessarily a good thing to be close to Attila, you know. He killed people who ticked him off. Killed his brother in 445 so he could rule the Huns as a king, not sharing power. He offed his own brother."

Maybe it wasn't a good thing to be close to Benito. Irem pushed the thought away and concentrated on the relics. She had Googled Attila last night while she soaked in the bathtub after the police had left, but hadn't read about the fratricide. She had delved into the Hun's second attack on the Roman Empire in 447, aimed at the south. He'd handily defeated the soldiers on the Utus River. Attila had suffered some serious losses in that campaign, but didn't quit, driving to the Balkans and then into Greece. Later, Roman Emperor Theodosius II tried diplomacy with the Scourge of God, and a treaty eventually was signed… and a hefty tribute paid.

"Attila was a sociopath," Lacy continued. "A monster, tyrant, terrifying brute."

"Oops, you got her started," Santiago said.

"Pillaged. Plundered. Just because he could. He loved destroying things. Okay, so some of the historical records are sketchy, but what there is all paints him the same way."

"Because the records are Roman," Santiago argued. "Attila's enemy. When your enemy writes about you, it isn't going to be roses and—"

"Attila was a piece of shit. His army killed twenty thousand in what's now France. And the Romans had paid him to do it. They hired Attila… then he turned and went after them next. Naissus, he wanted the gold. He broke the walls, and the Romans couldn't stop him. At one point when the Romans stood up to him, they outnumbered the Huns four to one."

"And Attila still beat them," Benito put in.

Lacy looked smug. "Like I said, a shitbird. He had lassos and nets, weapons the Romans weren't used to. Better military tactics. And madness, I'm sure. Rome had no answer for his tactics. Some of Attila's own men were so fearful they deserted. And when he caught the deserters… he impaled them."

Santiago brushed his hands against his pants. "But historians say there was a human side, that he supposedly was a loving father."

Lacy snorted.

The Hun was a real bastard, Irem thought. *Tu bastardo.* Attila and his force had looted Padua, Milan, Aquileia. He would have conquered all of Italy if Pope Leo hadn't sent a delegation that pleaded for mercy... and brought a good deal of wealth to buy peace. Although some think the weather was involved in their exodus. Tree rings showed a few years of cold, wet weather that would have played havoc with all the horses, might have contributed to the Hun's decision to back down. Attila died in 453... to poison, too much food and alcohol, venereal disease... the cause debated. The cause could likely be defined if Benito found the bones. He supposedly was buried in a big sarcophagus crammed with treasure, the tomb builders executed so the grave would never be found.

"Never" might be incorrect. Perhaps Benito, Santiago, and Lacy were truly close to finding it. Irem wanted a piece of this so bad. She could keep her mouth shut about Benito and the man with the gun if it meant she'd get her piece.

"*Lei e di grande aiuto,*" Benito said, putting a hand on Santiago's shoulder. He looked at Lacy. "Both of you. I would still be digging in the first chamber if I did not have your help."

"But—" Santiago said. "There's a 'but' coming, right, Doc?"

"I worry that you work too fast. When I am not here, I think you speed through this. I can tell by the edges, and the amount you have dug. Too fast, Santiago. Look at all the dirt piled up against the walls. You've not taken it out. You dig too fast. You're not taking enough care."

Irem saw Santiago bristle. Lacy shook her head and kept working.

"What's too fast, Doc?" Santiago rubbed at a spot on his jeans and looked from the skeleton to the armor pieces. He folded his arms across his chest and made a huffing sound. "Fast? You've been holding us back, it feels deliberate, and—"

"Easy, Sant—" Lacy urged. "Don't—"

"Don't what? Piss him off? I ain't gonna piss him off. I'm working my ass off for him." Santiago closed his eyes. "For us. Working my ass off for us. Doc, look, we are working fast. I admit it. We're slaving at this. But it's not *too* fast." He nodded toward Irem. "And we shouldn't be talking about this with—"

"Irem is family to me," Benito said. "What you say to me, you can say to—"

"Okay. Fine. Have it your way. This is your show." Santiago had a sharpness to his voice. "We're taking great care with all of this, Doc. But, yeah, we're working fast, maybe cutting a corner or two."

"Or three," Lacy whispered. "Little corners. Only little bitty corners."

"We want to get behind the wall *now*. All the carvings on that wall… the Latin says Attila is back there. And I found the way."

"What?" Benito's face showed shock.

Irem sucked in a breath and felt her heart race.

"Yeah, that's the surprise, not the helmet. I found the way behind the wall. I'd be there today, right now, but there was this body to finish. Because we are taking care with this whole site. But we'll finish this body today, in another few hours. Then let's go behind the wall. Let's get provenance for this site, get it protected. Let's reveal the Scourge of God. A great wedding present, huh? Then let's get more diggers down here to finish and get us onto the next one."

"The next one?" Irem asked too softly for anyone to hear.

"Attila is *the* prize, Santiago," Benito said.

"Sure. A great prize. Let's nab it. I'll pay off my loans in a heartbeat with books and lectures when I get back to California. In fact—"

"We'll talk about this later." Benito's face looked harsh in the light. "This way behind that you've found—" He looked at the pieces of plywood on the floor. "*Madonna mia!*"

The air tasted thick again, and Irem felt her chest tighten.

"I said I found the way behind the wall." Santiago stepped over to the pieces of plywood that extended across the floor up against the carved wall. He bent and picked them up. "Had a helluva time bringing this plywood down through the tunnel. Did it to surprise you." A square yard of earth had been worked on, revealing steps leading down into a well of darkness. The wood had hidden the opening of a stairway.

"They come open on the other side, Dr. Abruzi," Lacy explained. "We took a look. A quick look. There's a room down there. A room on the other side of this wall."

"How could you—" Benito's face was red.

"We didn't go all the way. We didn't dig. We just *looked*." Santiago set his hands against his hips. "And then I brought down plywood to make it a surprise... no easy matter... and put it over the hole. Like I said, I wanted to surprise you."

"I didn't," Lacy said. "Surprise you, yes. But I didn't want to futz with the plywood. I thought that was silly. But we really did want to surprise you." A pause: "I helped Sant dig out the dirt covering the top steps. And I did help him haul some of the dirt out of here. It was only a foot or so thick, most of the stairs were open under it. Yeah, we haven't hauled *all* the dirt out that was covering this skeleton, but give us a break, Dr. Abruzi."

"Like I said, we just *looked*," Santiago repeated, the words spaced staccato short. "Saved the honors for you, Doc."

Benito pulled out his flashlight and shone the beam down into the hole. "How did you find the stairs?"

"How do you think?" Santiago had a smug look on his face.

"The metal detector," Benito said.

"Yeah, we thought there was another skeleton up against the wall, jewelry on it. That's why we had marked it out. But it was coins, not jewelry. They're inlaid in the steps, the coins. See? A pattern to them. That's what the detector picked up."

"*Madonna mia!* You should have waited, Santiago."

"I did wait, Doc. Just a quick peek, that's all I took. And you can thank me, by the way."

"Thank you, Santiago. This is—"

This is seductive, addicting, dangerous, Irem thought.

"—your dig. Yeah, I get that. But you're not here all the time. Lecturing at the university. Today a luncheon. Day after tomorrow a wedding. We work when you're gone those hours. Maybe work faster when you're gone. Okay, yeah, definitely faster. But like I said, that section, I thought it was another skeleton. Finding those stairs was a miraculous accident and—"

"So we're finishing up this chamber. Today, I hope," Lacy said. "Or more likely tomorrow to get the dirt and artifacts hauled out. Shoot some video on your camera." Irem could tell Lacy was trying to ease the tension. "We couldn't sleep last night, started real early, around four. My fingers and toes are crossed we get this fellow here done." She brushed a strand of hair out of her eyes. Her face was smudged with dirt. "And, yeah, we're working fast. But we're not really cutting many corners. Not any significant ones." Softer: "Just itty bitty ones."

"We've not broken a single piece, not cracked a finger bone," Santiago said. "But we are anxious to see Attila. Go ahead, Doc. Go down the stairs and say hello to the Scourge of God. You can be pissed at me all you want. *Incazzato* as you say. But *I* found the way to your prize. *I* got you in the history books. *I* did that."

"*Us,*" Lacy whispered. "You got us into the history books."

Irem fought for breath. This time it wasn't a panic attack. It was anticipation. Her heart thrummed loudly in her ears as she crept over to stand next to Benito and gazed at the coin-dotted steps his flashlight beam touched. Some of the coins had been cut in half. There was a pattern to them. Letters? They looked familiar. Latin. She mentally translated them, one word every other step. From her vantage she could only clearly read two words: *Numquam floret.* It never blooms.

Benito audibly pulled in a deep breath and started down.

TWELVE

LACY GRABBED THE SMALL VIDEO camera, and Santiago took a pair of flashlights. Irem watched the Garcias follow Benito down the steps, their footfalls careful in an attempt to not walk on the coins, and pant legs making a whispery shush-shushing sound. Then they were out of sight, their excited conversation drifting up and sounding like a breeze rustling dry leaves. Irem stared at the steps, seeing moving globs of light. She should go after them.

Would go after them.

She studied the steps she could read from her vantage, at the Latin words the embedded coins spelled out:

Numquam floret.

Attila the Hun could be so very close.

She could touch history, *be* history with this discovery.

The Field Museum, her brother, the colors and sounds and beauty of Rome, the square-faced man with the gun... all of that was pushed to the back of her mind.

Attila the Hun.

The Scourge of God.

She would go after them, of course, down the steps, which she thought should be covered and protected, not walked on. The others had been too excited to consider that perhaps. Her heart slammed in anticipation. But she held back. She'd wait a few minutes and let them revel in whatever discovery was at the bottom. It was their dig after all; she was just a guest.

A guest alone in *this* chamber.

Her mouth went desert dry at the possibilities beyond those steps.

Attila.

Dear God, could the bones of Attila the Hun really be down there on the other side of this wall? She wanted to call her friends in the archives at the Field, call Lev, text everyone. She wanted to follow Benito and Lacy and Santiago right now. But she still held back.

Irem thrust a hand in her pocket and felt for the key that Benito had given her—her ticket to the best carnival ride in the world. Amazing that she was here, under Rome, in history's belly. Invited. World-shaking news if the warlord's remains were here. Irem was part of this.

She reached in her other pocket and retrieved her cell phone. Irem was well aware no signal would reach here. She wanted it for the camera. Benito had told her "no pictures," though clearly the Garcias had been filming the dig for the archaeologist. What would it hurt for her to take pictures, too? It would be something wonderful to show her fellow archivists back in Chicago, her own record of this historical find. And with the archaeologists down the stairs, they wouldn't know. Her secret. Souvenirs that would take up no space in her apartment.

Irem hurried, snapping picture after picture of the wall with the carvings, making sure she got all of it. She didn't need the flash because the pole lights blazed over the excavation. Then she took pictures of the latest skeleton, close ups, and the array of jewelry on the canvas, then a few of the helmet, and one of the top step with coins forming the Latin word *numquam* before she put the phone back in her pocket. The coins bore the visage of Attila—so Santiago had said, and she'd taken a few close ups of them. She felt guilty and utterly pleased at the same time.

She put her phone back and took one of the small, bright flashlights, turned it on and shone it down the stairs. Irem stepped gingerly, reading in a whisper as she went.

"*Numquam floret quo ambulau. Flagellum Dei*," she said. "It never blooms where I have walked. The Scourge of God."

"Beyond it being a dead language, Latin is an odd one." Benito was at the bottom of the stairs looking up at her. "I was wondering if you would join us, Irem."

"I didn't want to intrude," she said truthfully. "This is your dig. I wanted to give you some time alone with—" With what? With nothing, it looked like. Give them some time alone with absolutely nothing.

"I believe the tomb builders were trying to set down one of Attila's famous quotes, what you just read on the steps: 'There, where I have passed, the grass will never grow again.' *Numquam floret quo ambulau* is close." Benito took her elbow and helped her down the last step, which was about two feet higher than the floor.

The chamber was roughly forty feet square, and Irem guessed it was about twenty feet deeper into the earth than the space above. The flashlights weren't adequate to keep the darkness at bay, everything the shade of dried mud and looking like the setting for a horror movie. The air smelled old and stuffy, damp, and she saw motes of dust hanging suspended in the beam of her flashlight.

"It's Al Capone's vault," Irem said flatly after she had stepped forward and pointed her beam at every corner.

"Huh?" This from Lacy, who was also angling her beam from one corner to the next.

"Al Capone's vault. More than thirty years ago Geraldo Rivera had a live television special, going down under Chicago into supposedly one of Al Capone's vaults. We watched a recording of it in one of my classes at Purdue. He spent most of the program tantalizing viewers with all the things that might be inside—money, stolen goods, bootlegging equipment, all together a possible fortune. His crew broke through a wall, went down a tunnel, and found nothing. Oh, it was a vault. Geraldo got that part right. And maybe once upon a time it had belonged to Al Capone. But there was absolutely nothing in it."

"Huh." Lacy said.

"Zippo. Nada. Then there was Zahi Hawass, who opened a mummy's tomb on the History Channel," Irem said, frowning. "All the buildup, and it was empty. Geraldo and Hawass should be here."

It wasn't *wholly* empty, she mentally corrected; it was filled with disappointment. It was like a lottery ticket—for that time between when you buy the ticket and the numbers are drawn and you discover you've wasted three dollars. In the between time you got to dream. Irem dreamed that way every week when she plopped down her money at a corner convenience store and picked the same numbers for the lottery ticket.

"A three dollar busted dream," she whispered, deciding she should have told the policeman about Benito talking to the square-faced man.

Benito clearly didn't share her disenchantment. He was grinning, and Lacy's eyes were wide. Santiago's face was angled down at the floor, and he paced along the walls, the beams from his two flashlights stabbing at the shadows. The archaeologists didn't look disappointed at all.

"Of course, it *looks* empty," Benito said. "The chambers above that we excavated also *looked* empty. To Santiago: "Please—"

"Sure, Doc." Santiago gingerly climbed the steps, the beams from his flashlights bouncing and making the shadows cavort eerily.

"Lacy, I want this recorded. Get pictures with my video camera."

Irem remembered his "no photographs" comment from previously. Apparently that only applied to her and his assistants and confirmed that the camera was his. Made some sense, she guessed. Normally archaeologists took pictures of everything in situ as a dig progresses.

Benito looked at Irem and crooked his head. "What did you think we'd find?"

"I dunno. I thought there'd be—" Irem let out a big sigh. "*Something* to see down here. I dunno. Treasure. Piles of it. A coffin befitting a king, and statues—maybe the Hun equivalent to shabtis. Or at least the remnants of something that showed someone had already been through here and looted. Put on a John Williams soundtrack. I wanted you to be right and—"

"I am right," Benito said.

"You've seen too many movies, Miss Madigan," Lacy told her. She pointed up, and Irem looked.

The ceiling was uneven like the floor, rough and scalloped in places as if a big ice cream scoop had been used to carve it out. Woody threads extended down from the ceiling, like wisps of hair on an old soul's head. One square patch near the center was devoid of the threads.

"Most of Attila's followers died in battle," Lacy said, as she aimed the video camera at the ceiling. "Or to venereal diseases, the stories go. Two skeletons from that last room showed slashes into the bone, probably from deep, heavy sword wounds. The other skeleton... not a mark on it, so maybe VD. But they were important, those skeletons. The helmet and jewelry tell us that. In life those people had been important."

"*Importante*," Benito said. "Attila didn't have the glory of dying from battle. He died on the night he wedded Ildiko. Some say a hemorrhage, or he drank too much and choked on his bloody vomit. Some say Ildiko poisoned him, and that his soldiers in turn killed her."

"Do you read George R. R. Martin?" This from Santiago, who was coming down the steps, flashlights tucked under his arm, metal detector in his hands. Before Irem could answer—indeed she'd read the Game of Thrones series—he went on. "Some fans think maybe he got the idea for Joffrey Baratheon's death scene from Attila and Ildiko."

Irem was still perplexed why they weren't disappointed in the empty chamber.

"Not much is known about her, Ildiko," Lacy supplied. She held the camera even with the flashlight and recorded the rest of the room. "But her name suggests she was Gothic, East Germanic. Anyway, Attila's body, according to historical records, was found drenched in blood, was cleaned, and put on display in a big silk tent. I've seen transcripts of accounts that claimed his warriors came in to pay their respects, a day of grief. They ripped hair from their heads and mutilated themselves... all to guarantee that their warlord was mourned by the sacrifices of his men and not the tears of his women. I think—"

Benito interrupted: "Some think he was buried in Hungary, although the accounts we studied strongly hinted at Italy, Rome in particular. Some say he was buried in the steppes and hundreds of horses trampled the grave to hide it. Another says a river was diverted to run over it and hide it forever so the wealth buried with him would never be discovered. What the tales have in common, and what is a consensus among historians, is that the burial site exists and could be one of the most significant lost treasures." A pause: "And that the site was very well concealed."

This far under Rome fit the "very well concealed" part, Irem agreed.

"Let's see if the bone shroud was right, Doc." Santiago passed one of his flashlights to Benito; the archaeologist held a flashlight in each hand.

Benito pointed with the beams to the center of the chamber, and Santiago turned on the metal detector, held it low, and started in an achingly slow sweeping pattern. Lacy filmed it.

"There are records—enough that many scholars are forced to agree—that Attila was likely buried in a triple-ply coffin. The bone shroud suggests that. One layer silver, another gold, and the outer layer iron," Benito said. "The silver and gold symbolizing Attila's status of a king, the iron denoting his power and strength."

"Iron," Santiago said. "A strong reading."

Irem sucked in a breath and watched him manipulate controls on the detector.

"Silver," Santiago said. "And gold." He stood and faced Benito. "Lots of gold, Doc. It's about five feet down."

"Oh God! Oh God! Oh God!" Lacy said. She patted her chest with her fist, the flashlight in it sweeping crazily. She spun and hugged Benito, almost dropped the camera. "This really is it, isn't it, Dr. Abruzi?"

"*Lo spero*. I hope so," Benito said softly. "Yes, I think very much so. Yes. Yes." His eyes were wide and glistening.

90

He mouthed something. Irem thought perhaps he was praying.

Santiago walked slowly around the room, the detector held just above the ground. It softly clicked. "More gold over here, about a foot and a half, maybe two, down. Scattered."

"The volcanic soil of Rome was perfect for all the catacombs," Lacy said, finally releasing Benito. "Easy to dig into, but hardening after a fashion when exposed to the elements. The Huns could have dug down here, maybe off a tunnel already existing, and —"

"Probably collapsed their large tunnel," Benito mused. "They could not have brought anything of significant size down through the serpent path we traveled to find this. That path? Maybe some previous treasure hunter was responsible for it. Maybe an underground stream carved it. Or maybe followers looking to pay their respects to their warlord were responsible. Hell, maybe even Huns who later came to bury those generals. Maybe they were buried after Attila." He paced. "Collapsed. Probably a large tunnel. Had to be a wide tunnel for horses to drag, or an arrangement like a well, pulleys and ropes." He scratched at the side of his head and looked at the square patch in the ceiling devoid of threads. "Maybe a well, and they lowered a coffin down through it. Maybe they brought it down this way. That is something to puzzle out later, eh?"

"Hey, Doc, I'm picking up a lot of gold. Here and here, and over here. Some silver. About four feet down. Mostly gold." Santiago turned off the metal detector. Irem couldn't see his face, the beams from the flashlights all pointed at the ground. But she could hear the excitement in Santiago's voice. "This could be the fucking motherlode, Doc."

"Language," Benito said.

"I'm just saying," Santiago kicked back at Benito. "I'm just fucking saying." Then he let out a whoop.

Irem shivered. Gold, silver, maybe Attila's skeleton, the find of a lifetime, and she stood on top of it. She was feeling myriad emotions — giddiness, excitement, and curiosity at what was under this dirt. Her breath came fast, and she wished there was a paper bag to breathe into.

The square-faced man had said something about Attila to Benito. Gave Benito money. What had the wad of money been for? Something related to this dig?

Was Benito selling some of the artifacts? Would he sell a piece of Attila? Suddenly that made sense. Benito could earn a significant chunk of change for a bracelet or two. No wonder he claimed ignorance of the man in the stingy-brimmed hat. Selling artifacts was wrong—illegal and immoral. On that age-old scale of one to ten... how wrong? Should she go to the authorities? Call Gregario?

Not just yet in any event. She wouldn't do anything that might jeopardize her chance to see Attila.

Illegal and immoral... she could tolerate some of that to be in the shadow of the Scourge of God, couldn't she?

THIRTEEN
OCTOBER 7

"IT NEVER BLOOMS WHERE I have walked," she whispered. "There, where I have passed, the grass will never grow again." The quotes had stuck with her, memorable and sounding foreboding.

"A lament of a dog walker?" Levent mused.

Irem held her phone out and took a picture of her brother. It didn't look like he'd aged at all since leaving the States, but that was only four years ago. He looked so young and happy—happier than he'd been in Chicago, boyish, his eyes brighter, and his smile genuine. Rome had certainly agreed with him, and she decided in this instant to never ask him to "move back home." He'd not left much family behind anyway... parents who disapproved, and, of course, her. Any other relatives were scattered in Turkey and Ireland.

"You're real funny, Lev. Should've been a comedian. The first saying was found inscribed in Benito's dig, written in coins, on steps... but he thinks it translates a quote attributed to Attila. The warlord supposedly said: 'There, where I have passed, the grass will never grow again.' And now I've got the phrases running through my head like some catchy pop music earworm."

"I still think it sounds like something a dog walker would say, eh?" Levent raised an eyebrow, and she took another picture. "How about you dwell on the street level, sis? At least for a little while. I get enough of the underground talk from my Benito. That's practically all he's been spewing lately. Attila this. Attila that. All he talked about last night. Did you know that the Huns ate raw meat? Put a slab on the back of their horse and rode for hours, the action and the heat tenderizing it. Benito told me that. He's obsessed with Attila and the tunnel with its musty air. The air is better above ground, sister dear. I tell that to my Benito sometimes—about the air being better. And so are the things to show you. Spectacular." He waved his arm like a music conductor.

Irem agreed that Rome above ground was spectacular, but she had a difficult time focusing on it. Right now her body was in the Pantheon, but her thoughts kept dipping into the underground, mentally traversing the serpentine tunnel to the dig site and imagining the scent of the old, close air. She touched the key in her pocket. She could be there—right now, "playing in the dirt," as Benito called it. As much as she loved her brother—and she dearly loved him with all her heart, she'd like to be looking for the Scourge of God's bones.

She'd come to Italy to shake off a bad relationship, and more to see her brother and stand up for him at his wedding. Not to play in the dirt. And yet—and yet that was where her thoughts centered.

When they'd come up last night, they were all giddy and chattering about the possibilities. Santiago and Lacy were practically out of breath from the excitement and said they were going to celebrate with a bottle of red wine at Osteria Bonelli.

"The tourists don't know about the place," Lacy had said. "Not the best of neighborhoods. The menu's on a chalkboard, in Italian, and everything's so good you lick the plate."

"And cheap with a capital CHEAP," Santiago had added. "Want to join us? We order for each other. It's fun. A quick stop at our itty bitty apartment—" Santiago pointed to a building across the street. Convenient to rent so close to the dig, Irem thought. But the building looked old and the windows narrow. A green and white striped canopy stretched across the front, dressing it up. "I want to change clothes. Then we'll stuff our faces."

Benito had accepted, but Irem declined. It was after eight, she was tired, and took a cab back to her hotel. Now she regretted that decision, as she might have heard more interesting tidbits about Attila the Hun and his forces. What was the saying: sleep was overrated. What had she missed by turning in early?

The archaeologists had told her they were going to finish the chamber with the generals today. Make sure that they'd missed nothing, carry away the bones and artifacts and some of the dirt, and then the day following the wedding go after what Santiago kept calling "the motherload" — digging the new chamber to see if Attila truly was there. She was invited.

She had a key in her pocket.

Benito had mentioned more than once that because of the Scourge of God there'd be no honeymoon for a while. Five feet down was a reading of iron and gold and silver. It would take a while to carefully dig that.

There were not enough days in her vacation.

Irem was a history junkie, and Benito and his bone tapestry and the Attila dig provided a nonstop heady fix that reached to some sweet spot deep in her heart. History was all she had now, she mused. Her relationship with Ronnie was history. Her and Levent's sojourns in Chi-Town... that became history when he boarded the plane to Italy four years ago.

Everything she truly loved was history.

Should she put her career as an archivist in the history column too? She'd been unhappy ever since the split with Ronnie... until she came to Rome. Why did she need to return to the Field and her no-any-time-in-the-near-future-chance-for-a-promotion job? She had no intention of living in Italy, not permanently. But maybe... just maybe... she could stay long enough to see the Attila dig through to the end with Benito, Lacy, and Santiago. She could find a job elsewhere when she went back home. There were other museums, and if she could put Attila on her resume the opportunities might be big.

Despite her attempt to concentrate on the Pantheon tour they'd joined, she only half-listened to the guide, her mind too muddled with everything else.

"The Pantheon is the oldest monument standing in Rome." His badge read Antonio Sarli. She guessed him to be in his early sixties, tanned face with lines reminding her of tree bark, crystal blue eyes, a good smile, and a heavily accented deep voice, which fit the surroundings. He brought to mind Paul Newman. When she looked at him straight on, she thought him the spitting image of Newman's headshot on a salad dressing bottle. Antonio's large hands fluttered as he pointed up at the dome. "The original structure was built in 27 B.C. as a temple to the many Roman gods. But Emperor Hadrian, nearly one hundred and fifty years later, ordered it demolished. What we are inside now was built in its place. And it remains the oldest structure in our grand city."

She noticed he had polished black leather shoes and cuffed pants that were probably stylish in an earlier era. Irem took his picture, and then a few pictures of the rest of the group.

There were nearly three dozen people in this tour, and she and Lev were near the front. They'd eaten breakfast at McDonald's across the street and were first in line when the Pantheon opened at nine. She thought the free admission a nice touch.

"You will note that it is a circle, this building, with an opening in the ceiling that reveals the sky. It is symbolic of the eye of heaven, all seeing, gazing down upon the temple and those within. Consider yourselves blessed today. The oculus was also a practical consideration, because with the way they built it, there would be no way to achieve full dome coverage."

He went on to detail the three levels of granite columns and bronze doors. Irem recalled a Tom Hanks movie, maybe *The DaVinci Code*, maybe *Angels & Demons*... something based on a Dan Brown book, where the Pantheon was pivotal in gathering clues to solve the mystery. The mystery in Benito's dig was more compelling.

"The dome's height is equal — precisely — to the circular diameter of this building. Nearly two thousand years ago the architects were able to be so exact." He paused. "And they had only rudimentary tools. The floor's gentle slope allows for the runoff of rain."

Irem was impressed with the architecture... but also with its cleanliness and condition, pristine despite its age and the millions of people who had walked through it. Another tour group came in, the guide speaking in French, perhaps giving the same spiel.

"This tour," Levent said, leaning close. "It is available in many different languages. Everyone who comes to Rome can soak up the history."

"History," Irem said. "There's a lot under the city, too."

"Ah, the Hun," Levent tsked.

Irem wondered if Santiago and Lacy were cutting corners to finish the generals' room so they could start on Attila *before* the wedding. Maybe Benito was hurrying, too; he'd been eager — and yet a touch reserved and agitated — when the metal detector revealed gold and silver in the apparently empty chamber. Maybe they wouldn't wait. Maybe they were digging that chamber right now. She hoped she wasn't missing something earthshaking.

"This is the heart of the city," Antonio continued. He'd been lecturing about the construction, and she cursed herself for being distracted. "Michelangelo visited this dome, studied it, before he began his work on St. Peter's Basilica. Truly, this is one of Rome's most endearing and enduring sights. Several important nationals are buried here. We will visit that section next."

"Like Raphael," Levent said. "The famous painter. He is buried here."

And Attila is quite possibly buried not far away, though probably fifty or sixty feet deep, she thought. She took more pictures of the guide and the architecture.

"So many things to pick from next," Levent said, as they headed back out onto the street. "I want to show you everything, which is impossible, of course. So a handful of things instead I will show you. Or — "

"Or what?" *Or maybe go below to the dig?*

"Maybe I show you only one or two things more. We take our time. We stop for a glass of wine."

It was her turn to raise an eyebrow. A slow day... a short day... maybe she really could go back down to the dig.

"If I only give you a taste of my city, sis, you'll have to come back... fear of flying or not."

"I made it here, didn't I?" she mumbled.

"Because you don't have a fiancé."

"I have a passport instead."

Levent tugged her to the Trevi Fountain next and used Irem's phone to take a series of pictures of her against sections of the fountain. Passing the phone to a friendly tourist, Levent joined Irem in some of the shots.

"This fountain," he explained, "*Fontana di Trevi,* is the most beautiful of all the Baroque fountains in Italy, maybe the world. There was a movie in the fifties —"

"*Three Coins in a Fountain,*" Irem supplied.

"Yeah, that one. It started a tradition." He reached into his pocket, pulled out three coins, and handed them to her.

Two, worth roughly a U.S. penny each, depicted the *Castel del Monte*, a thirteenth century castle. The third was larger and showed the statue of Marcus Aurelius on horseback; it was worth almost sixty cents.

"Last year," Levent said. "A million and a half dollars in coins were thrown in the fountain. Crews come every night to sweep them out."

"What happens to the money?"

"Years ago thieves took a lot, before the city made that illegal. Now it goes to a worthy endeavor, *Caritas.* It is a Catholic non-profit that spreads the money worldwide, mostly for disaster relief and to ease poverty."

Irem looked at the coins in her hand.

"Toss them in, sis. One at a time."

Less than a dollar, the coins wouldn't go far for charity. But she obliged him.

"It is said that if you throw one coin in the Trevi Fountain you will come back to Rome again. Toss in two, you will find romance here. Three... well, three means —"

"What's next on our agenda?" Irem stepped away from the fountain and took another picture of her brother. *Something nearby, so we can be done and I can go underground?*

Levent grinned. "Now we will go to the Piazza della Rotonda. It is close. Lots of pretty little shops. You must buy something lovely to wear that is made here in my city. This blouse you have on today —"

" — it's a cap sleeve —"

"It's Pantone four forty-eight C, opaque couché, not good for your complexion, muddies you out. All earthy tones and no pop of good color. Does nothing for your beautiful bourbon-colored tresses."

Bourbon colored? Irem had always thought of it as plain brown. She liked the sound of that: bourbon-colored tresses.

"Opaque couché... that olive green is very pretty in nature, or as upholstery for an antique armoire, maybe even a man's suede jacket. But a pretty woman's blouse —"

"A cap-sleeve top."

"Whatever," he said with a feigned arrogant sigh. "I'm taking you shopping. There are restaurants, too, and so if we time it right, we will eat lunch in the neighborhood. Something quaint with tables on the sidewalk. Something adventurous. Maybe that glass of wine. Or maybe two. And then to an art gallery. I insist on the gallery. One in particular you must see."

Adventurous? Irem would have been happy with a return trip to the Golden Arches or another fast food joint that was equally comfortable. Still, she figured that shopping in the Piazza della Rotonda might be a good opportunity to get that knickknack for her mom and a refrigerator magnet for Rowan. And if they didn't dawdle, she still might have time to go under the city.

How long would the entire Attila dig last? Weeks? A month? More? She'd ask Benito about the timing, and then figure out how to fit it into her life. The leave of absence notion surfaced again. This was a bucket list-worthy item that would overflow the bucket if it yielded up the famous Hun's skeleton.

The square was lively and filled with boutiques, cafés, and bars. In the next block a string quintet played outside a restaurant. A few of the shops appeared elegant, some shabby, or shabby-chic as her friends would say. All over it was alive with color—the various skin tones of the shoppers... from black to deep brown to sun-tanned to parchment white; the shades of the buildings; bolts of vibrant green cloth in one window; bright red apples on a cart. She heard color in the conversations, too, so many different languages, obvious words of affection, biting profanity, the singsong of vendors, and the chant of a robed man on a corner. The neighborhood's contrasts assailed her. It was primitive and modern, clean and dirty, rich and poor, and so teeming with life she couldn't register everything. Irem breathed deeply, taking the perfume and everything else deep inside.

She could see why Levent loved the city. But there were things to appreciate in Chicago, too.

"This neighborhood is a good place to sit on a bench, pull out a sketch pad, and people watch," Levent said. "I come here often."

"So's Grant Park," Irem cut back. "We used to people watch there. I remember an abstract you did of a mime. I still have it, framed, in what passes for my living room."

Levent hooked his arm in hers and directed her south. The awnings and shop fronts were vibrant, and Irem wondered if he mentally ascribed names and numbers to each hue. They stopped in the center, in front of a large fountain.

"Let me give the historian some history," Levent said. "Two hundred years ago all of this was considered a bird market. Owls, parrots, so many birds were sold here. There were also fruit peddlers and pastry stalls. At night lighted paper lanterns hung everywhere. And there were flowers everywhere, too. Before my time, but I've seen pictures."

Irem noted that there was still an abundance of flowers.

"It was said to have a gay appearance." Levent laughed. "Back then it meant happy."

"It looks happy," she said. "And it smells wonderful." Fresh-baked bread mingled with amaryllis. She held the scents.

"This is called the *Fontana del Pantheon*, built by decree of Pope Gregory XIII in the fifteen hundreds." She noticed there were five steps leading up to the fountain on this side, two on the other, due to the slope of the ground. She climbed the steps, Levent behind her.

Irem touched her fingertips to the water. "Gorgeous, but it looks a little mismatched. The thing in the middle —"

"Thing?" Lev put on a face like he'd bitten a lemon. "Thing? It's called an *obelisco*, an obelisk. It was added around seventeen hundred under Pope Clement XI. It was one of the first fountains I sketched when I moved here. "The obelisk is Egyptian, twenty feet tall, red marble. Supposedly it was constructed for the Pharaoh Ramses II for the Temple of Ra."

"I'm impressed."

"With the obelisk?"

"With you, knowing so much about it."

"I have become a student of Rome." A playfully smug look was splayed on his face.

"So how did it get here?" Irem took pictures with her cell phone, making sure she got some with Levent in the foreground. Then she turned and took pictures of the colorful shops that stretched away.

"Like other things from Egypt, it was brought here in ancient times. It was set up in the Iseum Campense, a shrine to Isis that used to be southeast of the Pantheon."

"Okay, so I ask again… how did it get *here*?"

Levent dangled his fingers in the water, stirring. "In the late thirteen hundreds they found it under a collapsed basilica near the church of San Macuteo and put it in the center of this fountain. That was in the early seventeen hundreds, as I said. They still call it the *Obelisco Macuteo*. Now shopping, eh?"

She bought three T-shirts off a sale rack, ecstatic with the find. Cooler weather coming to Rome, the summer fare was deeply discounted. The beige one was printed *Bella Italia*, beautiful Italy, with nine photographs of various tourist attractions displayed like a Tic-Tac-Toe board. The red one had Roma in a brush font above a picture of the Colosseum, and the third was pale green with Italy's flag across the chest. She decided she would wear one of them with a pair of skinny jeans to her parents' bar proclaiming she'd been to visit her brother. Maybe it would make them feel guilty.

In another shop Levent bought her a chic silk blouse in a shade he called cobalt turquoise one ninety-one. He took picture after picture of her as she modeled the various pieces she tried on.

"Now this blouse… it complements your skin and hair."

Bourbon-colored tresses, she thought.

"Gay men are experts at dressing women, I think. We know how to make you beautiful. Although it takes only a little effort with you, sis. You are so very beautiful to begin with."

She felt her face redden. Even in Chicago he'd been effusive with compliments. "You come back to Chicago and come shopping with me at Macy's. After Benito is finished with his dig, and after you've honeymooned. Come for the jazz and help me with my wardrobe, Lev."

"Sure. I will go shopping with you. Nordstrom and Macy's." He looked wistful. "When I come back for the Blues Festival." He paused. "Oh, what did I agree to, dear Irem?"

"I'm holding you to it."

"*Certo.*" He let out a huffing breath. "Sure. Yes. I promise. I will come to Chicago. With Benito in tow. For a week maybe. For you and the blues and to put better things in your closet."

"And to see Mom."

He gave a slight nod and changed the subject. "Now, *da questa parte, per favore.*"

"Getting all fancy on me with your Italian. Okay. I'm guessing by the arm wave you've someplace to take me. Lead on. I'll follow."

The morning disappeared, and Levent announced lunch was his treat and therefore his choice, and so selected the Scusate Il, where he ordered something on the simple side for her: Ritardo Brucshetta con prosciutto di Parma, which was basically grilled bread with Parma ham. He chose Carciofi fritti — fried artichokes and grilled, smoked scamorza cheese. Dessert was a few doors away at Ciucculà; strawberry ice cream cones with chocolate glaze. The menu clearly said ice cream, not gelato like the other places they'd strolled past. Irem thought it the most delicious strawberry ice cream she'd ever eaten.

"I'm not taking hapkido ever again," Irem said as they headed in the direction of the Spanish Steps. "Not even to go for a higher degree in black. But I'm joining a gym as soon as I get back." *When I eventually get back.* "Work off some of these pounds I'm no doubt putting on. I hope dinner tonight will not be too — "

Levent draped an arm around her shoulder and gave her a half-hug. His other hand carried her shopping bag. "About dinner tonight. I thought I'd take you to — "

Irem pulled away and faced him, so fast he bumped into her. "I thought Benito was cooking. He went on and on down at the dig about how much he likes to cook and — "

"That was before the big breakthrough yesterday. He'll probably work most of the night, come back to our apartment, grab a few hours of sleep, and then off to our wedding. That wedding cake he was going to bake? That phone call I made when we were walking to the Pantheon — "

" — when you were so engrossed you almost got hit by the tour bus?"

"I called Biscottificio Artigiano Innocenti, and with only one day's notice they agreed to deliver a wedding cake. It won't be one of those tiered fancy things. But it will be beautiful. It was not too much of a reach for the bakery; they were already going to deliver dozens of cupcakes for us. Benito is — "

"Busy with Attila."

Levent nodded sheepishly. "My Benito, he is obsessed, as I told you. I was afraid he'd postpone the wedding because of his search for old bones. Fortunately, he is also obsessed with me. Perhaps because I threw three coins in the Trevi Fountain." He stood tall and tipped his head. "You tossed three coins, too, dear sister. Maybe that handsome policeman, eh? Three coins in the fountain."

Three coins? Irem pictured more coins than that. In her mind she saw the ones embedded in the steps below ground, the ones with Attila's visage.

She could be gingerly stepping on the Attila coins right now.

FOURTEEN

SHE WAS DISAPPOINTED LEVENT TUGGED her somewhere else. So much for a short touristy day.

"I remember when you were a freshman in high school, working on some history paper, and Mom made you drag me to the Field so she could have a Saturday to herself."

"You remember that?"

"Crystal," Levent pronounced.

"Wow. You were seven, I think."

"Half your age at the time, yeah. I was a real pain in the ass. But you were a good sport."

"Didn't have a choice, did I?" Irem smiled.

"For me the Field was all about Sue. I had dinosaurs on the brain when I was a kid." He paused and turned his head as if listening to something else. "Well, dinosaurs and anything that sparkled. I glued sequins on my tennis shoes the night before Sue. Sequins on my T-shirts, on the one I wore with you to the museum. On my shoulders like dandruff." He sighed. "But they fell off in the rain on the way there."

Irem laughed. "Okay, I don't remember the sequins, but otherwise the Field visit is a crystal memory for me, too. I humored you, took your picture next to Sue."

"Sue's bony calf. You didn't back up far enough to get the whole dinosaur skeleton in the shot." He drew his features together, and they looked pinched. "I still have the photograph."

"No shit."

"I didn't take much when I left Chicago. Two suitcases of clothes and one carton of keepsakes, including a photo album the size of a paperback book. Didn't want to pay the extra baggage fees. I figured if I liked Italy as much as I thought I would, I'd start over, live simply, minimalist, buy what I needed here. And if I didn't like it, I wouldn't have to pay extra baggage fees for a return trip. Start over in Chicago or New York City, San Francisco. But I liked it here."

"I'm glad you like it here," Irem said. But she didn't wholly mean it.

"When we come for the Blues Festival, Benito and me, we'll have to go back to the Field. Give you another chance to get a better picture of me next to Sue. Back up this time to get all the bones in. And my Benito can see where you work."

"I'll use a real camera," she said. "Not my cell phone. I've got a nice Canon Rebel that I should have brought with me." She poked his arm with her index finger. "But Sue? You liked the gems better than Sue. I remember that."

"The Grainger Hall of Gems. Ahhhhhh. I was caught up with all the color and the shine. I still like sparkly stuff. All the jewels and gold and jade. Hey, does the Field still have that ruby and diamond necklace?"

Irem nodded.

"I could have spent all day looking at those pieces."

"But I was there to see the mummies, Lev. That's what my report was about."

"They creeped me," Levent said, visibly shuddering. "Cringy, you know. You always liked very old and brittle things. You and Benito. Oh, and old things... are the Ghost and the Darkness still there?"

"Still there."

"And the McDonald's?"

"There's the Explorer Café. No Golden Arches."

"I remember you pitching a fit about that, a McDonald's in the Field. You thought there ought to be something historical. An Egyptian restaurant or somesuch."

Irem didn't reply. For whatever reason, she'd been more adventurous with food in her younger years.

"You and Benito have a lot in common, Irem." Levent's tone was serious. "I bet if my Benito was straight, you two would be perfect." He paused: "I want you to find love, sis. But I'm very glad my Benito's not straight."

Straight? She thought back to the man passing Benito money. Straight... more certainly crooked. But just how crooked?

"Maybe that cop, eh? Gregory—"

"Gregario," she corrected.

"Good looking. Three coins."

The streets around the Pantheon were too narrow for buses, a veritable maze of walking paths that begged Irem to explore. She saw clumps of people behind professional guides, who stopped and gestured at places to take pictures of.

"A local guide, that is best," Levent said. "Tells you things about the city you'd otherwise need a book for. Although there are phone apps that help. That's how I learned my way around."

"Phone apps?"

"Come with me." He grabbed her hand and tugged her into a corner art gallery, steered her to the right-hand wall and stepped behind her. "Look."

Irem did. "Wow."

The wall was covered with striking impressionist and abstract paintings, the colors vibrant and thick, swells raised above the canvas. She wanted to touch the paint and feel its texture, but knew that would be inappropriate. So instead, she just looked. The largest was of flowers twisted and warped and enchanting, as if the artist had selected the most beautiful shades in the world and put them all on this one piece of canvas. Others were renderings of tourist attractions, melted bottles of wine, children with overly large eyes and narrow limbs, and stained glass windows that appeared to glow.

"These are amazing." Then she noticed they all carried the same signature: Levent Kartal-Madigan. "Holy crap. These are yours!"

"Some of mine. I have more at another gallery. Which of these do you like best?"

"All of them. I knew you were good. I just didn't know how good."

"My sculptures are even better, but this gallery shows only oils and watercolors." He stepped to her side. "Which do you like best?"

"The big one, with all the flowers. The colors are... wow. Do you mind if I take a picture of it?"

"Please do." He retreated to the back of the shop and came back a few minutes later with a piece of paper. Levent thrust it at her. "That painting, it is yours. She will mark it NFS... not for sale. You can come back and get it before you return to Chicago. The manager will wrap it up so you can take it on the plane."

"I can't accept this, Levent."

He looked hurt. "I insist."

"Wow."

The next several blocks floated by.

Levent gestured grandly. "There it is... the bottom of the Spanish Steps. Almost three hundred years old, those steps. Restored from time to time, all the people walking on them."

Irem thought of the steps underground.

"Early, this was a place where artists and poets met. Do you understand why I will never live anywhere else?"

She didn't answer. Irem looked up the staircase, a mix of straight flights, terraces, curves. The Spanish Steps covered a steep slope between the Piazza di Spagna at the bottom where they stood, and the Piazza Trinita dei Monti at the top. No coins with Attila's face on these.

"Lots of fountains around here," Irem observed. They stood next to one and she took a picture.

"Let's be at this," she said, as she hurried to the steps and started the climb.

Levent counted each step.

"We've walked sixty-nine steps. Sixty-nine more to go," he announced when they'd reached the halfway point. He pulled her to the side and took a few deep breaths. "We'll wait a minute here, okay?"

The backs of Irem's calves were agreeing with him. Maybe she was burning off more calories than she was consuming.

"When you come back," he continued, "it must be in May. They decorate the steps with pink azaleas then. *Sixteen Candles* pink, eight four oh oh two. The scent is amazing. You can get drunk on it."

"You're coming to Chicago first." She wasn't going to consider a second trip to Rome until she'd seenw if she could stomach the return flight to Chicago.

"And look, there." He gestured down and to the right. "That's called the Via de Condotti. Very stylish, designer clothes and perfumes there. Versace, Armani, Dolce, Gucci, and the like. Nice to look at and famous labels, but why spend so much? That district we walked through... the prices are better. The clothes... I think they are just as good. As for the labels... who sees them except the person who undresses you?" He laughed. "But what do I know about clothes?"

"Apparently more than me."

"Well, yes. I know what colors you should wear," he admitted. "John Keats lived and died in that house." He pointed again. "It's a museum now, but it's not Italian. That's for another visit, eh?"

He gestured off to the other side. "Babington's Tea Room, dates back to the late eighteen hundreds."

"Hey, Lev, after we get to the top, how about we go to the Conservatori?" Irem smiled. "Or are you tired of that place? Me... I'd like to get another look at it. See Benito's artifacts again. I didn't get much of a look the other night." She'd intended to beg off and go underground, but the guilt set in halfway up the steps. Besides, after he'd gifted her that painting, she couldn't leave him. This was her brother's day. But the Conservatori could be a compromise, a hint of her Attila fix.

"The Conservatori? Awesome sauce. Race you the rest of the way to the top, sis."

An hour later they were in the plaza at the Conservatori.

"I think if I lived in Rome, I'd want to be an archivist here." She had pictures on her phone of the tapestry, and she'd backed them up to the Cloud; her safeguard in case something happened to her phone during this trip. She discovered last night that she'd not gotten the entire cloth in one frame. Besides, a photograph wasn't the same thing as seeing it up close. "I want to see that shroud again," she admitted.

"I'm glad you wanted to come back. Certainly you got only a small look at it the other evening. You could spend days here. I have." Levent gestured to the statue outside the main building. "This is Emperor Marcus Aurelius."

"I know that." Irem instantly regretted those three words. Better that she let her brother give the history lesson on this trip; ignore the plaques on the statues.

"But did you know that this is a copy? The original is kept in the Capitoline museum."

"I did not know that."

He shook his head. "So much of what people see in my city is copies, the originals either gone or protected. In the Middle Ages the Christian Church ordered so many statues destroyed. Like ISIS destroying statues and buildings in the Middle East. Like the Romans destroyed the Temple in Jerusalem. Obliterate the art and artifacts of other people's religions. They didn't smash this statue—the real one—but only because of a mistake... they thought it was an image of Emperor Constantine, who supported Christianity. And so they did not want to ruin something they thought had Christian ties."

"I did not know that either."

Levent beamed. "I can teach history to the historian, eh?" He paused: "I've missed you."

"I've missed you, too." How many times had they said that to each other?

Eight nuns in conventional habits walked past, two by two almost in military precision. Irem photographed them against the museum in the background.

"This day is wonderful, sis. And the day after the wedding, you and I—"

"Don't you think the day after the wedding the two of you—"

"Benito will be underground, I told you." He swung around to face her. "Irem, this Attila deal. It is *enorme*. Huge."

I know that. I love you to the moon, but I'd rather be down there right now than standing here even though I think your fiancé is shady. But this is our day.

"Benito, he can't stop on this dig. My Benito, he is driven. Not until he has the truth, Attila's moldy bones in his hands. Not until it is verified and protected. My Benito is revered here, but with this… he'll be known throughout the world. Books, lectures, maybe a movie. Probably a movie. If we did not have an entire day planned tomorrow—the wedding ceremony, reception, dinner and dancing—he would be digging tomorrow, too. He thought about it; we talked about it, argued about it. I won. Tomorrow he stays up top. All day and night. You and I can explore more on the streets the day after the wedding." He pivoted to come to her side again. "It will be like old times, us together." A pause. "Except for when you go out to dinner with the good looking cop."

They strolled through a half dozen galleries, taking their time in a stretch of baroque sculptures by Bernini.

"Really, honestly, how much do you know about Benito?" Irem brought up the topic again. "Everyone has secrets just as you said. How much do you know about his past?"

Levent shrugged. "I have secrets, too. He doesn't know everything about me. Benito doesn't know I had a falling out with our parents. Although I'll tell him eventually. He doesn't know that I tried a relationship with a girl. That I doubt I will ever mention."

111

Irem's eyebrows rose. She didn't know that. "Really?" She drug out the word and gave it an extra syllable.

"My second month here. Tina Gardini was her name. Red hair, a little plump—sensuous curves you could say, incredible eyes. Luminous. I told her she had luminous eyes. She was in one of my art classes, and she kept hitting on me. I was not at all sexually interested in her, but I enjoyed her company. She'd posed nude for me. A woman's breasts do nothing for me. It's just excess fat that our society has turned into a sexual focus."

Irem was surprised her brother was making this confession to her.

"But I was curious. I hadn't met any men yet to interest me. I was curious, and she trembled when I touched her. I was flattered. We went out casually, twice, maybe three times before—"

Irem touched Levent's arm.

"—we, uhm, connected. I didn't tremble, sis. It was... nice... okay... but nothing special. I didn't *feel* anything, really. She was a friend, and I loved her in the way you love a friend. I needed something special. Someone special. I needed someone to make me quiver—"

Irem sucked in a quick breath and squeezed his arm. At the end of the hall was a tall man with a square face like a jug. He held a stingy-brimmed hat in his hands, the hint of a beard, and he stood admiring a large painting. At his side was a slight woman Irem had seen somewhere before. Holding her hand was a small boy.

"What's wrong, sis? I'm telling you too much personal stuff or—"

The hall was well lit, and so she could see the man's face in profile. He might be... and he might not be... the man who'd shot at her. Certainly stingy-brimmed hats were owned by many men in Italy. It had been dark, he'd had a raincoat on, everywhere shadows, hadn't been able to make out many details.

Still... there was something about him that was raising all of Irem's proverbial hackles. He might be the guy.

And the woman; she was familiar. Not the boy, but the woman. Definitely the woman; she'd been with the vintner Hamadi that night at the reception in front of the bone shroud. Was the boy her child? She seemed so young to have a child that age. And the man with the hat? She didn't get the impression that the three of them constituted a family.

"Sis?"

"I'm fine, Lev. You weren't oversharing. Not at all." Well, he was, but Irem wouldn't tell him that. "Maybe I had too much wine at lunch. I'm going to visit the ladies room. Give me a few minutes. I'll meet you in the place with Benito's big shroud and those Romulus and Remus masks."

Irem scurried around the corner, her chest tight, and her mind whirling. She slipped into the bathroom; she had it to herself.

Chill, just chill. Breathe.

Just her mind playing tricks, had to be. The woman… young, plain, had been with Hamadi's entourage on the night of the reception. The man? Was it the same man who'd shot at her? It couldn't be the same man, she decided. He couldn't be the thug. It became clear in her mind — as she took deep, even breaths — that the thug who'd given Benito money was a man of the night and shadows, not one to stroll through a museum in the daylight, and certainly not one to be in the company of a young woman and a little boy.

Irem decided to take one more look at them, get a picture on her phone. But when she returned to the hall, it was empty.

FIFTEEN

"NO TARDARE. WE CAN REMAIN here only a little longer, James." Sophia smiled at the boy. He was engrossed in studying an ornate column rather than the nearby art. He'd only glanced at a few of the pieces since they'd arrived. Hamadi had suggested the trip, as he wanted his son exposed to Rome's vast, historical culture. She doubted the vintner knew the boy was more interested in the building itself rather than what was inside it. She'd brought him here a dozen times, and each visit was always the same; he was fascinated by the architecture.

"Why are we in such a hurry today? I like it here, Sister Sophia. I want to stay all day. I could live here, I think. Yes, I would like to live here. You could stay here, too." James poked out his lower lip; Sophia thought that when the boy was petulant he actually appeared like a five-year-old, rather than his normal too-mature self.

"I have a hair appointment, James. I am going to look fancy for the wedding tomorrow."

"The wedding tomorrow is silly, Sister Sophia. Two men should not get married." The boy paused, appearing to think. "Neither should two women get married. It's in the Bible. Levi— Levi— Leviticus! I remember you reading it to me. 'You shall not lie with a man as one lies with a woman. It is an abdomen.'"

"An abomination," she corrected.

" '—an abomination.' I memorized that verse." He drew out abomination, as if tasting each letter. "I've been memorizing Bible verses."

115

Sophia countered. "Also in the Bible, Ruth says to Naomi: 'Entreat me not to leave thee, or to return from following after thee: for whither thou goest, I will go; and where thou lodgest, I will lodge. They people will be my people, and thy God, my God.' I do not think God cares whether his children are gay or straight."

"I know, John 3:16. Right, Sister Sophia?"

She beamed. "That is right, James."

"I wish I was going to the wedding tomorrow, Sister Sophia." The boy tipped his head up and stared at the ceiling. "Not to see two men get married. That would be boring and silly and wrong according to Leviticus. But to see the church. I have decided that I will be an architect when I grow up."

"A reasonable profession," the tall man pronounced. "You should make good money."

"I don't care about making money. I want to make buildings," James said. "I have been drawing buildings. I could see the church tomorrow Sister Sophia, and—"

"You will instead have a good time at home with Taavi, eh?" Sophia looked past James to the tall man holding the stingy-brimmed hat. "Taavi will tell you stories and sing songs."

The tall man scowled.

"And will you take me to the movies, Taavi?"

"*Certo.* Certainly," Sophia said, answering for Taavi. "We should be leaving so I can make my hair appointment."

James thrust his lip out even farther. "I like it here, Sister Sophia. I like this building."

"You like it everywhere," Taavi said.

"Tell me again about the dead false god we walk on," James said, as he reluctantly took Sophia's hand. She guided him down the hall. "The one people used to pray to before they learned better."

"This wonderful museum was built atop an ancient temple dedicated to the Roman god Jupiter. Michelangelo was called upon for renovations, especially to the Corinthian pilasters and the columns on the ground floor. The building's façade—"

"That means 'face,' right? Façade."

"Yes. It was updated in the early fifteen hundreds by Michelangelo and—"

"—nearby they used to sell cattle, right? I remember you said that the last time we came here. Moooooo."

Sophia shuddered. The boy was so young to remember so much. Gifted to be able to memorize random facts and songs and scripture. God had granted him—perhaps inadvertently—an amazing mind. She prayed every night that James continued to learn and to grow spiritually.

"Was Michelangelo gay, Sister Sophia? Did he marry another man?"

"I think I will get my hair cut, just a little," she said to change the subject. "What do you think? To my shoulders? It will always grow back if I don't like it."

"Some people think Michelangelo was gay. I heard that somewhere. I remember things I hear."

"I have worn my hair plain for too long, don't you think, James? Shorter, just a little. I will get curls, too."

"Color it purple, Sister Sophia."

"That's a good idea, James," Taavi said. "I'd like to see Sophia with hair the color of grape juice."

Sophia gave them both a withering glare and walked faster, her heels clicking against the hard floor. She would get her hair done, which she knew would please Hamadi, who encouraged her to look "fine and fancy" for the wedding. But it was a wedding she did not support. She was of James's view regarding men marrying men.

Sophia considered herself a tolerant soul and honestly believed that God loved all his children, gay, straight, whatever. But she was not as accepting as God. She'd enjoyed the company of the archaeologist and his painter fiancé on the occasions they'd crossed her path. Intelligent, charming, likeable men. She really did like them. And she loved that the archaeologist had been so instrumental in furthering Hamadi's grand plan with the discovery of the shroud map.

She really, really, really did like them, she told herself.

But she really didn't like the idea of the marriage.

John 3:16… words to live by.

Wither thou goest, Ruth… more words to hold in her heart.

And yet for her young years, Sophia was old fashioned, the product of the convent she'd tried to make her home. She would attend the wedding without approving of it. And she would be "fine and fancy" for this civil union, and she would dance with Hamadi if there was music at the reception. Sophia figured she might even enjoy herself. Makeup? She would even use a little of that. And earrings that dangled and sparkled when the light touched them.

And then some days after the wedding, Hamadi and she, perhaps with Taavi or the twins, would make another late foray to a burial ground. She was disappointed that the vintner was arranging for one *during* the wedding—she would have chosen to participate in the illicit expedition over attending the marriage ceremony and the reception after… if the choice was hers. But Hamadi was the force behind all of this, the orchestrator and financier of their very important endeavor. Sophia had to follow his wishes. Everyone in his circle had to follow his wishes.

So she would look forward to the next excursion. She focused on that to lift her spirits. It was such important work.

"*La prosimma volta,*" she whispered. She would go on the next foray, and the one after that. The excitement became so thick and palpable she felt as if she bounced along on the cushion of it as they left the Conservatori and headed toward the statue on the plaza. It was dangerous, grave robbing, and she hoped they could visit all the burial places on their list without discovery. They risked arrest if they were caught, although Hamadi's wealth might ease that and keep them away from legal trouble. Perhaps. They were so careful, always, she knew. And the danger was thrilling, and the work was necessary. And the robbing… they would only take one thing.

She prayed Hamadi would again give her the honor of collecting it.

SIXTEEN

IREM STARED AT THE CLOTH. From one angle it still looked like a bleached Art Deco couch throw. The colors were strong, but the palette rather drab. She wondered if Levent was mentally ticking off numbers and names of each shade. She stepped to the other end and looked at it from a different angle, seeing an elaborate pattern of threads. Once more she was reminded of the notion thatshe could buy a bolt of it at the Needle Shop on Lincoln in Chicago.

The plaque beneath it said it had been discovered by Dr. Benito Abruzzi, listed it as five hundred and fifty to six hundred years old. She had thought it might be even older.

How the hell had he used it as a map to find the Hun graveyard under Rome?

She stood in front of it and studied the center, seeing the image of a wolf or a dog, but then noticing twelve faint and smaller dogs in an arc above it. Below the main wolf lay a mythological beast and the suggestion of a rearing horse. Swiveling the other way, as she had a few nights past, she saw a running man. Little skulls dotted some of the sections. Did the skulls mark the Hun graveyard? There were several clumps of tiny skulls.

"My legs are stiff, standing in one place so long. Are you done looking?" Levent pulled out his cell phone to check the time.

She shook her head. "Give me a few more."

"Already gave you a few. C'mon or he'll be gone for the day and you'll miss the surprise. C'mon. You're done here." Levent put on his mischievous grin and tugged her into the hall. "While you were in the ladies' room, I made a call. The man who restored that tapestry and worked on some of Benito's other treasures is downstairs. He's agreed to let you see pictures of the restoration stages. It took a little persuading, but I mentioned Benito and the dig sponsor and—"

The artwork on the walls and the sculptures on the pedestals were a blur as she followed her brother down one hall after another until they reached an office and connected with a petite young security guard, who motioned them toward a wide door.

"You and Benito. This stuff interests you." Levent toyed with one of his curls. "I would rather look at all the beautiful pieces on display in this magnificent museum than pictures on a computer." He made a *pffting* sound. "But this interests you."

"I'm thankful he's letting me look at the pictures on a computer. I'm an archivist, this fascinates me, and I—"

"Yeah, yeah. You love old moldy things. I know." He poked her in the arm. "I find some of it curious, too, how they restore things. I am especially interested in the restoration of paintings."

Irem followed the security guard down a short corridor and then a flight of stairs to the basement, passing a series of offices and workrooms before coming to a well-lit room dominated by a low, wide table. The place smelled like hospital disinfectant mixed with linseed oil, not heavy, but noticeable. A loom on the far end held a stretched tapestry of the Madonna. Levent had been close behind Irem, but suddenly scooted ahead and walked toward the center of the room, hand out.

"Gustavo Portanova." Levent shook hands with the rotund man sitting in the middle at the long table, a laptop and printer in front of him. "Irem Madigan, *mia sorella.* Irem, Gustavo restored that shroud of bones you're so curious about."

"I will be in the hall when you're ready," the security guard said as she left.

A conversation in Italian followed between Levent and Gustavo. Irem understood only a few words because they spoke so quickly. Levent had told her at the reception that Gustavo had picked up the work on the tapestry after the previous restorer's death.

"*Il lavoro di arazzo conservazione può essere lungo quanto diverse settimane o mesi... Ed è complesso.Tuttavia, mi piace quello che faccio.*"

Levent whistled. "Gustavo talks like lightning. Basically, he says the work of tapestry conservation can take as long as weeks or months ... And it's complex. However, he says he loves what he does. He loved working on Benito's shroud."

Gustavo was a few dozen pounds overweight, face florid, and his nose had tiny veins hinting that he drank too much. He had an unruly shock of mud-brown hair streaked with gray and bushy eyebrows that practically met in the middle. Irem thought he could well be one of those heart attacks waiting to happen and that the shroud would have another death connected to it.

"Gustavo speaks only Italian, so I will have to translate for you." Levent stepped back from the table and gestured to the impressive laptop, an Acer with a twenty-one inch curved screen. Expensive and enviable.

Irem peered over Gustavo's shoulder and looked at the screen. She wrinkled her nose, the restorer wore a lot of cologne, and that scent mixed with something that smelled like a spicy gyro.

"He says these are images of the shroud when it first came in. They take many pictures and then they document the restoration process." She stared closely, then a finger as thick as a sausage stabbed a few keys and the images flashed across the screen in a slide presentation. "He says he is showing you this only because I was persistent and because you work for the Field Museum. Gustavo worked with the Field a dozen years ago on the restoration of some Chinese silken tapestries purchased from a collector in Florence. He restored the pieces before they were shipped to America, and a representative from the Field made a documentary of Gustavo's work."

Irem wondered if she'd seen those silk tapestries. The Field had so many treasures, not everything on display all the time. She certainly hadn't seen everything the Field owned. When she got back to work, she'd walk through the museum's Cyrus Tang Hall of China and look for tapestries.

"That was before I started work there," she said. "I've only been at the Field seven years." Levent did not translate her comment. "Can he tell me what exactly he did to Benito's shroud? To restore it? That first picture he showed looked pretty dreadful. And I'd like to see that first picture again."

"*Certo*," Levent said. He proceeded to translate back and forth. Irem hoped he was catching everything the restorer said.

Another stab of the sausage finger and the tattered cloth reappeared.

"*Inizio*," he said.

Irem knew that meant "the beginning." She quietly slipped out her cell phone and turned on the video function, holding it in front of her and hunching her shoulders and back like a turtle as if to hide it. She shivered, like she was a spy fearful of being caught. There was just something not sitting right. But then a lot of things hadn't been sitting right since the night in the rain. She watched the back of Gustavo's head... if he turned around he'd spot her phone. For a reason she couldn't explain, she didn't want him to see her recording this.

Levent translated more of the rapid Italian: "The piece had suffered major damage, including a half meter-long rip on one side, which the previous restorer repaired. That was all she'd done to it before her unfortunate death. Everything else Gustavo managed. There were a few patches where the material was missing, looking like insects had eaten it."

"I can see that," Irem said.

"And there was centuries of dust, dirt, ashes accumulated. Gustavo thinks the bone shroud is—"

"*Siecento*," Gustavo said.

"Six hundred years old," Levent translated.

Again the finger stabbed the keyboard and another image came up; this one had been taken by someone else, as it had Gustavo in it, painting a small section of the cloth. The restorer continued to talk, and Levent soaked it in and then gave Irem the English version.

"Gustavo says he stabilized the entire piece, cleaned it, put it on the loom, and then he recreated what he calls the lost areas. I'm thinking he means filling in the holes. More details in the fabric emerged, all the little skulls appeared, and patterns in different threads."

"Stabilize. What does that mean? How did he stabilize it?" Irem thought if she returned to work on her doctorate she'd take classes in antiquity restoration.

Levent translated her question and waited until Gustavo flipped through more pictures, words in Italian firing from his mouth like machine gun bullets, and never taking his eyes off the screen. Twice Levent asked him to slow down so he could better understand.

"All of this is intriguing, sis. He says there was more than the large rip, there were small tears. Usually there are tears in ancient fabrics. He stitched those closed… finding thread as close to the texture and color as possible. Then he backed it with linen to give it strength, all of this done by hand. The backing, I guess that's the stabilizing."

Irem carefully continued to film the computer screen and tried to imagine the restorer's thick fingers doing such delicate work. But she had to admit the shroud hanging on the wall upstairs looked amazing.

"Gustavo considers himself a conservationist. His first aim is to conserve. But in this case the museum asked him to restore the shroud. There is a difference in the work." She had picked up the word *conservatore*. She'd remember that one. *Conservatore*… conservationist. "The linen backing is important to fight fabric fatigue, to help the little repaired tears from spreading. Then he filled in the missing material. Several thousand tiny stitches, Gustavo thinks he made. Finished, it was restretched on the loom where the Madonna is."

"*Tredici,*" Gustavo said. "*Tredici!*"

"Okay, I get the thirteen. Thirteen what?"

Irem waited as Gustavo spewed more Italian. Levent worked to keep up with him. The restorer turned his head, and Irem shoved the phone into her pocket, turning it off. The man might not have cared that she took video, but she didn't want to risk any impropriety.

"He mixed thirteen different colors of paint to match the palette in the shroud. These colors he tapped over the stitches so they blended in with everything else. In four places images were missing sections, and Gustavo had to create pieces. Only noticeable, he says, if you have a magnifying glass and know exactly where to look."

Exactly... *precisamente*. Maybe Irem could remember that word, too.

"Conservation... the shroud would simply be saved and the holes filled in with linen or silk dyed to match. To preserve... you spend much more time, fix the patches in place with silk thread, bolster the integrity of fabric with backing. Museums, they take this approach, where a collector wants it untouched if possible."

"Most museums," Irem said. "And it depends on the piece."

"Gustavo says what he did was to give life back to an elaborate cloth that was dead. He fixed the wounds and warps. He listened to the cloth, what it told him, discovered its colors."

"The age," Irem broached. "Why does he say six hundred years?"

"*Siecento*," Gustavo said again, shaking a finger at her.

Irem glanced around the room while the restorer went on, his voice coming across as bored, the inflection flat, like he'd passed through his stint of being polite and was now tired of lecturing about this.

"Fifteenth century works are not as complex as those from later years, the patterns and the colors, the weave, the material. All those things factor in. Gustavo is apparently quite good at knowing the time period of fabrics, be they murals, tapestries, shrouds, a woman's dress. The later a piece, the more colors used. And the style. A fifteenth century flower is not the same as one from a hundred years later or a hundred years earlier, he says. This shroud took him three months to restore. Others have taken him a handful of days. A few, nearly a year."

Irem decided to press a little. "All those threads, the patterns in different colors. Reminds me of the colors in a medieval map, like one I saw of Cambriae Typus."

"What's that, a Typus?" Levent asked.

"It was a temporary exhibit about a year and a half ago at the Field, the earliest published map of Wales as a separate country from Great Britain. It was from the fifteen hundreds."

Levent continued to render her sentences into Italian as she talked.

"You see, the thick patterns on the shroud upstairs, it reminded me of the pattern on the Cambriae Typus map, threads that represented the River Severn, and—"

"*Carta geografica?*" Gustavo sputtered as Levent went on. He waved his wide hand and cut them off. "No *carta geografica.*"

"He says it's not a map, just a burial shroud of some scholar or instructor from the *Studium Senese*, the University of Siena." Levent had trouble keeping up and obviously missed some parts. "An old university, the first public one in Italy, opened in twelve hundred. Probably some teacher or administrator from there." He paused while Gustavo seemed to talk even faster. "Gustavo recognized a small symbol fashioned of tiny skulls, the symbol for the *Studium* centuries past. It also helped him date the fabric, and—"

"Does he know the name of the scholar who was wrapped in it?"

"No, I asked him that. But Benito might know."

"Do you think he'd print out a few of the pictures, the original, and the one he finished? Printouts? Tell him I'd like to show off his work to my friends at the Field." She didn't need them; she already had them on her phone. But printouts would be handy now so she could look at the details in a scale much larger than her tiny phone screen.

"*Mai,*" Gustavo said after Levent posed her request.

"Uh, no," Levent translated. "He says no pictures."

The restorer's eyes narrowed, and he thumbed off the laptop.

"Gustavo says he has work to do before he leaves and that he graciously gave you time because you work for the prestigious Field Museum and because of Benito." Levent lowered his voice. "He's shooing us away. I want to breeze you through the Capitoline Picture Gallery before we leave. Paintings from the sixteenth and seventeenth centuries. Masterpieces there, sis. Caravaggio, Rubens, even Titian."

Irem dutifully followed him up to the second floor; Levent was so joyful in this place. She looked at the masterpieces and tried to pay attention—for him--but her thoughts kept drifting to the Scourge of God and the shroud that Benito said had served as a map. Interesting that the restorer was so adamant that it was not a map. One of them was wrong.

Who had been buried in it? And was that important? Was that man related somehow to Attila? Irem wanted to know.

The next two hours with Levent sped by. At the end of it she barely registered the taste of the pizza at the restaurant they stopped at—sausage and pepperoni, her favorite.

"Don't you think it odd that Gustavo got all anxious when I asked about getting a few printouts of his restoration?"

Levent shrugged. "The woman who started the project was much friendlier. She would have given you all the copies you wanted. Too bad she couldn't have seen it through, eh? But good thing Benito's sponsor knew of Gustavo. The Conservatori didn't have to search for another lead fabric restorer; one appeared the next day."

"Odd that a vintner knew someone expert at restoring tapestries," Irem agreed. That bothered her; she didn't like coincidences.

"I noticed the grouping of little skulls," Levent said. He took a long pull on his soda. "I remember Benito saying the skulls marked Attila's grave. But how he figured out where to dig... isn't my Benito amazing?"

"Amazing."

"Excuse me... too much to drink. Ask for a refill for me if she comes back, okay?"

Irem pulled out her phone when Levent strode to the restroom, calling up the earliest shot of the tapestry and panning around until she spotted a grouping of skulls inside three stitched rectangles. The color of the thread had faded, but it was definitely metallic: gold, silver, and a shimmering gray. She thought it might represent the gold, silver, and iron caskets the Scourge of God was said to have been buried in. Metallic threads traced back centuries, she knew, as far back as ancient Egypt and China. She forwarded through her video and noticed that the embroidered rectangles had disappeared.

"Amazing," she snarled. She glanced at the other groupings of tiny skulls and the embroidered designs around them in the raw shroud… the designs also all missing in the restored version of the cloth. Did they represent other important graves?

No wonder Gustavo didn't want me to take pictures. He not only repaired the shroud, he altered it. I'm betting purposely. No accident. This is dangerous, Lev.

She recalled Benito's conversation from their late dinner: "The restoration inadvertently removed most of the clues, made it unreadable," he'd said. "Tragic and fortunate at the same time, eh?" Another dark thought entered. Maybe the original restorer hadn't died of an old-age malady.

Or her husband of a heart attack.

Or her assistant of a drug overdose.

"Dear God," she whispered, as she started texting. *Happy to meet you for dinner on the ninth, Ari. Seven? I can find the place.* Irem figured she'd have a lot to talk about with the good looking policeman. It was time she told someone about Benito and the square-faced man.

Levent returned and stared at his empty soda glass.

"Waitress hasn't come back yet," Irem said.

"Just as well. It's eight. Benito should be home soon."

"And tomorrow you'll be married," Irem said.

"You're giving me away!"

"I gave you away four years ago when you left Chicago." She smiled sadly and hurried out and onto the street.

SEVENTEEN
OCTOBER 8

THERE'D BEEN NO REHEARSAL, but there really wasn't a need. There was no walk down the aisle. Benito in a dark brown suit... Levent told her it was Quinacridone burnt orange twelve-eighty; Levent in raw sienna thirteen-forty; she in her ochre gabardine dress that had been repaired, all gathered at the front near the altar. Some university professor she'd never met wore black; he stood up for Benito.

Irem had her hair done again, and makeup, at the same salon she'd stopped at the other day. She wore the pretty, but uncomfortable, pompadour heels. A spray of flowers on her wrist delicately added to the scents in the impressive old church.

A small gathering, she'd been told. But a glance at the pews and she guessed there were easily two hundred people—some in finery, some in blue jeans, about two-thirds of them men. She wondered if Tina Gardini was out there. A photographer positioned to the side constantly took pictures without being intrusive.

Everything was in Italian, the background music—more Vivaldi--the whispered conversations of the guests, the minister's service, the vows; Irem didn't even try to understand any of it. She just reluctantly signed a document as a witness toward the end, crying inside at the possibility that Levent was marrying into something scary.

At the conclusion, an organist played *Pachelbel's Canon*—a German classical piece, the one thing not Italian about the ceremony — as Benito and Levent strolled toward the back of the church, hand and hand.

The photographer continued to take pictures.

Irem sat with Lacy and Santiago at the reception in the church's basement, joining them after she'd posed for several photographs with her brother upstairs. She overheard the young archaeologists discussing "the dig." It was bound to be a more interesting conversation — and in English — than what the other people shared, whom she suspected chattered about Benito and Levent, politics in Rome, and the politics of gay marriage... she'd picked out just enough Italian words to get that impression. Besides, Santiago and Lacy were at a small table in the corner — away from the bulk of the guests.

"Did you get to Attila yesterday? Did you dig down and find a casket?" Irem looked at the selection of cheeses and meat slices she'd put on her plate and started making a sandwich of them. "I wanted to come down, see where you were, the progress, but I was with Lev. I'd promised him the day. We went to the Steps, shopping." She paused before making a confession. "He's my brother and I love him and all I could think about was —"

"Attila," Lacy supplied in a low voice. "It's all I think about."

"We finished what we call the generals' room," Santiago said. "We really wanted to start after Attila last night. But it got late. We talked about going today. We have the floor marked out, where we think the casket is. We're ready."

"But the wedding," Lacy said.

"And the reception here," Santiago added glumly.

Lacy frowned. "And dinner and dancing at the club after this. An all-day affair. I just know it's gonna go to midnight. And I know I'm gonna eat enough calories for an entire week."

"Midnight? Later than that, I'm betting. But maybe we could skip the club. Maybe he wouldn't notice if we're not there."

Lacy gave Santiago a withering look. "He's already pissed at you. At us. We don't need to do anything to make it worse. We're going for the whole damn thing. And we gotta get them to come up to our place for the present before they call it a night. It's gonna take at least three people to lug that down the steps. Can't put it off another day. All the other days belong to Attila."

"We should've never paid the antique store to lug it up. Should've given it to 'em a month ago when we bought it."

Lacy's eyes were daggers. "Should've done a lot of things, right?"

"Should've stayed down to the wee hours at the dig," Santiago said. "Attila's so close."

"Don't you think Dr. Abruzi would rather be digging up Attila tonight than dancing?" Lacy ran her thumbs along the edge of her plate. "He loves Levent, but he's obsessed with the dig. And he made us promise we wouldn't go down today."

Irem swallowed her bite of sandwich and leaned forward. "Pissed? You said Benito is pissed at you. What happened?"

Santiago shook his head and waved his hand in an "it's nothing" manner.

Lacy rolled her eyes and answered: "Dinner at Osteria Bonelli two nights ago... good thing you didn't join us. We had a little too much wine. Loosens the tongue, you know. Sant admitted emailing a few pictures from the generals' room to the chair of our archaeology department, and a shot of the carved wall. We weren't supposed to take pictures, but we have a bunch anyway. Hundreds. Just never took any in front of Dr. Abruzi."

"I only emailed a few," Santiago whispered. "Okay, a dozen. But nothing that screamed 'Attila.' Just stuff that let her know we were onto something important."

"Sant thought he'd impress her, thought it would buy us an extension on our hands-on studies here."

"And it did. We've got the spring semester here guaranteed. And that means summer, too."

"Except," Lacy said, drawing out the word, "Dr. Abruzi got pissed. Big time. Didn't want any word getting out. No photos. Said our secret isn't a secret anymore. We can't take our laptops down under anymore. Or cell phones. He's pissed. Said maybe he won't keep us for the spring semester after all. But the wedding gift might help. Put us in his good graces again. We spent more than we should have on it."

"I never told the chair we were going after Attila," Santiago hissed. "In the email to her I only — "

"You didn't have to come right out and say Attila. You emailed pics of Hun skulls, that helmet. You don't think it screamed Attila? It screamed Attila. And the caption I saw you write: THIS IS BIG. That, dear heart, screams Attila the Hun. And, worse, after half a bottle of wine you told Dr. Abruzi about your THIS IS BIG comment. Big? Big trouble."

"Just being honest. Doc was on his phone to that fat vintner. It was just my way of admitting what I did. Coming clean, you know. He was talking to the vintner. I wasn't sure he even heard me. Except he did hear me."

"Yeah, he heard."

"Shit. I screwed up. Me and my tiny brain," Santiago mumbled. "At least I didn't tell him I sent some pages of our notes. I just mentioned the pictures."

"*In vino veritas,*" Lacy said. She stuffed her mouth with an appetizer that didn't look appetizing to Irem.

"And in the emails I made no mention of what our next site would be."

"Just that there was going to be a next one," Lacy countered.

Instantly Irem remembered her video of shroud restoration and the other groupings of tiny skulls.

"Doesn't matter," Lacy said. "You've made Dr. Abruzi pissed *and* paranoid."

"*I'm* a little paranoid now," Santiago countered. The husband and wife talked as if Irem wasn't there. "Good thing he can't hear us talking now."

"Hear us?" Lacy gave a lopsided grin. "All day yesterday he watched us constantly. Hell, maybe he's had our apartment bugged."

"Okay, that's being too paranoid," Santiago said.

"Am I?" Lacy gulped down the punch. "No kick in it," she said. "But I expect there wouldn't be, a church and all." She gave a wink. "But the dinner and dance after this... there'll be lots of alcohol. And he certainly won't be pissed after we give him that antique rolltop desk. That set us back. Hopefully that will make everything right again."

"Buying brownie points," Santiago grumbled. "Money well spent."

"I took a close look at that bone shroud," Irem whispered, steering the conversation her way. She had their attention now. "I saw images of it before the restoration, and I saw groupings of skulls marked. It really is... was... a map, right? There are more graves. What's after Attila, Santiago? You've extended your stay through the spring—if Benito gets unpissed. What are you digging after you finish this site?"

The couple was quiet, and the conversations of the other guests swirled around them.

"Alaric," Santiago finally said. "We're going after him next. Benito says you're family. I think you're cool and all, and it's almost too bad that you'll be back in Chicago before we start on that dig... provided he keeps me and my big mouth around. Attila is a motherlode for sure, and it'll take us a little time to finish it. But Alaric... as excited as I am about Attila... Alaric will be a goldmine."

Irem wondered if Rome would give Benito and his assistants some sort of percentage of the value of their finds... a tiny percentage... but a tiny percentage of a goldmine was a hell of a lot of money. Plus Benito had a salary from the university. Archaeology wasn't a terribly lucrative field—typically, just like he said. But all of this... all of this would net Benito a fortune, especially when he parlayed it into lectures, books, and more. Levent married into money, although she knew he'd married for love. But what all had he married into?

Out of the corner of her eye she saw the thin woman from the Conservatori sit across from the vintner. The little boy was not with her, nor was the tall man with the suggestion of a beard. The young woman was far from plain today; she'd cut and styled her hair and wore a knee-length teal lace dress. Long dangly earrings sparkled.

"Alaric had ties to Attila," Santiago said, pulling her attention back. He talked low, barely above a conspiratorial whisper. "You could probably get all this with a Google, but—"

"Okay, sure. Never mind," Irem said.

"But Santiago is a walking Google, and you've asked him about one of his favorite obsessions—the Visigoth king," Lacy cut in. "He'll give you the Alaric-lite, won't you dear heart?"

Santiago grinned. "Yeah. I like talking about this shit. Alaric was the first king of the Visigoths. He took an army into Rome in—"

"410," Lacy provided. "I know that much." Apparently, Irem thought, Lacy was also a walking Google.

"Yeah. Yeah. 410. Sacked Rome, and probably caused the fall of the Western Roman Empire. It was the Huns who'd forced Alaric and his Visigoths into the Roman Empire, where taxes, not enough food, and ill-treatment from the Romans made things so untenable that Alaric rebelled. So that's how Alaric is linked to Attila."

"Rampaged is a better word for it," Lacy said. "Ransacked Rome. Rampaged and ransacked."

"The city's treasury, mausoleums. Alaric reportedly left Rome with wagons overflowing with gold and silver."

"And pepper." Lacy stuffed a cupcake in her mouth and talked muffled around it. "Pepper was valuable at the time, and he had more than a ton of it."

"He was going to take his men into Sicily next, but he died the same year he sacked Rome. People have been looking for his tomb... more for the gold than for the historical significance, I think."

"And Benito thinks he knows where it is." Irem didn't pose it as a question. "Because of the shroud."

"He was right on Attila," Lacy said. "Last night we staked out where we know a big rectangle of gold and silver is. Gotta be the casket. Gotta be Attila, right? Gotta be.

Gotta be. We're going for it in the morning—hangovers be damned. Going for it before he sends us packing. Dear God, I hope our wedding present makes things better. Go for Attila. Then we'll start clipping the newspaper headlines."

"He was right on Attila," Irem said softly. "With the bone shroud." Her foot tapped anxiously under the table. She stared at her sandwich and cake; she'd lost her appetite, so engrossed in the possibilities. "So maybe he'd be right on where Alaric is, too. Is that what you're thinking?"

"I'm betting on the Doc," Santiago said. "The Doc and the shroud. A bunch of Italian scientists have been concentrating on five sites they think Alaric could be, all of them in or near Cosenza in the far south. Claim there might be upward of one-point-three billion dollars of gold... US dollars, I put that into. Billion. And that doesn't count the historical significance."

"And the prestige," Lacy whispered. "We could live anywhere, write our own tickets as they say. Do anything. Tours, a lecture circuit. Attila *and* Alaric? Fucking amazing, yes."

"Holy crap," Irem said.

"Doc says they're wrong, the other diggers. Says we'll prove Alaric is right outside of Rome. But he won't let us start on that site—"

"Understandably," Lacy cut in.

"Until Attila is locked up. Finished." Santiago took a drink of punch and made a sour face. "And he's being so damn slow about it. We could've started digging for Attila last night. It's like he's dragging his feet, prolonging this. Maybe to savor everything. But if word leaks out to the public—"

"—which better not happen because of your emails, Sant."

"I don't want to risk losing this opportunity, Lacy."

"Who was buried in the shroud?" That question had burned in Irem's brain, and she mentally kicked herself for not asking Benito. "A scholar, right? Do you know his name?"

"A scholar, yeah." Lacy finished her cupcake and licked her fingertips. "Dr. Abruzi told us the name of the guy, and I've typed it in my notes. An obscure teacher at the University of Siena some hundreds of years ago who was big on ancient burial places."

"The secret ones," Santiago whispered. "He was said to have embroidered his own funerary cloth, taking to his grave his notes on where all the important bodies are buried. Except Benito found his grave... and the cloth."

"We're writing about it, the search for Attila and Alaric," Lacy put in. "When we're finished digging... books plural, probably. The first is sitting at fifty thousand words already. Halfway there, I think. Bookssss." She drew out the "s" like a serpent's hiss. "I've been taking so many notes. I figure a book about each site, and one separately on the shroud. Maybe a book about Benito. Bookssss. But that's for when we're finished digging. We're going for the big money ones first, Attila, Alaric —"

"That's enough," Santiago cautioned. "Doc is looking this way."

That was more than enough for Irem. She had no desire to go drinking and dancing tonight. She wanted to go back underground.

Irem glanced at Levent's table. There was an empty seat next to him; he'd expected her to sit there. She'd join him for a while. Eat her sandwich and drink another glass of the overly sweet fruit punch. Then she'd slip away and feed her obsession.

She had a key to Attila's place, and it felt like it was melting a hole in her pocket.

Eighteen

"It is the imperial form," Uziah Donkor said. He stared at the characters carved into the wall, the images crisp, as if put there only yesterday.

"Perhaps," his twin, Rauf, observed. He held the lantern close. "*Semkath. Resh. Nun. Tau.* But there are places where the earlier alphabet shows, as if the passage was written by two different people."

"Or written at the time when the forms were changing?"

"I suppose. See, there's the earlier. There and there. *Waw,* looking more like the number seven in the imperial alphabet. *Yudh,* looking like a bisected Z in the early alphabet. All in the same string. I see Syriac as well. On close inspection, I say definitely more than one hand did these carvings. At least three. And the carvings start roughly a dozen feet down, at this landing. I wonder if there was significance in that." He passed the lantern to Uziah and drew out his cell phone, holding it near a string of characters and taking pictures. "Steal only memories and photographs, as we will never trespass here again," Rauf said. "No one will ever trespass here again."

"And one thing," Uziah added. "We will take only one thing."

"If it is there," Rauf said, replacing the phone and taking back the lantern. "If this is the *true* place. But the variance in words does not settle with me. I find it conflicting."

"You overthink things, brother."

"Maybe."

"It is a second burial, remember? Unknown who is responsible for moving the remains to beneath the city."

"Responsible? Long dead souls who wrote in a long dead language," Rauf said.

"Which you can read far better than I."

"Languages have always come easy to me, Uziah. Mother gave me her artist's soul. Father gave you his keen mind."

Uziah shrugged and looked away from the carvings and down the ancient steps. The edges of them were sharp and the surface flat, evidence of scant foot traffic. "It feels as if I am inside history and that by going deeper I am starting my ascent to heaven. I believe this is the right place. The *only* place the bones could be. The air... when I breathe it deeply, it feels like this is most reverent. I have enough faith for both of us. I cannot wait to see what is at the bottom."

"Reverent? The air feels old, Uziah. Just old. And damp like a marsh. But I am hopeful we can prove the divine."

The men had dressed too warmly for this venture, heavy jeans, flannel shirts, and jackets, hard leather shoes with thick rubber soles, thin latex gloves like a doctor would wear. In unison they took off their jackets and tied them around their waists, Uziah having to adjust his backpack in the process, and Rauf to set down his shovel. Rauf's backpack was not as cumbersome, as most of its contents had already been placed.

Sweat beaded up on their faces.

"October," Rauf said. "It should be cooler."

"Especially here." Uziah grunted in agreement and stepped off the landing and headed down the second set of steps, lantern held in front. Uziah walked slowly and evenly, as if marching. Rauf's footsteps syncopated the rhythm.

The twins dressed similarly, short hair styled in the same manner — although it was not intentional — identical in build, weighing only several pounds apart. From more than a dozen feet away colleagues often found it challenging to tell one from the other. Uziah, however, had a thin scallop-shaped scar along the left side of his face; it showed bright white against his mellow-brown skin, a souvenir of skin cancer surgery. The lines at the corners of his eyes were a little deeper.

"It is good to be just us this time," Rauf said.

Uziah had thought that also, although he had not voiced it. He considered Hamadi a fine associate, in spite of their diverging personalities not allowing for true friendship. Uziah barely tolerated the vintner when he was puffed up and full of himself, but honestly enjoyed the man's company when the two relaxed over a bottle of wine and talked of things beyond their important cause. He felt uncomfortable in Sister Sophia's presence. She was earnest and eager, and while she was driven, Uziah did not believe she'd had enough years on this earth and enough life experience to understand the ramifications of their mission. Besides, she was wholly Roman Catholic and questioned the beliefs of their early-Christian sect. Taavi? He considered the jug-faced man simply muscle.

His brother provided the best company. Uziah thought of Rauf as a mirror, a copy of himself. Although their doctoral studies differed, their interests were close, their hobbies and their core beliefs the same. He was most at ease in Rauf's presence and was, therefore, thankful that Hamadi and the Sister were attending the wedding festivities and not participating in this venture.

And he was doubly thankful that the archaeologist had stalled the Attila dig just long enough. They'd needed time to find this one sacred spot. Unfortunate that it was so near the archaeologist's chambers, but good that they could come here before Abruzi found the warlord's remains.

If the warlord had been uncovered first, the tunnel above would be bustling with government people. This precious find might be unattainable—at least for many, many months. Now they would be able to go in and out, destroy the vault, and let the archaeologist continue his pursuit of the famous Hun.

Just he and his twin for this day's miraculous find.

"You know, there are more than forty noted burial places under this part of Italy," Rauf said. "Mostly Christian, mostly beginning in the catacombs in the second century. Part in response to overcrowding and land shortage above, but mainly because in the earlier times Christians were persecuted, and using catacombs allowed them to bury their dead in secret." Rauf rubbed his thumb against the wall. "There are separate Jewish catacombs, too, not as numerous, but equally important."

"Important to the Jews," Uziah said. "I read that nearly a decade ago the Vatican asked to become involved. But I did not follow the story."

"I did. It was with only part of the catacombs. The Divine Word Missionaries, priests and brothers, administer the St. Domitilla Catacombs."

"Ha! If only the Vatican knew about *this* place." Uziah was happy no one in a religious hierarchy knew of this secret.

"No one will know of this place when we are finished," Rauf said. "If this is true, the remains the shroud pointed to."

"But we will remember this place. God has led us here."

"God and Hamadi."

The stairwell narrowed like a funnel, and at the bottom Uziah had to turn sideways to slip inside the chamber beyond, maneuvering so his backpack did not brush against the walls. He held his breath and shone the lantern around, the room looking like a cave with rounded walls, as if a giant with a gelato scooper had dug out a chunk of Roman clay. The chamber was no larger than a den, and the wall was spotted with more carved letters. He might take the time to read some of it, in spite of the language being difficult for him. Now he was more interested in what sat roughly in the center, on an earthen pedestal.

Rauf had been speaking, but Uziah had been so caught up in his surroundings, he'd paid no attention.

"I said," Rauf spoke louder, "didn't you expect something larger? A proper casket?"

"Brother, this *was* considered a proper casket. Simply different from what we saw the other evening in the old cemetery."

"This is an ossuary." Rauf propped the shovel against the wall, stepped behind Uziah to open his backpack, and removed a silk pillowcase. "Definitely an ossuary. I thought there would be something larger. I want a picture of it."

"A second burial explains the ossuary. In Talmudic times the first burial was likely in a hewn tomb, an elaborate coffin or sarcophagus."

"You are correct; this is the true place we were looking for," Rauf said.

"A reinterment a year or so after the original burial, I suspect. After the flesh is gone and the bones would fit in an ossuary."

Rauf shuddered. "I would not want this for me."

"Perhaps the second burial was customary in this case," Uziah said. "Perhaps, more likely, to hide the remains, to keep them safe from pillagers."

Rauf snorted. "But not safe from us."

"We are not pillagers," Uziah growled. "We are *protectors*." He reached for the box. "We did not need the shovel. I did not care for all the digging the other night. It bothered my back. Heaven smiled on us that we do not have to dig again."

In unison they opened the lid. Then Rauf moved the lantern near.

"It looks uncomfortable, does it not, brother? All the bones stacked together."

Uziah nodded. "I give you the honors."

"*Šhukran.*"

"'*Afwan*," Uziah said. He watched as his brother put his hand inside the pillowcase, reversing it and using it like a mitten, reaching into the box and removing one bone.

Rauf pulled his hand out, tugging the pillowcase up around the bone and folding the silk carefully. He placed the bone in Uziah's backpack, hooked the flap closed, and then the brothers put the lid back on the ossuary. Rauf took a picture of it.

"It is like we were never here, yes?"

Uziah shook his head. "We were here, in the heart of history. If all my other memories fade, I will never forget that we were here." He pulled the right glove off, kissed his fingertips and touched them to the lid, then put the glove back on. "I want to read the walls, but I will need your assistance. This took us so little time to accomplish. We have time to read."

"And to breathe this holy air," Rauf said. "Let's start here," he suggested, shining the light on a curved section of wall. "It is the early characters." Rauf placed a charge of plastic explosives, set the timer, and began to recite the writing.

Uziah chimed in when he recognized words. Uziah was almost sorry Sister Sophia had not accompanied them. She would have relished touching the bones, and she would have loved to hear these very old words.

Rauf set a few more charges around the room as he continued to read.

Almost sorry, Uziah thought again. Sister Sophia would not have approved of the explosives.

NINETEEN

IREM HAD SPENT ONLY A little while at the head table with
Levent, Benito, and the university professor she couldn't
recall the name of. Finished with her seriously delicious
cake, she'd slipped away and told Lacy she was going to her
hotel to rest before the remainder of the wedding festivities.

"If Lev and Benito ask about me, tell them I'll show up
later for drinks and dancing," she'd said. "Make that I'll *try*
to show up if I shake this headache. Migraine."

It hadn't been wholly a lie... not the part about going
back to the hotel.

"What the hell am I doing?" Indeed she went back to
her hotel... to change into jeans and a long sleeve T-shirt,
thick terrycloth socks, and tennis shoes. Out of habit, she
put the Do Not Disturb — *Non Disturbare* — sign on the door.
She stopped at a convenience store for a flashlight and extra
batteries, and a small bottle of lemonade. She didn't want
to wait until tomorrow to go underground. She wanted to
take a look *right now* — admittedly all alone — so she could
get more pictures and so she could think in all of the quiet.

Think about Attila the Hun and everything wrapped
around him.

Without Benito nearby.

She vowed not to spend more than an hour or so down
before coming back up to change into something suitable
for dancing the night away. Levent would be pissed if she
missed the dance.

Alaric? Santiago had mentioned the Visigoth king,
tantalizing her with yet another historical treat. But that

143

didn't feel real to her, a fantasy, a scratch-off lottery ticket that wouldn't pay out. Attila? She thought that was closer to becoming a reality. Irem shared Benito's belief that the famous Hun was behind the carved wall.

She checked her phone and saw a text from Gregario; that he was looking forward to dinner tomorrow. Dear God, was she really going on a date with an Italian policeman she barely knew?

There was a message from her mother, wondering how the wedding was; she'd tell her in person when she returned to Chicago... whenever that would be. Irem stopped herself from texting her friends at the Field. She wanted to tell someone about the bone shroud and the dig. How much longer could she keep this a secret? Santiago had already shared pieces of it, and apparently had made Benito angry.

With every step she took down to the tunnel, she thought about Attila and the tapestry that had pointed Benito to the dig site. Irem decided she'd show the video of the shroud restoration to Gregario; the local authorities needed to know *something* was going on, that maybe the three deaths were more than accidents and natural causes. But how soon would she show him? Tomorrow over dinner? Did she want to touch history so badly that she'd suppress her morals and look the other way for a little while longer?

She bypassed the tourist route and used the service entrance Benito had shown her, remembering the passwords L-E-V-E-N-T and A-B-R-U-Z-I. Too easy, Benito needed to throw some numbers or symbols into the mix.

Irem ran her fingers along a wall, feeling the tickle of vibrations from something heavy driving on the street far above her. Where she knew that claustrophobic Levent would seize up down here, she found it oddly comforting, the silence and the shadows cocooned her like a favorite blanket. It helped that she was alone.

At the Field, Irem had been chided about being an epistemophiliac, someone overly preoccupied with history. Episto, her buddy Marilyn had nicknamed her. Irem dearly loved going through old manuscripts and archiving documents and other antiquities for the museum... her work was more of a passion and an interest than a job. But she'd never been truly *excited* by any of that. Intrigued, amazed, she felt those things, respectful of the past—always, curious about the people who'd left the objects behind, mindful of the history. But excited? This Attila dig was oh-Dear-God-I'll-pass-on-some-of-the-wedding-celebration-and-risk-my-brother's-ire exciting.

Irem recalled a poster she had seen in a business window on Wacker Drive: *Life is not measured in the number of breaths we take, but by the moments our breath is taken away.* Her breath had been taken away the moment Benito told her they were digging for Attila the Hun.

And then taken again when a man shot at her.

She reached the narrow iron door, pulled out her key, and froze. The lock on the gate was gone. Had Lacy and Santiago also sneaked away, beaten her here, too enticed by Attila to stay at the reception?

No, they wouldn't have removed the lock; they would have relocked the gate after passing through. Irem panned the flashlight beam around and spotted the broken lock on the ground just inside the gate, the thick shackle of it cut as if by a bolt cutter. She nearly retraced her steps to get to a higher vantage point where her cell phone would work, call someone and alert them.

Then her brother would know she'd skipped out because of a dead Hun.

And Benito would know she'd ventured down here alone.

And maybe ruin the wedding luncheon.

And her curiosity would not be sated. Who had broken the lock? Thieves? Did they steal any of the artifacts from Benito's site? Were they still here?

Benito's words from dinner came back, when he called archaeology a cutthroat business. "Santiago worries that if someone discovers what we do, who we work to dig up, they will try to steal our find by any means." With everyone at the wedding festivities, this would be a prime opportunity to steal.

She slipped through the gate and aimed her beam low. Irem hurried as much as the cramped confines of the tunnel allowed. She decided she hadn't lied to Lacy at all—she had a rotten headache that throbbed in time with her steps.

Her beam caught a crumpled cigarette pack. Whoever the trespasser was, he didn't care that he might be leaving something behind with fingerprints on it.

Moments later she paused at a crack in the wall, one of the spots she'd noticed on her previous foray where she'd wondered if it had been blocked over. She'd been correct, and someone had cut through to create a narrow opening; inside was a short, thin passage and chiseled steps going what looked to be a long way down. Her beam didn't reach the bottom. Irem debated a moment whether to proceed to the Attila site or investigate this. Was anyone down there?

She didn't hear anything. They'd probably come and gone and left this damage and the cigarette pack behind.

Attila's site or—

This closer curiosity won out, the black belt and a jolt of impulsiveness bolstered her and tamped down any notion of applying common sense.

She took a deep breath, edged inside, and was struck by the age of the place. It felt ancient, and the air was murky with dust particles that made it look foggy. She silently padded down the steps, stopping at a small landing and glimpsing symbols carved in the wall. It was a language, but nothing she recognized. Although she couldn't read many languages, she could recognize them because of the documents she had archived. She pulled out her phone with her free hand and took pictures of the writing, kept the phone out and hit record so she could get a video of her descent. She breathed shallowly, not wanting to add even a whisper to the silence. Farther down a hint of sound intruded, and she held to the step.

Insects? That would hardly make sense. Rats? The trespasser? Maybe the trespasser hadn't come and gone. Maybe he was still here.

Turn back?

Hell no.

Down a handful of more steps she saw the bottom and a faint glow. She turned off her flashlight to remain unnoticed. She listened closely and made out a voice, the language odd and rich sounding, and wholly unfamiliar. The *trespassers*—two male voices—were shuffling around. What was down here?

Was this the "back door" to the Attila dig? Another way to get behind the ornate wall? But the symbols carved in the wall, the ancient language, didn't match Benito's site. This was something different.

Maybe Benito's dig was safe, and these people weren't interested in Attila the Hun. Maybe she should leave and alert her new brother-in-law.

Hell no, no, no.

What if this was Alaric's tomb? That thought shot to the top.

Santiago had mentioned the Visigoth king. Could he be so conveniently buried near Attila the Hun? Cutthroat archaeology, maybe the trespasser was after a prize under Benito's nose... digging now because everyone was occupied with the wedding festivities.

Everyone except Irem.

Had Santiago's emails been discovered by someone other than the department chair in California? Had those emails led trespassers here?

She certainly didn't want the trespassers discovering her, doubting they'd take her presence kindly. But she *had* to know what they were up to and what was at the bottom of these stairs. And she had to know now.

Irem hesitated only a moment more and recorded as much of the conversation as managed to filter into the stairwell. It was primarily one speaker, but the other would interject a few words in unison.

Who were they? And how had they come to discover this place?

Had this location been marked on that old tapestry? Maybe removed during the cloth's restoration? Irem felt dizzy with the possibilities.

Just go a little farther, and then leave. Gain more information.

She crept down a few more steps, stopped at the very bottom, held her breath, and extended her cell phone, recording, hoping it would be her eyes on the men and whatever was beyond. She prayed they wouldn't see it as she turned it back and forth, proud of herself for spying. The voices stopped, and she pulled back.

Then she heard a rustling sound, maybe from the fabric of clothes.

"Finished. That should be it, then," one of the men said. "*Finito. Tamm alaintiha' man. Fini. Peperasmènos.*"

"We have more time," another argued. "The charges are set for thirty minutes. Read this wall, too. Take a few minutes more." The speaker appeared to effortlessly slip from one language to the next. What was their nationality? Maybe her phone had captured pictures of them.

Charges? Explosives?

"Better I take more pictures and we read it later. I am nervous, Rauf. So much explosives you used. I want to be well away from—"

Explosives! Irem took a few steps up, careful to not make a sound. She had to call Benito, the police—Gregario.

"Fine. Fine." There was more rustling. "Fine, I said. A few more pictures of the words. They will be destroyed."

"Take your pictures then. Hurry."

Better that she get to a higher vantage point right now and avoid being caught, call Benito, accept the chewing out that she deserved for cutting out of the reception. To not risk discovery by the men whom she knew nothing about and might be dangerous. Were certainly dangerous—explosives!

Thirty minutes! One of them had said charges were set for thirty minutes.

Could bomb experts get down here in time to disarm everything? The Attila dig could be jeopardized. Benito should know about these people!

She climbed faster, breathed shallowly, was careful and felt her way.

"I'm leaving," the nervous-seeming one said. His agitated voice carried. "I will meet you above when you are finished."

Irem increased her pace, feeling her way as she got farther from the dim glow of light below—which was brightening. When she reached the narrow landing above, she risked turning her flashlight on again, aiming it up so she could safely climb the rest of the way. Her breath caught. She hadn't noticed the clumps on her way down, but then she hadn't aimed her flashlight high. Farther up on the walls were large blobs of what at first glance she thought were clay, but they had small rods in them, and devices that were most certainly timers.

"Shit!" she said, not meaning a sound to come out. It looked like a lot of explosives.

"*Muta 'addin!*" came a shout from below.

Irem didn't know what the words meant other than that she'd said "shit" too loud and had somehow been overheard or spotted. Sure she had a black belt in hapkido, but she didn't know what they had — guns? Like the man on the rainy sidewalk? They'd planted explosives after all.

She dropped her phone into her pocket, still recording, and ran up the remaining steps, registering how sharp they were, untraveled. Outside the crack she spun to her right and shot forward into the tunnel, but her toe caught on a jagged section of floor and she tripped, her knees landing hard. The flashlight went flying from her fingers, skittered across the floor, and its light winked out. Everything turned blackest black.

Shit. Shit. Shit. Irem reached for her cell phone again as she jumped to her feet and ran. She used the light from the phone, but it was faint, kept her fingers against one wall to guide her, trusting to her memory of the corridor. She slammed into an edge, twisting, and nearly fell again. "Shit." She managed to catch herself, but flickers of pain radiated from her left knee. Hurt to bend it, but no time to check it out. Explosives!

Irem was forced to a slower pace, bumping against the wall as she went, like a pinball bouncing off rubber bands, and hearing the slap of footsteps behind her. She turned off the cell phone light so they wouldn't see her. She pressed herself against the wall, held her breath.

The black behind her lightened to gray; the men behind her had a light.

Black belt, she could turn and face them. She'd taken down the pickpocket easily enough.

She turned on the cell phone again and kept going. But she twisted her leg when she stumbled once more, her knee worse for the misstep. More pain throbbed when she put a little weight on her leg… a little more weight… in that instant if agony had a color it would be bright neon yellow. She'd felt nothing so awful ever before and tears flowed.

Oh God, oh God. She'd ripped something or broken something. *Oh God, oh God, oh dear God.*

"Stop now!"

A lighter gray intruded on the darkness, and she glanced over her shoulder to see the bobbing glow from a lantern, the beam wide and brightening as the man holding it jogged closer. She couldn't make out any details about him, wasn't about to take the time. She turned forward again, taking advantage of the increased light to better see the walls of the corridor.

"Stop!" he hollered. To someone else: "Rauf! It's a woman. The American from the Conservatori! I will catch her!"

Like hell you'll catch me, she thought, hobbling faster, the pain shooting in jolts from her knee. Her leg wholly locked and she pitched forward, catching herself and then rushing forward in a staggering gait with one leg straight, putting nearly all her weight on her good one. The light around her became brighter still, and she knew the man was catching up, his footsteps louder, and she could hear him breathe.

Time to trust the black belt.

Irem again dropped the phone into her pocket, spun on her good leg, and raised the injured one, intending to strike her pursuer and knock the air from him. It was a simple hapkido kick, aimed at his chest, and it found a mark. But in the process she struck the lantern he'd been carrying, dashing it against the wall, hearing something shatter, and the clunk of metal and glass hitting the ground.

The color of pain in her leg became dazzling white, and she clenched her jaw to keep from screaming.

Then everything happened at once. Absolute darkness swallowed her, and a competing ache blossomed when the man blindly flailed away and landed a lucky punch to her chest. He was strong, and the impact pushed her back. Off balance, she tottered and fell, dropping against the stone, not quite flat, her shoulders and head striking the wall. She heard him shuffle forward and felt him trip over her. He grunted, and there was the rustle of fabric from his erratic movements. It sounded like he might have fallen, too.

"Rauf!" he boomed. "Come with a light! Rauf! I am blind! Hurry! Get your ass up here!"

She pulled her good leg close and pushed against the wall to stand, her shoulders against the rough stone of the corridor. The back of her head felt sticky; Irem figured she was bleeding from the impact. She was suddenly nauseous... a result of her pain? Dizzy, she sucked in a deep breath and focused only on the sounds. She wanted to edge past him and reach the gate... and from there find her way toward a lighted tunnel and escape.

"Rauf!" he bellowed, as he bumped into her, the scent of some musky cologne strong. She heard fabric swishing as he flailed, felt the air move from his swings, and then felt another punch connect as she maneuvered past him. He must have gotten up because this time he hit her squarely in the sternum, and it added to the miasma of pains that threatened to claim her. He must have also hit the wall because angry words rumbled in the darkness; Italian profanity mixed with a language she didn't recognize.

Irem held her breath and slipped farther away from him, the sound of his cursing and the rustle of his clothes. She stepped on broken glass, but that sound didn't matter because he was shouting "Rauf!" again. "Where the hell are you?" And in between the words she swore she heard more feet pounding. The other man.

She forced a faster pace despite her pain, and a fear rose—worse than what she'd felt that night down in the subway when she'd been mugged. In a foreign country, under the city; these men weren't simple thieves. *Faster!* She'd been an idiot to go down those ancient stairs. Her damned curiosity could well be her demise. *Use the dark, don't pull out the phone.*

Irem considered herself a strong woman, and up until this point not a stupid one. That proverbial notion of living to fight another day sounded damn good. Faster!

"*Fessacchione!*" The second man shouted as he came up from the steps, flashlight leading, but its beam not reaching her.

Irem kept going—even though she realized in the darkness she'd gotten herself turned around and was heading toward Benito's dig rather than toward the gate that would lead to a way out.

"I'm over here! Rauf! The woman, she got past me. No, no, no. The other way."

"Let her die to the explosives, then."

"Rauf! We have time to catch her. We have minutes! We must find out what she knows."

"You mean find out who else knows."

Footsteps coming loudly, a light coming up behind her.

Shit. Shit Shit. Irem knew they would trap her, unless....

Hope tickled in the back of her dizzy brain. She bit down on her lower lip to stifle a whimper and hobbled along the slope, feeling her way. This way was twisty, like a serpent, and after the first coil, she thought maybe this plan might work. If it didn't, maybe her brother would never know what happened to her. Irem trusted to her memory and prayed she could find her way through the night-black maze of Rome's belly.

Find her way to Attila's chamber, where hopefully the explosives would not reach.

She prayed the Hun tomb would not become her final resting place.

TWENTY

IREM HAD SPENT A FEW hours in the emergency room the night she'd been mugged in the Chicago subway. She wished she was in an ER right now. The stabs of pain from her knee had stopped an,d it was one constant insufferable sensation. The ache in her chest couldn't compete with it, but it contributed to her misery. And she was so nauseated that she swore the essence of everything she'd eaten since coming to Italy was trying to make a spewing reappearance. Breathing deeply hurt, so she took as shallow of breaths as possible while warring against the dizziness and clinging to the stairway that led down to the room that might hold Attila the Hun.

She expected to die, but she wasn't going to just lie down and wait for it.

Although she'd stumbled around in the inky black and knocked things over, she risked using the light from her cell phone again and managed to find the pieces of plywood that Santiago had used to hide the stairs so he could surprise Benito. The thought came to mind of the blind chicken finding kernels of corn. She crept down those stairs and placed the plywood across the opening above her, turned off her light, and prayed she'd concealed herself. She kept the phone recording.

Dear God, don't let them look under the plywood. And don't let the explosives reach this far.

Irem had been able to stay ahead of them despite her limping gait, but only because she was familiar with the serpentine course and knew what room she needed to find. Likely they'd look in all the chambers, and that would slow them. But she knew they'd eventually come here because she'd heard one of them say:

"We can afford no witnesses. The *cagna* must be dealt with."

Cagna, that word had been in her Italian language book. It meant "bitch."

Yeah, she was pretty sure if they found her she was going to die.

Why the hell hadn't she simply stayed longer at the wedding luncheon?

A good sister would have stayed at the reception. A good sister would not be in this predicament. She wouldn't be sick to her stomach, in agony, and terrified.

Fuck my curiosity, she fumed. *And fuck Italy and Attila the Hun.*

"*Figlio di puttana!*" The Italian version of son of a bitch came to her muted through the plywood.

"*Ya gazma yib ig-gazma!*"

How many languages did these men speak? Why can't they talk in —

"How did we lose her, Rauf?"

Finally, English.

"Somewhere. We lost her somewhere. Maybe you were wrong. Maybe she ran the other way. Maybe she is outside and going for help."

"*Cazzata!* She had to come this way. We would have heard the gate grind. And she wasn't running, she limped."

She listened to them shuffling around, knocking over Benito's equipment. One stepped on the plywood, and her chest tightened so hard she couldn't breathe. Her fingers nervously twitched against the coins embedded in the steps. They said something else in a language she couldn't recognize, and then the man on the plywood moved away.

"We have no time," the one called Rauf said. "The charges. The tunnel will blow, and I do not intend to be buried down here with all of the saints and sinners."

"We do have time," the other argued. "A little. *Sufficiente.*
Maybe there is more to the archaeologist's dig. Check the
other chambers again."

"*Minchione!* I am leaving — with the bone. Time? We are
out of it."

"But the *cagna* — "

"The nosy bitch? We can find her. She is American,
works for the archaeologist. We can find her, I say. *If* she
found a way up. If instead she is still down here, hiding,
she will be crushed. We will use the rest of the explosives.
Everything. We will blow it all up. Then we'll manage the
others."

"The American children."

"I'm leaving before I join the dead here. Coming,
brother?"

"Yes."

Irem needed to leave, too... get to high enough ground
so that her cell phone would get a signal... call the police,
Gregario, about the plastic explosives, and warn Benito,
Santiago, and Lacy about the two men of many languages.
But she needed to make sure those men were gone.

Hope flickered that she might actually make it out of the
underground alive.

How much time before the explosives detonated?

"No witnesses," echoed in her throbbing head. But so
did the worry of being trapped in the tunnels with C4. She
waited until she was certain they had left, then cautiously
reached up to move the plywood, and felt herself instead
sag against the stairs, her arms limp as the dizziness she'd
been dancing with wholly took over.

Irem tasted cake, the slice she'd had at the reception
was mildly sweet, shot through with a raspberry paste that
she'd held on her tongue until it melted. The icing was some
sort of buttercream, she guessed, but better than anything
she'd had before. Like a child, she had eaten the layers first,
leaving the frosting for last. Almost asked for a second piece
of that cake... but she'd wanted to slip away from the head
table and go under Rome.

The shroud appeared crystal in her head, then all the threads unraveled and instead she saw an image of Attila... or what he might have looked like. She'd seen sketches and various representations of the warlord, and all of those flitted through her mind like a slideshow; everything so clear, even though a part of her knew the only thing in front of her eyes was blackness. A face came to the fore — handsome, with a long nose, flashing eyes. Not Attila. The policeman. Gregario. Ari.

The cake had been so good, all the flavors of it settled pleasantly on her tongue. The music piped in had been soft, quasi-classical, a soundtrack... the Indiana Jones love theme, fitting for an archaeologist's wedding. She heard the strains weaving between her ears, spiraling around the pounding in her head, the trill of a woodwind that came louder and made her tremble.

Made the steps beneath her tremble like someone was violently tickling her. Like the sensation she felt touching a wall when something heavy drove by overhead. But this was longer and more pronounced, and her teeth clacked together.

All the images and sounds vanished, and Irem huddled in the blackness, cramped on ancient stairs. The air was damp and dead feeling, and her mouth and throat were dry, all trace of the exquisite cake a memory. She worked up some saliva while she explored with her fingers — the only parts of her that weren't hurting, finding the embedded coins that all together spelled out: *Numquam floret quo ambulau. Flagellum Dei.*

The men must have left — she didn't hear anything except her breath, ragged until she calmed herself. She risked pulling out her cell phone, using its light. The battery so low, the light nothing more than a suggestion. She turned it off and opted for the utter blackness. She needed to preserve whatever breath of battery remained so she could get to higher ground and call for help.

Warn them about the explosives.

The trembling she'd felt... maybe they'd already gone off. All that plastique.

Irem edged upward, all her weight directed to the right side of her body, finding the top step and reaching up with her fingers to touch the plywood. She waited a few moments, wanting to be certain the men were gone.

Irem held her breath and slid the plywood aside. Crawled out of the stairwell, and likened it to swimming in oil—everything was inky black. She remained on her hands and knees and crawled around, fingers brushing against rubble, a wooden tray, the edge of a depression where Lacy and Santiago had dug to find a skeleton, one of the warlord's generals, they'd thought. She tried to remember what the chamber looked like with the tripod lights blaring, and after a few minutes of bumping into things, she found the small generator, fingers dancing until she figured out how to turn it on. The noise hurt. One of the tripod lights blared, the others broken; all of them had been tipped over.

Trays that had once held recovered artifacts were smashed, likely stepped on, and the jewelry and armor pieces scattered. If the men had been thieves, they would have taken the valuable bracelets and armbands. Maybe they'd been in too much of a hurry to take things. Flashlights were scattered on the ground, water bottles strewn haphazardly, Santiago's CD player on its back, drawer opened and disc cracked.

Irem took it in quickly, noting all of Benito's equipment in disarray, too. She crawled around and took two flashlights, stuck a small one in her pocket and turned another one on, clicked off the generator, wanting to conserve the archaeologists' power and cut the noise. She braced herself on the generator and used it to help her stand. Her left leg burned, but it was constant and endurable, not the ice pick jabbing sensation from before. Maybe it was still as intense, she thought, and she'd only inured herself to it. She still couldn't put much weight on it, so she hobbled forward as fast as she could, one hand against the wall, the other holding the flashlight, the beam bobbing crazily from her awkward gait.

Hurry. Hurry. Hurry.

The bouncing beam of her flashlight revealed cracks in the stone—walls, floor, ceiling—in places the pattern looking like a spider web. Had it been like that before? Stone dust hung in the air, making the way ahead appear hazy, and she had to sidestep some fallen chunks. Her stomach roiled. Around one curve, and a quick stop at the portable toilet, back in the tunnel, and then around another bend, the air tasting different here, like it was burnt. One more twist of tunnel took her past all of Benito's excavated chambers.

The explosions had already happened, Irem realized. She'd either not heard the noise or had blacked out when they'd occurred. She leaned against the wall and with her free hand pulled out her cell phone. A quick check of the time — 1:00 — then turned it off again.

Please let there be enough juice for a call when I get higher.

One o'clock. That was good. She'd only been down here less than an hour; everyone would still be at the church reception, and so she would soon discover how pissed and pleased Benito and Levent would be. Then the A.M. registered, and she froze.

Irem had been unconscious for roughly a dozen hours.

"Shit."

No wonder I'm so damn thirsty. She considered turning back and grabbing one of the water bottles. Somewhere she'd dropped her lemonade. But as quickly as that thought surfaced, she forced it back down. It had been difficult enough to limp along to this point.

I need to get my ass out of here.

Benito needed to know about the men and explosives… and no doubt needed to chew her a new one for cutting out of the reception to feed her Attila fix.

Levent would be doubly pissed by what she'd done. If she hadn't told Lacy she was going back to her hotel, her brother might have been looking for her. It wouldn't have registered that something was wrong when he couldn't reach her on the cell… Irem had a habit of turning it off. And she'd foolishly put the *Non Disturbare* sign on her door.

It had been selfish of her, coming down here, and her injuries were the price she paid for that and her overactive curiosity. At least she was breathing, and if the men had found her she might not be.

"No witnesses," one of them had said.

What the flaming hell had been so important they needed to blow the chamber to pieces to cover it up? In their eyes something there was more important than Attila the Hun. They'd mentioned "the archaeologist." They knew Benito was digging here. They'd also mentioned the other Americans, which had to be his assistants. Irem needed to warn all of them.

Around the next curve, and she thought maybe they'd be right on the "no witnesses" part. Her bobbing beam of light bounced off the collapsed tunnel a dozen feet ahead. The amount of explosives had obliterated all traces of the stairway and chamber the men had trespassed into... and had brought down the main tunnel — and her only way out.

"Shit. Shit. Shit. *Porca troia*," she said, effortlessly remembering more profanity from her Italian book. "Fucking *porca troia*."

Maybe she'd get out of here in a half-dozen hours or so, when Lacy and Santiago came down here to work, probably Benito with them. Attila wouldn't let any of them stay in bed overly long. They'd find her after they dug out the rubble. She could survive down here for that long, right?

They would be able to dig out the rubble, wouldn't they?

Irem didn't want to wait to find out.

I gotta get the hell out of here.

Lumbering forward, still dizzy, hurting, furious at herself, she set the flashlight at the base of the rubble, levered herself up, and tugged down stones from the top. She started at a frantic pace, pulling one chunk free after another. Irem continued clawing, angry and frightened and aching... but it didn't hurt quite so much anymore.

She gagged on the stone dust and felt her finely manicured fingernails break. Her left hand froze up momentarily, all sensation leaving it. Irem shook out her hand and cursed, redoubled her efforts with her right hand. She slipped down the rubble and climbed it again, struck her head against the ceiling and wondered if indeed she ought to wait until Lacy and Santiago came down in a handful of hours.

Then she went at it once more, finding some feeling returning to her left hand, the fingers working, grabbing stone after stone and pulling it down, tumbling down with them. She pulled the other flashlight from her pocket and moved the beam across the stones. She'd made some progress.

Irem hooked the flashlight under her arm and climbed again, dug and dug until her fingers bled, then she paused to catch her breath. Her arms felt so heavy and it had become onerous to lift them.

"Don't quit," she hissed.

She kept at it until she thought she'd pass out from the exertion. Then Irem sensed the slightest movement of air and reached forward into the darkness, her arm extending through a gap in the rubble. A little more work and she had made a hole big enough to squeeze through. Shining the light down, she saw the iron gate.

"Thank God."

Irem pulled herself through and slammed her teeth together when she fell down the other side, jagged bits of stone slicing at her and piling onto her pain.

Holding the flashlight close, and with considerable effort, she got to her feet again. She galumphed forward, crying joyfully when she grabbed onto the iron gate, holding on, letting the tears flow and gulping in air, despite the deep breaths hurting.

Irem didn't want to guess how long it took her to find the service door and make it up an impossibly tall staircase. She fell several times, once lying still for a while, dozing apparently because her cell phone read 2:43 A.M. when she risked turning it on again. Finally she pulled herself along with the handrail, worried that she might fall again and break something.

Outside!

Dear God, thank you. Thankyouthankyouthankyou.

Heavy city air had never smelled so wonderful, even though it was laced with smoke. The streetlights and fluorescent lights of bars across the street cut the dark—as did the spinning blue lights of two firetrucks parked in front of the corner building where Lacy and Santiago's apartment had been. The burned husk still smoldered.

Irem sagged against the bricks behind her, retrieved her cell phone, the bar barely showing. The colors of streetlights and the flashing lights of the firetrucks spun like a child's kaleidoscope, the patterns changing and brightening. People milled about on the corner, the colors swirling around them and distorting their silhouettes.

Someone pointed at her, the arm snaking out like a stretched rubber band, said something.

" —*l'ospedale.*"

"Look, a woman is down."

"*La polizia.*"

"*Come ti chiami?*"

"She is injured."

"*Chiamate un'ambulanza!*"

Irem pushed back her wooziness and punched in 1-1-2 on her phone. "*Ambulanza,*" she said with as much voice as she could summon. "*Per favore.* I need an—"

Suddenly it was blackest black again.

TWENTY-ONE
OCTOBER 9

"FIVE TWENTY."

"What?" Had Levent just named a color and ascribed a number to it?

"Five twenty-one, Miss Irem Madigan who works at the Field Museum in Chicago. You asked me the time."

"The time. P.M."

"*Sì.*"

Irem registered the hospital bed, the antiseptic odor; saw the drip of something that flowed down a tube and into her arm. She also registered the police officer she'd met after the pickpocket incident: Gregario Ricci, *Agente Sceito.* Ari. What was he doing here?

"What is this?" Irem nodded to the IV.

Ari shrugged. "Medicine. The nurse said you were dehydrated. Maybe it is fluids. Maybe it is medicine."

Irem tried to sit up, but she felt so heavy. Tried again and managed to swing her legs over the side of the bed, her feet dangling just above the tile floor. The sheet fell away, and she saw that she was in an ugly pink and blue hospital gown and that her knee was heavily wrapped.

Gregario leaped up and came around to the other side of the bed and gently put his hands on her shoulders.

"I have to get out of here."

"You cannot go anywhere, Irem. The doctor, she will be in soon I was told. You must —"

"Whoa." Everything felt fuzzy... her fingers, her head. Her tongue was thick and her mouth dry like a sandbox.

It felt like she was swimming in a mass of cotton candy. Surprisingly, her knee didn't hurt; she barely registered it. "Dehydrated. Yeah. Could you—"

Before she finished the sentence he reached to a small table, poured a cup of water, and held it to her. Irem wrapped the fingers of both hands around it and greedily drank. She handed the cup back, and he filled it again. She drank that, too.

"Better, *sí*?"

"Thank you, Gregario."

"Ari."

"Thanks, I—" Irem stared at him, perfectly dressed in his uniform. "How did you know I was here? Why are you here? How could you possibly—"

"The apartment fire yesterday evening and into the morning hours," he said. "I was summoned to that. You were across the street."

"Oh."

"Arson, definitely. Perhaps terrorism. The police were summoned, and I was assigned."

"Oh. I was—"

"Found across the street, as I mentioned."

"Yeah. But I—" The memory of coming up from the underground slammed into her, and she vividly pictured the firetrucks, the lights, and the smoke. "I wasn't in the building."

"I know. Fortunate you were across the street."

"I'd been at Benito's dig. Came up… and now it seems I've been in the hospital all day. I have to get out of here. Talk to Benito. My brother. Lacy and Santiago Garcia. I have to—"

"You're not going anywhere," Gregario repeated. His voice had a hard edge to it. "You are scheduled for surgery tomorrow morning."

Irem's mouth dropped open. "I can't. Surgery? I don't have time. Surgery? What for? I have to talk to Benito. There was an explosion. Surgery?"

"On your knee. I was not so impolite as to ask the doctor what will be done. I leave that question to you. As for the underground explosion, we are aware of that. Police were underneath earlier today. All of the tunnels are closed. Now that you are awake, a detective or two will arrive soon to ask you about the explosion and what you were doing under the street. We will need your help with the investigation."

Irem took a deep breath, discovered that it hurt, and let it out slowly, breathed shallowly instead. She closed her eyes and tried to put all her thoughts in order. Then she gave Gregario an abridged version of the events.

"I discovered that someone had broken Benito's lock on the gate, trespassed, and had opened a mysterious sealed chamber. Idiot me, I went down and heard men talking, waited too late to leave, and saw a shitload of plastic explosives. Then they chased me. Two of them. Honestly, I know they wanted to kill me, probably think I'm dead under the rubble. Geeze, I hope they think I'm dead. I've got a fucking target painted on my—"

"These men—"

"—were hellbent on catching me. I got turned around in the dark, hid in Benito's dig, and eventually they went away. I really thought they'd find me. I really thought I was dead. But I know that one of them... his name is Rauf, I heard the other one keep calling this guy Rauf. Anyway, one of them was worried about the explosives, so they left. I guess I passed out and woke up sometime after everything had gone boom."

She really needed to tell Benito about this.

He raised a hand. "Save your stamina, Miss Irem Madigan." His pleasant voice had returned. "Tell the story later in detail, when the detectives arrive. One or two will be here soon. And if they do not speak English well, I will translate. The explosion, perhaps related to the fire. My department has much work to do."

She held out the empty cup, and he refilled it. "Surgery, eh?"

Gregario nodded.

"Great."

"Fortunate you were across the street and not in that apartment building."

"Yeah, you mentioned that before. Where is my phone? I called for the ambulance. I remember that. But I don't remember anything after that. Until I woke up here. And I don't remember talking to anyone in the ambulance. Don't remember the ride, getting here. Chunks of my memory are all foggy. But my phone... I might have dropped it. The phone is important—"

Gregario looked disappointed. "Americans and their cell phones. I thought you were different about cell phones."

"It's *really* important."

He gave an exaggerated sigh. "Perhaps it is with your clothes... what was left of your clothes." Gregario looked over his shoulder to the door. "The doctor, she should see you, now that you are awake, and—"

"The phone," Irem repeated. "It's *really* important. The men I mentioned underground. One of them named Rauf. I recorded those men talking, down under the street, the ones who planted the explosives. I probably got video of them stored on that phone, certainly pictures of the walls and the plastic explosives. It's all on the phone."

Gregario stepped back. "I agree now. The phone is truly important, Miss Irem Madigan. I will leave to see what happened to your belongings, Signorina Rossi."

"Who?"

"They've logged you here as Signorina Rossi. Equivalent of your Jane Doe. No ID on you."

"Just Irem, okay?" She reached out to grab his arm. "It's *my* phone, Ari. The detectives will want to take it. I have a lot of things on that phone, of my trip here—"

"Yes, they will take it. But they won't keep it. You will get it back—provided I can find it—and they will not strip its contents. We don't work that way. We will copy. We won't steal." He smiled and stepped to the doorway. "You do not move. *Sì?*"

"*Sì.*" But the moment after he left she eased off the bed and stood, the tile cool against her bare feet. She bit her lip when the pain in her bandaged knee knifed through her. Irem realized that she had a wrap on her arm, too. She managed to maneuver the pole with the IV drip and hobbled into the bathroom, desperately needing to empty her bladder.

Finished, she stood in front of the mirror.

"Oh crap. I look like crap. Crappity crap." Something that resembled a shower cap contained her hair. Her face and neck were a mass of purpling bruises. More bruises on her arms, not as dark and not so numerous. "I look like absolute hell."

Like a tank rolled over me, and backed up for good measure. Her lip was split, and she spotted stitches along her right jawline and near her right ear. Irem was suddenly embarrassed that the handsome policeman had seen her like this. *I have to talk to Benito. Lev. I need to see Lev. He's probably worried sick about me.*

She hobbled back to the bed and was able to lever herself up into it when Gregario returned with a doctor and a nurse. He carried a large clear plastic bag that had her torn and filthy shirt and pants in it, shoes, jacket, and at the bottom… her blessed cell phone.

Irem reached for the bag, but the doctor stepped in front of Gregario.

"Irem Madigan?" The doctor looked and sounded Indian, was thin and small and had a warm expression. "English, correct? American?"

"Yes. Chicago."

"We did not find any identification on you."

"I'd left all that in my hotel room. I'm Irem Madigan, not Signorina Rossi."

"We will keep you listed as Signorina Rossi."

"At my insistence," Gregario said. "The men who tried to kill you might be smart enough to check hospital listings."

The doctor moved closer. "You were brought in exceedingly early this morning with a concussion, cracked ribs, torn meniscus, and many contusions. The *terepia intensiva*—critical care unit—administered a morphine-four drip. Here, you are on a Dilaudid IV now, but we will discontinue that within the hour and give you Tramadol, and Zofran for nausea."

Irem felt numb by the information, hadn't realized she was in such rough shape. She needed to let Levent know she would be all right.

"There is an opening in the orthoscopic surgery suite at nine in the morning, and you are scheduled to have your meniscus repaired. Then I want you here for two more days, starting rehab immediately. We'll fit you for a brace, of course, and you can use crutches or a cane, whichever you prefer and works best for you. We will recommend an outpatient facility for continued rehab."

"Oh God." Irem's stomach clenched. "Dr. —"

"Dr. Lakshmishree Byrraju."

Irem decided not to muddle the pronunciation. "Two days here?"

"Correct. If you believe that is not long enough—"

"Oh, no. That's plenty long. Too long. I have to let my brother know that I'm here. Really, I need to get out of here. I have a hotel room. I'm paying for a hotel room that I'm not staying in. I have to—"

"After two more days you can go back to your hotel room. Or call them now, have your things put in their storage and check out while you are here. Save yourself paying for a room you are not using. With hope, they will agree. Most hotels here are good."

"I'll get Lev to pack, check me out. I don't want to pay for something I'm not using."

"I understand, as I would not want to pay for that either." Dr. Byrraju sounded sympathetic. "Surgery at nine tomorrow morning. Rehab will start in the afternoon. Two more days here." She gave a slight bow, spun on the ball of her foot, and left.

The nurse came forward and checked the IV and spoke rapid Italian.

"The nurse says she will remove the IV when that bag is finished, and that a light dinner will be brought," Gregario translated. "The detectives, two, are on their way, probably twenty, thirty minutes." He reached into the bag and pulled out Irem's phone.

She grabbed it as the nurse retreated to the hall. "C'mon. C'mon." Irem worried over it a moment, her fingers a blur on the keys. "I have no charge. And no charger. No. No. No charge. Piss."

"Perhaps I have a charger that will work with your phone."

She looked up, exasperated, and talked rapid-fire. "Dead. *Morti*. I got all the stuff from the Conservatori, and the restorer. I want you to see it. You *need* to see it. About the tapestry. I have pictures of the tunnel and the explosives, the men. Sure, I uploaded most everything to the Cloud… but not the men with the explosives. I hadn't done that yet. Damn battery went dead—*morti*. Levent might not know I'm in the hospital. I need to tell him I'm okay… gonna be okay. I need to call my brother, get him to go to my hotel room, get me some clothes and my charger, check me out so I don't keep paying on that room, borrow his laptop and—"

"About your brother, Irem."

"I need to tell him I'm here. I have to talk to Benito—"

"Dr. Benito Abruzi?"

"Yes."

"He knows you are here."

"I have to talk to him. And Lev, I—"

"Your brother, Levent Abruzi, is here." Gregario's face was suddenly grim.

Irem quavered. She didn't think he meant that Levent was out in the hall waiting to see her. "Lev—"

Gregario slipped into Italian. "*Terapia Intensiva con il cranio fratturato.*"

"What? Tell me where is Lev?"

"The apartment fire late last night… many people died, many were injured. Your brother was in the fire. Suffered very bad burns and a fractured skull. He is in the critical care unit. Dr. Benito Abruzi is there with him."

Irem felt dizzy. Her fingers dug into the mattress, and she fell back.

TWENTY-TWO

SOPHIA HELD THE WINE ON her tongue: a Sauvignon Blanc. The elegantly fluted bottle had been pulled from a case gifted to Hamadi by a fellow vintner who lived somewhere in the Bordeaux region of France. They traded vintages from time to time. Sophia savored the citrus, melon, and floral notes, thought it slightly smoky. Perhaps there was a touch of peach as well. A fine wine, *certamente*, though not in the same league as Hamadi's whites. In fact, she'd never tasted wine as good as what Hamadi made.

But perhaps she was biased.

"I can tell that you study it, the wine," Hamadi said. "You've become a student of many things since leaving the convent, Sister."

"*Si*, I study the wine," she replied. "The world has become my teacher, dear Uncle."

"Someday all the world will be my teacher, too." James sat at the dining table directly across from Sophia. He beamed at her and raised his glass of milk as if in a toast. "But now you are my teacher, Sister Sophia. Correct, Papa?"

"Correct, James," Hamadi said. "Until next fall when you enroll in a private school."

"For the gifted," James added.

"Yes," Hamadi said. "For the gifted."

"But Sister Sophia will continue to teach me. And sing with me and play croquet and take me to the Conservatori."

They dined formally tonight, dressing as if they were going out to an expensive restaurant, but staying in to continue James's lessons on etiquette and to explore cuisines. They would speak only English at the table.

Music played softly in the background, surrounding them from numerous speakers high and barely visible along the walls. The piece was Gioacchino Rossini's *La Cambiale di Matrimonio* from 1810. Sophia was well read on Italian composers and knew that Rossini had been one of the first to heavily incorporate emotions into his pieces. His most popular was *The Barber of Seville*, but Sophia favored *La Cambiale* over that; she sensed an innocence and determination in it. Fond of opera, she might suggest that they take James to a performance next week. Arias of Giuseppe Verdi and Giacomo Puccini were scheduled at the Sacristy of the Church of St. Agnes in Agone on Rome's famous Piazza Navona. James could appreciate both the music and the building... the architecture would enthrall him.

"You look very nice tonight, Sister Sophia," James said.

"Thank you, James." Sophia wore a calf-length skirt and three-quarter sleeve blouse by Italian designer Massimo Giorgetti. She used to feel uncomfortable in costly garments, but had become more tolerant of them, appreciating the fit and construction, and understanding that her uncle was beyond simply wealthy and so certainly could spend some of his money on her.

James and Hamadi wore matching gray suits. "And you look quite handsome, James, Uncle."

Hamadi nodded as an attendant came forward and poured him more wine. Sophia put a hand over the top of her glass.

"Not yet. I will enjoy another after the meal," she said.

The attendant lit the tapers on the table, scenting the air with vanilla. He gave a curt bow and retreated to the kitchen, returning a few minutes later with a plate of appetizers: bruschetta—toasted bread topped with diced tomatoes, basil, and garlic. Sophia watched James grimace as he ate; the boy was not fond of a heavy application of garlic, but never outright complained about what was set before him, always acting appreciative even if his facial expressions gave him away.

"Papa, may I offer a prayer for the archaeologist's special friend?"

"Of course."

James finished the piece of toast, bowed his head, and spoke clearly. "'Is any one of you in trouble? He should pray. Is anyone happy? Let him sing songs of praise. Is any one of you sick? He should call the elders of the church to pray over him and anoint him with oil in the name of the Lord.' May Dr. Benito's special friend be healed."

"Very good, James," Sophia said.

"May he not be punished for being gay," James continued. "May the hellfire that burned him—"

"You are kind, James," Sophia interrupted. "We all pray that Levent Abruzi's suffering is eased."

She did not want to debate same-sex marriage with the child over the evening meal and was relieved when the salad arrived—Romaine, artichokes, with lemon vinaigrette and parmesan cheese. The main course was almost too quick after that.

"This is delicious," Hamadi pronounced.

James took a bite, grimaced again, and then politely smiled. "What is it?"

The attendant answered: "Crusted flounder, pan fried and seasoned simply with fresh ground pepper, lemon, and served over orzo."

"Flounder. That's fish, yes? I should like fish. Matthew wrote: 'Once again, the kingdom of heaven is like a net that was let down into the lake and caught all kinds of fish.' Jesus and Peter were fishermen. I should like fish, Papa. This is a nice meal. But I like chicken better. What about the Chicken Marsala? That is very tasty. I thought we were—"

"Tomorrow," the attendant returned. "At the market today the flounder looked too good to ignore. Tomorrow Chicken Marsala will be prepared."

James grinned and worked on the fish. "What about dessert?" It came out soft.

"Triple chocolate cake," the attendant said. "Would that be to your liking, young James?"

The boy nodded and ate the fish faster.

"It was not hellfire that burned Levent Abruzi," Hamadi told the boy when he had finished his own plate and signaled for another glass of wine. This time Sophia edged her empty glass forward. "It was an apartment fire, orchestrated by man and not God... although it was in the name of God. Lives were lost. Levent Abruzi, a great artist and a friend of mine, was severely injured. God was not punishing him. God did not set the fire."

"'Therefore confess your sins to one another and pray for one another, that you may be healed,'" James quoted. "I pray that Dr. Benito's special friend, who is your friend also, will be all right, Papa."

"I am certain he will be, James," Hamadi said.

Sophia was not certain. She'd gone with Hamadi to the hospital late this morning, and even though she did not venture into the critical care room, she saw Levent through a window. She would not have said that to James. In fact, Sophia wondered if it would be more fortunate for the young artist if he died.

The attendant carried a silver tray with three pieces of chocolate cake on it. Sophia noted that James fidgeted happily. "Sir, one of your associates has arrived, Dr. Uziah Donkor. Should I escort him in or ask him to wait?"

"James, take your cake to your room. There is boring business to discuss. Send Uziah in immediately."

The boy took his glass of milk and cake and dutifully excused himself from the table.

"Bring a glass of wine for our visitor," Hamadi said. "And a large slice of cake. Uziah appreciates chocolate."

The attendant returned with Uziah, set a plate of dessert for him, and poured wine for everyone. Sophia accepted her rare third glass. "Will there be anything else, sir?"

Hamadi shook his head. "I will clean up myself tonight. Enjoy the remainder of the evening."

Sophia nearly joined James, as she knew Hamadi and Uziah would talk about unpleasant things. But there would be a good purpose to some of the conversation, and she did not want to miss that part. She slowly ate the cake. It was scrumptious, made for taking tiny bites to prolong the rush of flavor.

Uziah took a seat and nodded approvingly at the wine and cake. "Rauf left a few hours ago for Sicily. He secured the relic from our delve yesterday, as well as the one retrieved from the grave field six nights past. He will spend one day at the university to catch up on necessary paperwork from his brief leave. Then he will begin the laboratory preparations, and I will join him and start in earnest on the next project."

"Very good," Hamadi pronounced. "I am pleased. And I will arrive there a day or two beyond that. I am anxious."

The men spent several minutes discussing the complexity of their studies, eventual ramifications, and whether to carefully leak this to the public, however if they did, it likely would be a few years away. Sophia listened attentively; her heart was glad at this discourse, and it bolstered her rationale for leaving the convent.

Pausing from the talk, Uziah broke off a large forkful of cake and chewed quickly. Two more forkfuls, and it was nearly gone. "This is excellent, Hamadi. Chocolate. So bad for my diet. I swear I weigh ten pounds more than Rauf. And if I am not careful, that will be twenty. We will no longer look so much alike."

"You will walk that off when you return to the university, I am confident. So large is that campus that the pounds will melt." Hamadi raised his glass. "To the great work that we shall achieve. And to the next foray into the earth."

Sophia also toasted to this. She dreamed that they would accomplish remarkable deeds.

Uziah washed the last bite of cake down with the wine. "We could have spoken of this on the phone, but I wanted to personally say I am sorry for the wounding of your artist friend. I could not have known that the painter would be in that apartment building. I believed he was with his new husband, still dancing, or perhaps fornicating. It was our intent, Rauf's, mine—" He paused and Sophia wondered

175

if he was mentally rehearsing what to say next. Did he fear Hamadi's temper?

"I understand," Hamadi cut in.

Relief showed on Uziah's face.

Sophia did not understand.

"I understand," Hamadi continued, "because the archaeology students needed to die, and their computers and phones had to be destroyed. They were talking too much to their California friends. Sharing too much. Their emails too revealing. They sought fast fame."

"One was writing a book," Uziah said.

"They could have brought unwanted eyes our direction. And Dr. Benito Abruzi will eventually understand about Levent." Hamadi drew in a great breath. "But I pray with my son James that the artist recovers. The artist was simply in the wrong place."

"I do not understand," Sophia admitted aloud. "I do not understand why our cause needed such bloodshed, especially after a wedding. There had to have been another way. Innocent people died in that fire. A baby was burned to death. And a child."

Uziah scowled. "But you support what we intend to achieve, Sister."

"Yes. Wholly yes."

"And you realize there are sacrifices," Uziah said. "You have broken laws with us. Six nights past we robbed a grave together."

"No one died that night," Sophia countered.

"We will rob together again," Uziah added.

"Yes. I understand that there is the greatest good to consider," Sophia said.

"As there was with this fire. A cleansing fire. Consider this, Sister." Hamadi rose and leaning on his cane walked to stand behind Uziah. "In 1095 the Crusades began. On and off during the next two hundred years nearly two million people were killed in the effort to recover the Holy Land from Islamic rule. During the thirty-seven years of the French Wars of Religion in the fifteen hundreds, nearly three million died. And the Thirty Years' War, which began in 1618 as

Catholics against Protestants, evolved into a political battle that left roughly eight million dead in Europe. Eight million."

Hamadi padded around the table and came to stand next to Sophia. She turned and looked up at him.

"The people who died in that apartment fire, Sister, like innocents in the religious wars before, were unfortunate casualties. But necessary. Even one of our own was injured in the conflagration. Correct, Uziah?"

He nodded. "One of our brightest graduate assistants from the university. She helped us to set the fire. She tarried too long and was burned. We were wrong to include her. We had not realized the risk. It will be a few days before she is released from the hospital, I think."

"She is crucial to our plans. But is she also a liability?" Hamadi posed. "Should she be removed to another country? Egypt perhaps? I have an estate there."

Sophia's fingers trembled. She had met Maritza, a fine young woman who had dined here and discussed Catholic doctrine and some of its similarities to the early Christian sects.

Uziah's voice was firm. "Maritza is not a liability. So loyal, she will not talk. This I guarantee. But we do need to watch her."

"Protect her," Hamadi said. "She will be well, yes? You said—"

"Yes. Minor burns. The police have no reason to question her. When I saw her earlier today we decided that if anyone asked about her presence in the building, she would say she was visiting a friend... one of the renters who died. We will keep Mari very close."

"At least for the next several months. Good," Hamadi pronounced. "You will protect her. The rest of the casualties we give to God to sort out, eh? The baby who died in one of those apartments... the baby will grow up in heaven. And what about the artist's sister?"

Uziah frowned. "Her presence below ground was disconcerting. Taavi said she followed him on the street several nights ago. He tried to kill her then, but she got away. She did not get away from me and my brother."

"Are you certain she's dead?" Sophia asked.

Uziah nodded. "She was crushed when we destroyed Cephas's tomb. Buried in the rubble. It was probably a quick death. Her body will be found if your archaeologist ever goes back to dig for Attila. We checked at the hospitals to be certain. No Madigans in any of them."

Sophia felt weak from the talk of death. "She may never be found, and never properly mourned and buried. Dr. Abruzi may give up on the dig, all the grief attached. Who does he have to dig with? And for? No one. Attila may stay buried forever."

"Like Cephas's tomb," Uziah said. "Too much explosives, too much stone falling."

Hamadi returned to his seat and regarded Sophia. "Are you all right, Sister?"

She nodded. "What we do is important and good, Uncle, and I believe God will forgive us for our trespasses. I accept it, that there are casualties. I accept it. I do not have to understand it. But I can accept it."

She drank the rest of her wine in one swallow and signaled for another glass.

TWENTY-THREE

"You sound American," Irem told one of Levent's doctors.

"I am. I was born in Hell." She gave a gentle laugh. Irem read her nametag: Dr. Robin Bianchi. "Hell, Michigan. It's about fifteen miles out of Ann Arbor. I was working at a hospital in Chicago when I met the most marvelous young cardiologist—Italian, he was part of an international residency program. We dated. He proposed. I followed him over here, and we got married. Been working at the same hospital for a decade now. I love Italy. And my husband."

"My brother loves Italy, too," Irem whispered. "He says he will never leave."

Irem was in a wheelchair, Gregario behind her. Dr. Bianchi stood next to them at the window of Levent's critical care room. The curtain had been drawn back so Irem could see inside. Benito, dressed in hospital scrubs and with a mask and cap, was at Levent's bedside. The hospital allowed only one visitor at a time. Irem would have to wait—and suit up to go in.

"Tell me how bad it is. It looks bad. It is bad, isn't it?"

"It's early yet and—"

"I *have* to know."

"Talk to his husband and—"

"*Please*. He's my brother. Family. You *have* to talk to me. You've been treating him, right? You know. You—"

"I am *one* of the specialists treating him." Dr. Bianchi sighed, the sound like dry leaves blowing across sand.

"Your brother suffered third-degree burns. What I can tell you about third-degree burns you could probably get off the internet if you Googled WebMD."

"Go on. *Please.*"

"I'll be honest. It's not good, Miss Madigan. Knowing might only make it worse in your mind."

"No. Not knowing would be worse." Irem noticed that Gregario took a few steps back and answered his cell phone.

Dr. Bianchi spoke softly. "Your brother has extensive third-degree burns. His lungs have smoke damage and damage from toxic substances, cleaning chemicals that were in the building. He has some heat injury to his trachea and upper respiratory system, which means he was breathing in direct heat or flame. Apparently he was near the heart of the fire." She smiled sadly at Irem. "Treating patients with extensive burns is difficult, especially when they sustain a TBSA—"

"What? What is a TBSA?" Irem kept her eyes on Levent.

"Doctor-speak. Sorry. Total Body Surface Area of eighty percent or more. That he also sustained inhalation injury complicates matters. The risk of infection is high, which is why he is in strict reverse isolation, why his husband is in there with a mask and gown, gloves."

"Infection?"

"With much of the skin burned away, bacteria can easily enter."

Irem sucked in a breath. "Are you telling me Lev might not make it?"

"I spoke a few hours ago with his husband, who is able to make health care decisions for him. You might want to talk to him—Dr. Abruzi—about possibilities and ramifications. Perhaps he will include you in any end-of-life discussions."

"He might die, Lev."

"The amount of burns, the inhalation damage. There is a chance, yes, that he won't make it. Age is a factor, youth is in the plus column. Health... a person who was healthy before the burn... that's another plus. Many people died in that fire. Your brother is fortunate to have made it this far."

"Oh God," Irem whispered.

Dr. Bianchi waited a moment and then continued as if she were lecturing to a class: "His lungs are compromised because of the heat, breathing is difficult. Blood flow to his extremities is compromised, and his hands and feet are at risk. If he survives, he might lose range of motion. Third-degree burns are called full-thickness burns, so deep that the muscles, tendons, ligaments, even the bone suffers. Organ failure is a possibility. If he survives there is good chance of permanent disability, lengthy rehabilitation, perhaps an amputation. There might be a temporary graft of cadaveric skin. Most certainly there will be constant special bandages and dressings, cleaning, removal of dead tissue from the burned area, debridement."

"Oh God. Eighty percent? Was Levent burned that much?"

"Eighty-five." Dr. Bianchi touched Irem's shoulder. "Your brother is young, and like I said he has that in the plus column. He obviously has a husband that cares a great deal about him. He has you. He is at an excellent hospital. I'd count that another plus. You will need a cap, gown, mask, and gloves. And do not stay long."

Dr. Bianchi glided down the hall to the nurses' station.

Gregario talked into his cell phone, and Irem listened detachedly, her fingers shook and she grabbed onto the arms of the wheelchair and squeezed. Apparently the detectives were downstairs. He ended the call and stepped up. She didn't want to talk to them. She didn't want to talk to anyone except Levent. This didn't feel real, couldn't possibly be happening, could it? Levent was in love, had just married, so young. A brilliant artist, this was not real. A bad dream, Irem thought, all of this was a nightmare, and when she finally woke up everything would be perfect again, and Levent would be happily whirling with a man old enough to be his father.

"I will retrieve the detectives and bring them to your room," Gregario said.

It was a nightmare, but a real one. Levent might never whirl again.

Irem could hardly breathe. "No, I—"

"They need your help with the investigation. You do not have a choice. Visit your brother first, and then come talk to us. We will be in your room, waiting."

"Sure. Okay." Irem heard Gregario retreat just as Benito got up and came into the hall, closing Levent's door behind him. The archaeologist looked much older than his forty-nine years, the circles dark under his red eyes. She suspected he'd not slept since getting up yesterday morning for the wedding. And she knew he'd only slept a couple of hours before that because he was at the Attila dig site.

They stared at each other. Irem needed to say something, but the words wouldn't order themselves.

"You cannot know how much I love him," Benito said. His voice was brittle and the words broke. "I'd give my life for his, Irem. If God would let me, I would trade places with him."

Irem would trade places, too.

Neither said anything for a few minutes, both watching Levent through the glass. Irem noticed the breathing tube. Was her brother on life support? She'd ask later, ask a lot of things later, talk to Benito about the men underground who'd set the explosives, who'd mentioned Benito's assistants, who maybe set the apartment fire, all of that later. Important and urgent and necessary... but meaningless at this moment.

The fingers on Benito's left hand closed and his knuckles turned white. He made a gulping sound and he shuddered. "I can't breathe," he whispered. "I don't want to breathe. He might die, Irem. What will I do?"

"Oh God," was all Irem could muster.

"I am scared, Irem. So very scared. They say third degree, eighty-five percent of his body. They say he might not make it. They say there's a good chance he won't. Thirty-percent chance to live, one said. A good chance of death. Nothing good in the words they give me. I am so very, very scared. He is my heart and soul, Irem."

Her brother's comment about the wine came back, replayed perfectly in her mind from the night at the Conservatori: "We had wine on our first meeting. I watched him roll his glass between his hands, and he peered over the edge of it as if teasing himself what it would taste like. I drank my own wine, too fast maybe, it tingled against my lips as if there was electricity in it, and I held the last of it in my mouth, savoring it, and he still hadn't taken a sip. Wine hadn't tasted so good as it did in that moment, and then I realized the electricity came from his eyes and our connection." Levent had shrugged. "Maybe there was nothing to the wine at all. Maybe the moment just made everything wonderful."

To have a love like that, Irem knew she would never find something as strong.

Suddenly she was angry, at her parents for driving Levent away because they couldn't accept him. He might well be in Chicago right now if they'd been tolerant and loving. In Chicago and safe. Angry at herself for not staying at the wedding festivities. Maybe her presence would have altered what had happened. Maybe if she'd been there he wouldn't have gone into the apartment building. Maybe he'd be dancing with her. Maybe this was her fault.

"Why was Levent there?" Had she asked that aloud? "In the apartment building? At Lacy and Santiago's?"

"Our wedding gift," Benito answered. His voice was so low she had to strain to hear him. "Lacy and Santiago had something for us too large to bring to the reception. They insisted we have it now, would not be argued with. And Levent went to their apartment to help carry it down the stairs."

Irem remembered the couple telling her about the gift — an antique rolltop desk — at the church... and that Benito was upset at Santiago.

"No elevator, that building. Probably a piece of furniture, something heavy, but not so large it wouldn't fit in a van, they'd said. I'd parked my van out front and waited. I would have gone up to the apartment, too, but I had to stay with the van, the spot I parked was not legal. They very much wanted us to have the gift on our wedding day. Maybe they thought it would smooth things over. Santiago and I'd had an argument the day before. They hadn't been gone long, Levent and Lacy, Santiago. Several minutes only, when smoke came out of windows, then flames. I tried to go in, but people were rushing out, pushing me. So many screams, and then sirens. Again, I tried to enter, and I must have made it inside. I woke up in an ambulance."

Irem noticed that Benito's right hand and wrist were wrapped. Looking closer, she saw a burn on the right side of his face, shiny salve on it. Other things registered as he removed the gown: he was wearing the same dress shirt and pants from the wedding, soot on the shirt, the once-beautiful leather shoes horribly scuffed. The jacket abandoned somewhere. He smelled faintly of smoke. She'd been so caught up with thoughts of her brother she hadn't paid any attention to the archaeologist.

"You were hospitalized? You were hurt, too?"

He shook his head and swallowed. His voice was a little stronger. "They treated me in the ambulance. Someone towed my van. I suppose I must discover where it is."

"Lacy and —"

"Dead, I was told. Lacy and Santiago burned in the building. More people burned, too. Many. Too many. People I don't know, people who are being grieved by strangers to me. Lacy and Santiago... their relatives are in California, and I don't know if someone has notified them. I must discover that, yes? Tend to that myself perhaps. Call their university."

Lacy and Santiago dead? Irem hadn't known them long, but she liked them, would have liked to become friends. Dead.

"Lev —"

"So many dead. Levent and a few others were pulled out still breathing." He paused. "I don't want to breathe, Irem, if my Lev dies. I don't want to live without him."

If she'd not been underground... if she'd instead danced with her brother...

Suddenly everything was again as dark as the tunnels, and her consciousness slipped away.

TWENTY-FOUR

DONATIENNE FOURNIER WAS SEVENTY-FOUR AND
had been walking down from her second-floor apartment
in search of the *propriétaire* to complain that her garbage
disposal had quit working. She heard a loud *crack!* followed
by *flammes partout*, "everywhere flames," and then an
explosion.

Fournier, an Italian citizen by marriage, said she'd lived
in the apartment for eleven months, moving in after selling
the house when her husband died. She had not noticed
anyone who didn't belong at the apartment building that
night, nothing suspicious, and that although a few of the
other tenants on her floor argued from time to time—the
walls thin—there'd been no serious trouble.

She told *Agente Sceito* Gregario Ricci that if her garbage
disposal had worked, she would be dead. Her burns were
superficial; it was being trampled by panicked tenants
trying to flee that put her in the hospital. The doctors were
keeping her one more night for observation. She hoped
they would keep her longer, as she did not know where
she would go. Everything she owned was burned, and her
mother in France was too old to help.

Gregario scribbled her comments in a notebook, as well
as recorded them. The senior officer believed in backing his
work up on paper in the event electronics failed him. He
gave her a card with a contact at the Croce Rossa Italiana,
who was arranging temporary housing for those displaced
by the fire.

The two *Polizia di Stato* detectives who had questioned Irem were also interviewing burn victims. They would work into the evening and then combine their information later. They would also analyze everything on Irem Madigan's phone. Local police were involved to a lesser degree, but this was being treated as a national crime, and possible terrorist strike.

There had been twenty-four apartments of varying size in the building—from efficiencies to three bedrooms, a mix of renters who had been there several years and short-term tenants. Gregario learned that roughly half of the tenants in the burned building were Italian; the remainder internationals who had booked rooms month-to-month, some of them tourists, some students enrolled in one of Rome's many schools. The multicultural survivors had been assigned to him because he spoke a smattering of several languages. His list: Fournier, French; Romano and Galli, Italian Americans; Palma, Tunisian; Greenwood, Canadian; Papadakis, Greek; and Fiafia, Samoan.

Aldo Romano was inconsolable. The thirty-one-year-old had third-degree burns over twenty-five percent of his body and had lost his American wife and their four-year-old daughter in the blaze. Their apartment—which they'd rented for the past year—had been on the third floor, and he'd noticed nothing suspicious before he heard what he thought was a canon going off. Then smoke came in under the door, and alarms in all the apartments wailed. He dashed into the hallway—thick smoke was everywhere, and flames—that was when he was burned. He managed to get back inside and close the door, rushed to the window with the notion of lowering his wife and daughter to safety, to drop them on the awning that stretched across the front of the building.

Aldo briefly noticed a van in front, which by the description Gregario determined had been Benito's, the archaeologist waiting for the piece of furniture to come down. Aldo called to his wife, and then was propelled forward by a second blast. It was he who landed on the awning; and he woke up in the hospital to the news that his family was gone.

"*Dovrei essere morto,*" he said. I should be dead.

The young American couple on the fourth floor was responsible, Belvender Galli claimed. Those two Hispanic Americans or the Muslim brothers, he said, who also lived on the fourth floor. Maybe they all plotted together. But as none of those individuals had survived, Gregario could neither prove nor disprove the man's claims. The Hispanic Americans had been Lacy and Santiago Garcia, who had worked for Benito Abruzi under the city. The Muslims had been studying at the Italian Chef Academy in Rome's Via della Camilluccia; it was unknown why they hadn't lived closer to the school's neighborhood. Perhaps lower rent in this building, Gregario speculated.

Galli said he had been in the *proprietario's* office, delivering his rent check a few days late. When he heard the blast, screams, and smoke alarms, the landlord rushed out and up the steps. Then came a second blast, and everything burned.

"*Sciocco coraggioso,*" Galli pronounced the landlord, who was among the dead. "He was a brave fool."

Martiza Palma didn't live in the building; an international student at the University of Catania in Sicily, she'd been visiting a friend, Luigi Rizzo, who lived on the fourth floor.

"I was thirsty," she told Gregario. "I wish Luigi had also been so thirsty. Sure, he had things to drink in his apartment, but the wine was gone. I wanted wine. I was going downstairs, was almost in the lobby when everything happened. A big boom, then smoke, fire, another boom... maybe three. All the noise, hard to tell. I fell, and burning things dropped on me. Someone helped me up, a man. We stumbled outside and fell together on the sidewalk."

She paused and drank from a glass of water. "Across the street and a block down was a small grocer's. That is where I had intended to go. Because I was thirsty for wine, I live. Luigi had given me euros to cover it, but he should have come with me. I'd intended to buy either a Barbera Bianca or a Syrah, very different. If he had also been thirsty for

187

wine, would have cared what vintage I bought, he would be alive, too."

Gregario turned off the recorder and put the notebook in his pocket.

"Wine will not taste sweet anymore," Palma said.

He looked in on Irem before he visited the other people on his list. He needed a break from the burn unit. Gregario both admired and was perplexed by the nurses and doctors who tended them. Respect for their efforts to save lives; mystified that they could treat such horrific injuries daily. Although he had seen plenty of ghastly things from his years on the police force, this many burns... he would not have the stomach for it.

Irem was sleeping, he saw her fingers twitch and her head turn fitfully, caught in a nightmare. Gregario nearly woke her to save her from the bad dream, but decided to leave her be. The detectives had questioned her for nearly two hours; Gregario had recorded everything on his phone so he could listen to it again.

She'd explained that she left the luncheon for the Attila site, wanting some time alone there, and had only planned to stay an hour. On her way she discovered a breach in a tunnel wall, a place that clearly had been broken into. Curious, she went down the steps, intending to report the intrusion to Dr. Abruzi. Two men were at the bottom, and she recorded them, heard something about explosives, and tried to retreat. Irem said they chased her and she managed to lose them in the archaeologist's dig.

She declined to comment about what Dr. Abruzi was digging for, insisting they talk to him. Irem also refused to reveal why she was so interested in the archaeologist's dig that she would leave her brother's wedding reception for it. Gregario assumed they'd gain additional information from Irem's cell phone, which she reluctantly surrendered.

Irem was not considered a suspect in either the explosion below the streets or the apartment fire, but the detectives were not happy that she clearly withheld some information. Not a suspect, but suspicious.

Gregario returned to the burn unit and noted that Levent was still unconscious, Benito still at his side, sleeping upright in a chair. He would check on Irem again in the morning; she had become his assignment. She was involved somehow... her brother in the fire, her new brother-in-law responsible for the dig under the city near where an explosion had occurred. She said two men had tried to kill her below the streets, perhaps because she saw something or recorded something, or perhaps solely because of her association with the archaeologist. Dr. Benito Abruzi's two assistants were dead. Days before that she'd called police to say she'd been shot at. Was that incident connected to all of this?

Indeed, not a suspect, but definitely suspicious.

Gregario was charged with following Irem, protecting her, and learning her secrets.

Rocco Greenwood, a retired wrestler from Ontario on an extended Visa, died just as Gregario went to visit him. Greenwood's burns had been listed as third-degree, seventy percent of his body, not as bad as Levent's. Dr. Robin Bianchi said they'd been hopeful Greenwood would make it.

Noe Papadakis was next. Papadakis had rented an apartment for two months, paid ahead, and had been two weeks into that lease. Newly retired, he wanted to take a leisurely vacation, and the second-floor studio had fit his budget and was in the heart of the city. He had just returned from the Colosseum and Ancient Rome Tour by Night, which he said had cost only forty-five euros because he had booked it through the internet. He was just starting up the stairs when two men "who looked so much the same they might have been twins" tromped down in a hurry. Miss Fournier came down the steps a moment later, and he paused to make sure she was managing the stairs all right.

"Then it sounded like a big man inhaled and sucked the sound away. There was an explosion and hell broke open. The fire was fast and angry and ate everything," Papadakis said. "It was like the fire burned from the bottom *and* the top, racing to the middle as if it wanted everyone to die. If I had been on the second floor, I doubt I would have made it out of the building. I was very lucky. I will be released in the morning. I will be going back home to Piraeus. My vacation is done."

Gregario put a star next to the men "who might have been twins." Papadakis said he didn't get a good look at their faces.

"Try," Gregario urged. "Picture them. It is very important. Close your eyes and think about them tromping down the steps."

"Round, a little, the faces. Middle-aged, I think. It was dark on the stairway, night, you understand, low lights in the building. Their clothes were dusty, and they wore hats. I thought that odd. Not that they wore hats, but that they appeared so very dusty. I wondered where one would go in downtown Rome to get so dusty. Cannot tell you more. Very sorry."

"If I showed you photographs? Could you pick them out?"

"I do not think so," he replied. "But I would try. I would like to help. That fire, that was no accident."

Sammy Fiafia said he couldn't sleep and so would happily talk to the senior policeman. Gregario focused on his notebook, avoiding looking directly at the young man, whose hair had burned away. Half his face was wrapped in bandages.

"I am fuckin' hurtin'," Fiafia said. "All over. Can you understand English okay?"

"I understand English fine. You are Samoan, correct?"

"American, really. Moved to the States after high school. I had a college scholarship; I was a standout Buckeye. I was drafted to play for the Raiders, offensive line seven years until I blew out my knee. Now I run sports camps and travel in the fall. Not coming back to Rome. Ever."

Gregario sat next to the bed and cringed when he took a close look at the man and saw that his left arm had been amputated at the elbow, the right arm heavily wrapped, a thick bandage was around his neck. He looked at his notebook again.

"They took the arm right away," Fiafia said, noting Gregario's stare. "I knew they'd have to, knew it when they loaded me on the ambulance."

"What can you tell me, about that night?"

"I was in one of the first floor apartments, a hint of an apartment, actually. Rented it for a month. An efficiency no bigger than my ex-wife's walk-in closet in her house in Albuquerque." Fiafia paused. "That's in New Mexico. The United States."

Gregario nodded. "Go on."

"I was in the fuckin' shower, earphones in, listenin' to my music. If fire alarms went off, I didn't hear them. I felt the building shake, though. Figured there was an earthquake, just a little one. Fuckin' idiot, I stayed in the fuckin' shower. Then I heard somethin' over the music, like a roar or somethin', and I turned off the water and pulled out the buds. There was groanin', the building groanin', and I heard screams, saw flames pourin' down the wall. I grabbed a towel and ran, but a piece of the fuckin' ceiling hit me. I figured I was dead, the ceiling on my arm, burning. But there were cops or firemen or somethin' and I got pulled out and tossed on an ambulance. I'm lucky I only lost my arm."

Gregario closed his notebook and turned off the recorder. The Samoan American hadn't seen anything suspicious. And, yes, he was lucky the fire only took his arm.

"Are you going to get the son of a bitch that set the fire?" Fiafia's voice rose.

"Yes," Gregario answered. "Them. We will get them."

"Them, huh? They should burn," Fiafia pronounced. "But burning in hell would be too good for them."

TWENTY-FIVE
OCTOBER 14

IREM HAD ESCHEWED THE DOCTOR-RECOMMENDED crutches.

The cane was copper-tinted aluminum, ugly, and the handle uncomfortably thick for her fingers. She'd purchased it at the pharmacy for eight euros, roughly nine US dollars. There were nicer ones, but she didn't intend to need this long, and so decided to be as frugal as possible.

The cane was hooked over the back of her chair, up against the wall in the restaurant. Earlier she'd propped it against the table, but the server had knocked it off with an attention-snaring clatter when he delivered their coffee... *caffè alla nocciola*, a frothy espresso with hazelnut cream that was said to be a specialty of the Neapolitan café. The noise drew the looks of the other diners. Irem moved the cane, noting that she'd forgotten to remove the price sticker, and tried to fold in on herself.

Several people continued to stare. Irem's face was still so bruised it looked like she'd had it painted at a carnival. Certainly something to gape at, she thought. *Maybe they think I lost a prize fight.*

And maybe a double shot of something alcoholic rather than coffee would do her better... despite the medication she was on. She took a sip. While she hadn't thought she'd like espresso, she admitted this was tasty and strong and would likely be followed by a second cup. She nursed it, holding it on her tongue, the perfect temperature. Conversations, all of them in Italian, became a susurrus that blended with the piped-in pop music; she made out only a smattering of the chatter.

"*Guarda che donna.*" She was pretty sure that meant "Look at that woman."

"*Donna triste.*" Irem got that one: "Sad woman."

"*Che le diede un pugno?*" No clue on that, other than it was said about her, as the speaker pointed to her face.

"Ignore them," Gregario said.

Gregario had picked the café because Irem thought the fancy restaurant on the sixth floor that he'd originally suggested would be lost on her tonight. It had taken his gentle, but persistent, prodding to get her to agree to an early dinner at a simple place. And she'd only relented because she needed company and to talk about her brother and the explosion in the tunnel.

And... she wanted her cell phone back. He had promised to bring it.

"Pizza *chiena* started in Naples, I think," Gregario explained. "A melding of pie and pizza. It means 'filled pizza,' and this... this is stuffed thick with cheeses and cured meats. Probably not very healthy. But... mmmm. Delicious?"

Irem nodded. She'd been released from the hospital two days earlier, and even though she thought she should be at the hospital right now with Lev, she desperately needed a day away from the place. She'd hoped the break might pull her out of the suffocating depression.

Impossibile. It hadn't, despite her charming company. She had to work to smile.

"Yeah, it *is* delicious. And it looks like there'll be enough for a doggie box."

He raised an eyebrow.

"Leftovers I can put in my itty-bitty fridge. It's empty right now."

Irem had found a minimally furnished efficiency not far from the train station. Short term, it was costing three hundred a week, a better deal than the hotel. Not fancy, the equivalent of two hundred and seventy square feet. First floor, no stairs. She'd hung the painting Levent had gifted her on the wall next to a two-seater couch that could flip open to a bed. There was a bus stop a half block from it where she could catch a ride to the hospital to check on Lev. Benito had suggested she instead stay at their apartment, as he would rarely be there, instead camping at the hospital, and it wouldn't cost her anything. But Irem wanted her own space. She had enough in savings to handle this.

"They've been keeping him in a coma, my brother," she began. "Said they probably would for another few days."

Gregario watched her but said nothing.

"Two months, Dr. Bianchi told me. Said if he survives — and she thinks he will — that he'll be in the hospital burn unit two months. *Months*." Another sip of the espresso. "Said then he'd go to a rehab facility for another couple of months, and he'd get some psych counseling."

Irem thought she might need some counseling to handle everything. She set the cup down and took a large bite of the *chiena*.

"I'm really hungry, and this is good. Maybe there won't be leftovers." She hadn't eaten since the cafeteria sandwich she'd picked at yesterday afternoon. Chewing slowly, she let the flavors soak in; she just had trouble appreciating much at the moment, including the policeman's company.

"Coma."

Irem nodded. "It's good he isn't conscious, I think. They took his right hand yesterday morning, cut off a few inches above his wrist. The doctors said the infection got so bad, gangrenous, they didn't have a choice. They'll know in a few days if they have to go higher, but Dr. Bianchi thinks they won't have to. Levent, when he wakes up, will wish he'd died in the fire. It's a good thing he doesn't know what he's lost yet. An artist... painter, sculptor, right handed. What will he do?"

"What will you do?" Gregario signaled for espresso refills.

Irem shrugged.

"Seriously, Miss Irem Madigan who works at the Field — "

"I have to figure some things out. I called work yesterday. They're giving me a leave of absence, up to six months if I want it, and I think I do. I'm good for another two and a half months here before I have to get a Visa to stay longer. Called the State Department, some officious-sounding fellow there is sending me paperwork and claims I'll have no trouble getting a Visa that would let me stay a lot longer. I've always been pretty thrifty. I figure I've got enough in savings that I could stay here a year, probably more, before I'd hit zero. I could sublet my apartment in Chicago. Rowan, my friend from the Field, knows someone looking for a temporary place. And that would give me more money to work with. The apartment here is a lot less than my digs in Chicago. I don't know how long I'll stay, but a while. For Levent."

Irem had talked to her mother last night, told her about the fire and Levent's dire condition. She figured her parents would make arrangements to come to Rome; they had passports. But her mother said she was very sorry to hear the news and that Irem should keep them informed. They didn't ask for the hospital's name or an address, and that to Irem meant they weren't even going to send flowers. Irem hadn't mentioned that she'd been in the hospital too.

"The circumstances, they are not good for your brother," Gregario said. "But I am pleased you are staying longer. You intrigue me, Irem. I want to know you better."

"You're kind." She stabbed at a piece of sausage that had seeped out of the *chiena*. "I'm not very good company right now. I'm angry and frightened. I'm messed up. I look like hell because of these bruises. People stare at me. You know, my brother might not have been in the apartment building if I'd been at that club the night of the wedding. Maybe he would have been dancing with me. Or maybe he would have left earlier to retrieve that wedding gift. Or left later. Wouldn't've been inside the building when it caught fire. The timing all different. Lacy and Santiago. Maybe—"

"It isn't your fault," Gregario said.

"Well... but maybe—" They finished the meal and pumpkin gingersnap tiramisu dessert without further conversation.

After the server cleared the plates and brought glasses of non-alcoholic sangria, Gregario pushed her cell phone across the table. Irem was quick to grab it.

196

"All charged," he said. "Your files have been copied for our investigation. I promise you nothing was altered or removed. Copies only."

"Thanks."

"I would like to talk business."

"Sure. I figured that."

"The fire was arson."

"Yeah. I figured that, too." Irem stared at him across the rim of the glass. "A real no-brainer."

"*Certo*, we believed that right away. The *vigili del fuoco*... what you would call the fire department... finished testing the ah... accelerants... burn patterns yesterday. Deliberatamente... set on purpose, an official ruling. Someone intended for a lot of people to die. The building, all of it a loss."

"Why, Ari? Do you think it was terrorism?" Irem didn't. She thought it was connected to the tunnels.

Gregario shrugged. "*Motivo*. Motive. That, myself and the detectives work on. Someone saw a man. Someone saw two men. Descriptions are— Oh, how do you say it? All over the place. The descriptions are all over the place. Fat, thin, tall, short, young, old. But one of the first to escape the fire said he saw two who looked near in build, like copies. Night, shadows. No faces, really. But dusty hats and similar build. And you saw two men below the street of near build. Explosives... fire... two men both places... perhaps it is related, the apartment fire and the destruction underground. In any event, *I* believe it is related. Terrorism? In this day it has to be considered."

Irem scooted forward. "I think those two men were responsible for both. The same two men. I feel it, you know. I recorded two men."

Gregario placed his hands flat against the table. Irem noticed a faint lighter stripe around his left ring finger. Had he been married? "The video you took on your cell phone was helpful, but not conclusive. So dark, and at no time while you recorded did they turn to show their faces. But I agree, similar in build, almost copies of each other in stature... from the back. The languages help us a little.

We know we look for men who can speak Italian, English, Latin, and we think Aramaic. And one language we are not able to identify or decipher. Perhaps it is a secret tongue like spies would use. The detectives still work on that. The mysterious chamber underground that you recorded ... That was some sort of a burial vault. We surmise the men destroyed it because they stole something and did not want their theft noticed. Buried under so much stone now. Even if it is excavated, the stone coming down would have destroyed whatever remained inside."

Irem started punching buttons on her phone. "Just a minute." She kept at it, sucking in her lower lip, her fingers fast. She disregarded the typos. "I have an idea." Irem typed a little more, and then set the phone down in front of her. "It's ten-thirty in the morning in Chicago, time difference and all. I sent Rowan the audio file of the men talking. She's a language expert. Maybe she knows what it is. Maybe the language isn't a secret code, just... rare. Rowan is into super obscure languages."

Next, Irem flipped through the pictures she'd taken until she came to the ones from the Conservatori for Benito's reception, her first night in Rome. "See the tapestry? The four people in front of it? Yeah, yeah, I know, it's their backsides. I was taking a picture of the tapestry, not the people. Anyway, the man with the cane is Hamadi Somethingorother. He's a vintner who catered the wine for the reception, for the wedding, too. The young woman? I don't remember her name. I don't remember if she was introduced. She attended the wedding with Mr. Somethingorother. Shamoon! That's it. Hamadi Shamoon. But those two men. Look, even from the back they could be the guys from the tunnel, right?"

Gregario took the phone and stared at the picture. "*Possibile.* I will ask the detectives if they compared photographs. Do you know these men from the Conservatori?"

Irem shook her head. "Hamadi. I was introduced to him. Wait... the woman's name is Sophia. I was introduced to her, too. But I wasn't introduced to the two men. Do you think they are the same ones—"

"The same men? *Possibile*, I say. But the lighting is different, the clothes different. But, yes. *Possibile*."

"Look at this photo." She thumbed to another one. "I got one of them mostly from the front, one of those men. You can see his face."

"Sort of see his face. We are investigating. Irem, we are looking at this. Very carefully. The detectives are using your photographs."

"I'm going out to the vineyard, Hamadi's. He invited me. I'll go tomorrow morning. I'll ask about the men and —"

"You have therapy tomorrow. Almost a full day."

How would he know that? Her medical schedule wasn't his business.

"A few hours of therapy, actually, in the afternoon. Today they told me I'm ahead of schedule."

Gregario frowned. "Miss Irem Madigan, you are an archivist. You are not a police investigator. Arson, explosives, this is dangerous. It seems two men tried to bury you under Rome. You will leave this to the *Polizia di Stato.* I will —"

"Come with me if you want, to the winery. I'm going tomorrow morning. I'd go right now, but I have to rent a car, and I doubt the vineyard is open in the evening."

He let out a sigh so big it ruffled the napkins.

"And, yes, I know it's dangerous. Before they tried to blow me up, I was shot at. It's all related. Maybe I saw something they don't think I should have." Irem scowled and worried at a frayed thread in the tablecloth. "The altered tapestry. Something wrong is going down. And my brother and I got sucked up into it. Just a whole lot worse for him." And Lacy and Santiago, she thought. The archaeology students were burned to death. "A major amount of suckage."

"The police —"

"Can hopefully figure out what it's all about. But I'm not going to sit at Lev's bedside and do nothing. And I'm not going to quiz my new brother-in-law about whatever illegal thing he might be involved with. The police can do that." She finished the sangria. "But I *can* go out to the vineyard and poke around. I was invited. I can do that. I *have* to do that." Softer: "For my sanity."

"Irem, you should take it easy until you are fully healed."

"I have to do something," Irem argued. "Free country, Italy."

"*La goccia che ha fatto traboccare il vaso.*"

"What?"

"I said, you will keep me very busy, Miss Irem Madigan. I will drive tomorrow morning to the vineyard of Hamadi Shamoon."

TWENTY-SIX
OCTOBER 15

THE SHAMOON VINEYARD VISITOR'S CENTER was a plain wood-sided building attached to a massive barn where grapes were stomped and festivities held, and at least once a month where Hamadi found a reason to hire a local band to play well into the evening.

Inside, the paneling gleamed under well-placed lights, everything shiny and spotless. It was more shop than anything, shelves upon shelves of wine for sale, all of it beautifully presented, signage in Italian, French, and English. A glass-fronted refrigerator held a variety of fine cheeses, a display next to it was stocked with crackers and breads. A few small tables were decorated with red and white checked cloths and candles set onto star-shaped crystal holders. The office proper was in the basement; visitors were never permitted there.

Sophia had barely opened for business when the couple arrived and stopped just inside the entrance.

"*Buongiorno! Benvenuto,*" Sophia greeted.

She noted that they took it all in like they had never been here before. She'd seen the woman in the past few weeks... at the Conservatori, and more recently at the archaeologist's wedding. Madigan, the American! But she couldn't recall her first name; it was something unusual. However, she remembered that her uncle said the name was Turkish and meant flowers.

Sophia knew Hamadi thought this woman dead.

That had been part of the dinner conversation a few nights past. Buried in the rubble under the city when the

201

brothers recovered the relic. Innocents die, Hamadi had said, and he was confident this woman was one of those unfortunate innocents.

But she was very much alive, appearing battered and tired, leaning on an ugly cane... and standing in the doorway. Sophia's chest felt squeezed. What to do?

At first glance one would think the woman had been assaulted, all those bruises on her arms and face; however, Sophia was aware the injuries had resulted from the cave-in. She *should* be dead, broken and buried beneath tons of stone. She should not be in the winery shop.

It would be easier if she were dead.

That she wasn't dead gladdened Sophia, who considered all life sacred. At the same time it also worried her. She thought, perhaps, that Hamadi should know about this. But did she need to be the one to tell him? And if she did, would he direct the brothers to come back to Rome and tie up this very much living loose end?

Irem! That was the woman's name.

If Sophia told her uncle, would she be to blame for the woman's likely demise?

"Good morning. Welcome." Sophia would speak English for Irem. "May I assist you?"

Irem came forward, awkward with the ugly cane. The man at her side looked official and wholly unfamiliar. He wore a soot-gray sport coat and pressed pants a shade darker, white shirt and maroon tie. Overdressed compared to Irem, who was in jeans and a short-sleeved sweater, but it was an "off the rack" suit that suggested middle class, perhaps a low-level businessman.

What could they want? Not to shop; they'd made no move toward the shelves. Sophia shivered, thinking the woman's presence a precursor to something ill.

"Allow me to recommend a wine for you today, *si*? The Colterenzio Sauvignon is exceptional."

"I met you at the Conservatori, going on two weeks ago," Irem said, paying no attention to the bottles.

"I remember," Sophia said. "But—"

"Irem Madigan. My brother, Levent... you were at his wedding. I saw you at the church, and at the luncheon, with Hamadi Shamoon."

"My uncle. Yes, the wedding of the archaeologist and the artist. So sorry to hear of your brother's injuries. The fire. *Terrebile*. My uncle and I visited your brother in the hospital. Tragic. But he is in God's healing hands. I pray for him." Sophia touched the cross that hung from her neck. "Did you come for wine? The Colterenzio Sauvignon—"

Irem gave a gentle laugh. *Damn the medication.*

"Perhaps a purchase now, to enjoy later. Or if you want a tour. I believe my uncle—"

"Yes," Irem was quick to answer. "Your uncle... Mr. Shamoon... he invited me to come here for a tour. Is he—"

"Away, unfortunately. I can arrange a tour for you. I am alone in the *negozio*... eh, shop... this morning. However, a vintner in the barn can—"

Irem looked disappointed. "No. No. I'd love a tour, the grounds look so beautiful. The air is so clean. I really would love a tour, but it isn't practical today. I recently had knee surgery."

It had taken Hamadi a while to recover from his knee surgery, Sophia recalled, but the woman was younger, thin, and looked fit, and so should not have as difficult a time. Still, Sophia imagined from Irem's expression that she was in pain.

"Perhaps you should come back when my uncle is here. You will be mended and he can give you a tour himself. He is proud of his vineyard. I know that Proverbs tell us that 'when pride comes, then comes dishonor.' But my uncle does not have pride in excess, and his vineyard honors the Lord. 'But with the humble is wisdom.' And my uncle is more humble than proud. Allow me to give you a complimentary bottle of our humble wine. Your trip here should not be such a *deluslione*... disenchantment."

"I can see why your uncle is proud of this place," the man spoke. He had a strong voice.

Pride. Sophia shivered. Another verse sprung to her mind, Psalms: *Therefore pride is their necklace; the garment of violence covers them.* If she told Hamadi about this woman, would violence cover her as well?

"Yes, that would be best if my uncle was here," Sophia continued. "You should return when he is back from his trip. Next week."

Again Irem shook her head. "No. Well, yes, I will come back when your uncle is here. I honestly would enjoy a tour. And I want to talk to him. But maybe you can help me now. I'm—"

The man stepped up and pulled a badge out of his pocket. "*Buongiorno.* I am *Agente Sceito* Gregario Ricci.

Police? Sophia sucked in a breath and realized that she appeared startled.

"I am just looking for a little information," Gregario continued. "Hopefully you can help us identify two men." He replaced the badge and withdrew a folded sheet from his inside jacket pocket. He walked to the counter, his heels clicking against the polished floor, and smoothed the paper out on it.

Sophia turned away from Irem and went to the counter, the fingers of her left hand rubbing her cross. "Police. *Non capisco.* I—"

"Nothing to worry about," Gregario said. "Just trying to identify these two men. He tapped a printed photograph. Miss Madigan took this picture."

It was from the Conservatori. Uncle Hamadi and she, and the two brothers. It showed their backs; the focus of the photograph was clearly on the burial shroud, which dominated the frame. A second photo he put out showed one of the men from the front.

"They were with you." The policeman pointed to the twins. "These men were in your company."

"*Si.*"

"So you know who they are?" The policeman posed it as a question.

"*Si.*" Sophia did not lie. Her stomach knotted and something acrid settled on her tongue. She did not want to talk to this policeman, did not want to give him any information. She wanted Uncle Hamadi to be here and deal with this, to lie if he felt that was necessary. Uncle Hamadi did not mind lying. But Sophia would not lie.

Irem Madigan must have indeed seen the twins in the crypt ... hadn't that been part of the dinner conversation? And, therefore, Irem — a *living* Irem — could tie the brothers to the ruined catacombs. That was why they had wanted her dead. Sophia would have to call her uncle, tell him about the policeman and Irem Madigan; tell him that she could not lie to these people. Her uncle would understand and do whatever needed to be done. The blood would not be on her hands. Not directly.

"These men —" the policeman pressed.

"They were visiting from Sicily," Sophia said. "Dr. Uziah and Dr. Nazih Donkor. They returned to Sicily."

Irem cut in: "No Rauf? Neither man is named Rauf?"

"Dr. Nazih Rauf Donkor," Sophia said. She pointed to the picture that showed the man's face, though not clearly. "He goes by Rauf." Could these people tell she was nervous?

"Sicily. Can you be more specific? Where in Sicily? Do you know where I can find them? An address? Phone number?" The policeman was persistent. He refolded the pictures and put them back in his pocket.

"Somewhere at the university," Sophia said truthfully.

"What university?"

Thou shalt not lie.

"The University in Catania. Somewhere there. They are importante people there. Dr. Rauf teaches at the university. Dr. Uziah is a researcher. I think he is connected to the university. But I am unfamiliar, really. Not certain. My uncle would —"

"Your Uncle Hamadi Shamoon. Where is he?"

"He is also at the university," she said. Sophia would not lie.

"With Dr. Rauf and Dr. Uziah Donkor?"

"At the moment? I do not know if they are together. Somewhere at the university," Sophia said. "Maybe Hamadi is with the brothers, with one or both. Maybe my uncle is somewhere else. A crystal ball, I do not have. I —"

She squeezed her cross. "I cannot tell you where he is at precisely this moment. But somewhere in Sicily."

"Did he go there to see them, your uncle? The two men? Specifically to meet with them?" The policeman's eyes were narrow, and that made her even more anxious.

Thou shalt not lie.

She rubbed at the cross. "Yes."

"Do you know what the doctors — professors — and your uncle are meeting about?"

"I have never been to the university, *Agente Sceito* Ricci. And I am not a bug on their wall. So I cannot speak to their meeting. I know they are friends, associates, and perhaps it is a visit of friendship." Sophia trembled; that was close to a lie. They were meeting about the project. But they were indeed friends and allies, and so some pleasant fellowship might be involved. And so it was not *exactly* a lie. And she had said "perhaps." She let out a breath. Not a lie after all.

Thou shalt not lie.

"You should come back next week when my Uncle Hamadi has returned." Sophia straightened herself. She brightened and met Irem's stare. "My uncle has too many canes, Miss Madigan. A collection, you would call it. They are all over the property. Several are here."

Sophia padded to a wall behind the counter, glad for a moment away from their eyes. She studied several canes arranged in an umbrella stand. She looked back to Irem, then the canes, pulling out a beautiful walnut one inlaid with brass swirls and topped by a half-curved handle.

"This is too short for my uncle, and so he does not use it. Pity, as it just sits and waits to be dusted. Here." Sophia passed it over to Irem. "It is not too short for you. It is perfect."

"It is beautiful. What a gracious gift." Irem accepted it and nodded her thanks. "If you don't mind my asking —"

I have minded you asking all these questions. I have minded you being here. She didn't reply.

"Are you a nun?"

"*Si.*" Sophia still considered herself that, still did many of the things she had while living at the convent. But she

206

had a different purpose here, and an opportunity to do something amazing and holy. "I am spending some time away from the convent." And likely would never go back.

"Thank you for this stunning gift, Sister." Irem offered a warm smile.

Sophia was again gladdened that the woman had not been killed beneath Rome.

The policeman turned away and eyed the shelves.

"I am sorry I could not help you more," Sophia said.

"You were fine. *Molte grazie, Suora.*" The policeman walked to the door, spun, and politely nodded to her. He opened the door and waited for Irem.

Sophia clutched Irem's shoulder, leaned close to her ear, and whispered: "Put your curiosity away. Go home to America. Stay safe. Go home now." Then she returned to the counter and arranged the pamphlets. She did not look up until she heard the car start in the parking lot.

Sophia would call her Uncle Hamadi and tell him of this encounter. But she would wait until this evening, after her vineyard duties were finished and her prayers said. Then she would call him, and after that she'd tuck James away and likely pray again.

Sophia would pray that Irem Madigan leave Rome as soon as possible... while she was still breathing.

TWENTY-SEVEN
OCTOBER 16

HER KNEE ACHED. AT FIRST seeming only stiff, she continued to walk on it.

Irem had skipped therapy, figured all this walking today was accomplishing just as much. Then the slow ache became a crescendo; she imagined there were a hundred angry bees stinging just beneath her skin. Irem clamped her teeth tight and leaned heavily on the beautiful cane, hoping it would ease.

It didn't.

Stupido. I am *stupido* with a capital stupid, she thought.

Irem had left her prescriptions in her apartment. When she'd rented the scooter early this morning she hadn't expected to be gone so long. A couple of hours at most, the scooter cheaper than a cab and more fun, more freedom, the weather still warm enough that all she needed was a light jacket. Cane hooked behind the seat, cell phone fully charged, she told herself that she was fulfilling a promise to her brother.

When she'd visited him in the hospital yesterday after therapy, sat at his bedside for the hour they'd allowed, she made a vow:

"I will get to the very bottom, Lev. I will find out what this is about. The tapestry. The vault that was blown to pieces. Because it's not about Attila the Fucking Hun. Because whatever is at the very bottom of this is why Lacy and Santiago and more than a dozen other people are dead and why you have no right hand, why you are hooked up to a damn machine that helps you breathe and keeps you in a fog. I will figure this out."

Levent was not awake to hear her promise; he was still in an induced coma. Irem hadn't seen him conscious since the luncheon after the wedding. She'd stood up for him that day. Maybe ferreting out this mystery would be standing up even taller.

An image flashed behind her eyes: Benito meeting with a man on the dark, rainy sidewalk. That same man minutes later shooting at her. Was it connected to the explosion and the fire? Would she find Benito at the very bottom of this? She prayed not; Levent loved him. The police were investigating Benito, and Irem was grateful for that, as she didn't want to pepper him with questions. She prayed he wasn't involved, for Levent's sake.

But if the archaeologist was?

Irem pushed that possibility aside and kept walking.

She had been gone well more than the few hours she'd expected. It had turned into an all-day sojourn, with the last vestige of the morning's painkillers a distant memory.

"Shit. I really hurt." But Irem figured her pain was insignificant next to what Levent might be feeling.

She let her own misery spur her. Last night she'd studied the images of the tapestry's restoration, the pictures of the damaged cloth she'd taken from the restorer's computer screen. The early images showed more embroidered skulls than the repaired product, along with wide metallic threads leading from them. Guessing which bones had represented the Attila site, Irem used an overlay map of Rome and its environs, playing with the sizes until she got a rough correlation for where she thought Benito had been digging. Then she looked at the other skulls and threads, finding one grouping so nearby the Attila site that it could well have been the hidden chamber that had literally been blown to bits. Who had been buried there?

More bones and threads corresponded to other spots on her overlay map, and she'd been to three of those locations already today.

Finding essentially nothing.

In one case there was a boarded-over restaurant she didn't want to break into... at least not during the day. In another spot an expanse of concrete; if something was buried under that parking lot, it was going to stay buried. The third was a massive building where a great many people were entombed. The caretaker there told her that most burials in the area were handled this way; the dead put to rest in vertical niches, one atop the other atop the next. It was an old building, but not ancient. However, it had been built over an earlier cemetery that stretched back well more than a thousand years.

It was an impressive structure, and Irem took pictures of it and the caretaker. Little photographs were affixed to some of the grave fronts, and small bouquets protruded from others. The caretaker gave her a tour and pointed out some of the more famous dead. There was nothing that stirred her, not on the Attila scale of famous, all of it looking pretty much the same, and seeing no signs of anything dug up or destroyed.

It was possible that she was reading the unrestored tapestry incorrectly, that the overlay was the wrong size or placement; that this was all in pursuit of that elusive wild goose.

She stopped at a convenience store for Twinkies, a packet of peanuts, a bottle of aspirin, and a can of soda. She feasted and moved on.

This place would be her final exploration of the day, as it was heading toward evening and she didn't want to be alone out here after the sun had set. She wanted to be on her little couch, leg propped up, pain pills swallowed.

On the outskirts of the city, it seemed to be nothing more than a field, although a weathered and beat-to-hell sign near the road proclaimed it a church cemetery.

There was a small stone building at the far edge, looking almost ancient and certainly not cared for. She ambled toward it, careful, as ground that at first glance looked flat was rather uneven. There was a scattering of trees, but not many, and most of those looked sad, sick, or dying, their limbs just about leafless. They clacked at her in the breeze, and Irem shivered at the sound.

What did she think she would find on this expedition?

"Something," she said.

Irem had wanted to find *something*. Anything that might prove the details removed from the tapestry had pointed to special places, tombs or... *something*. And that something was ultimately why her brother was in the burn unit.

It was entirely possible that there was nothing to the tapestry, that her imagination had taken her for a fruitless ride. But three deaths were attached to that piece of cloth. There was *something*.

She looked back at her scooter, parked at the side of the road. Irem had walked quite a distance from it, the field bigger than she'd thought. *Turn back. That small couch is comfy in my tiny apartment. Go put my feet up and crash.* Irem nearly followed her own advice, but a car pulled up next to her scooter, a man got out, and headed toward her.

"Crappity crap," she groaned.

He had broad shoulders, although he walked a little stooped, and he had a fast gait. Maybe he was going to shoot her or strangle her. He couldn't drop a ceiling on her, not out here. She reached into her pocket and found her cell phone, brought it out. She'd call Gregario, not that he could get here in time. Perhaps she should have asked him to join her today. She studied the man; a few kicks with her good leg would probably take him down.

"*Buona sera!*"

That sounded friendly; Irem stopped punching buttons. The man wore jeans and a deep red sweatshirt, high-top tennis shoes. An older man, a careworn face, not yet in the senior citizen category. Maybe fifty. Fiftyish.

"*Come Si chiama?*"

"Irem Madigan." She answered his question and put her phone away. "My name is Irem Madigan. I didn't think I was trespassing. And I'm sorry, but I don't speak much Italian."

"*Mi chiamo Antonio Borghi.*" He stopped about ten feet from her. She didn't see any weapons on him; no threat. "I speak small English."

Irem relaxed a little more.

"Trespassing. You do not trespass here. Are you American?"

"*Si.* Chicago."

"Ah! Cubs baseball," Borghi said. "The World Serious winners."

"World Series," she corrected him. "*Si.* Cubs baseball. And the White Sox."

"The Chicago Bears. Not so good, that team."

"No, not so good. But it is good that I'm not trespassing." Irem thought quickly. "This field, I thought it was a cemetery. I saw a broken sign back there about a church cemetery."

"Cemetery. It was. Is. Oh, what is word? Gravefield. Now a gravefield. Markers are gone. Broken. Dust. Church is gone. That is why I come down here. I see you walking. Wonder if you are misplaced. Eh, lost. You look for someone buried here? The *lavoro d'ufficio*, I think they are gone. And you... are you hurt?"

She touched her face. "I had an accident. The bruises look bad, but I'm all right. You said *lavor—*"

"The *lavoro d'ufficio*."

"Records?"

He shrugged.

"Paperwork about the graves?

"*Si.* Gone, the records."

"Are you the caretaker?"

"*Custode*? No. My grandfather was," Borghi said. "The final caretaker. Then the world, it finally gave up this place. Someone comes still and chops the grass, from the city I think, though not often enough. When I was small, Grandfather would bring me here. I was, oh, three, four, and we would walk... no stones or markers then, either. Just pieces. I do not believe there were markers standing when my grandfather was small. So old, this place. But my grandfather knew this land and its stories, about the bones in the earth, and as a child he attended the old church that used to be here. He would tell me the stories about this field and the dead."

213

"You live around here?"

"I live up that hill." He pointed behind him, and Irem noticed three houses perched on the hillside, poised as if they were ready to slide down in a strong wind. "My grandfather's house. Mine now. I looked out the window and saw you stop, saw you walking. I drove down here. As I said, I was concerned you had misplaced yourself."

"I wasn't going to hurt anything."

"No. No. Not to worry. Just... oh, the word... *curioso*. I came down to see if I could help."

"Curious."

"*Si.*"

"Why I came here?"

He nodded.

"I'm not sure why I'm here. I'll be leaving. Didn't find what I was looking for. Don't know what I expected to find anyway. Just saw it on a map."

"Must have been an old map."

"Very old, and —"

"Not many people stop here anymore. Sometimes nuns. Very old nuns. Sometimes other old religious. No young people. Not that I have seen. But almost two weeks past, someone came and disturbed a place. That would not have been old nuns. The old nuns would not have done that."

"Disturbed?" Irem glanced at the field with more scrutiny, not noticing anything.

Borghi pointed and walked south. She followed him. "Disturbed. Dug. Disturbed someone sleeping forever in the ground. Fool to dig here, there is nothing to find. This place, it is too old. Everything is gone, even the memories. Maybe all the bones, they are dust."

"Old."

"Ancient."

Irem shivered. "Was someone famous, from a long while ago, buried here?"

Borghi smiled sadly. "Maybe. I would like to think yes, that I walk on holy ground. Maybe I do. Maybe you do, too. But maybe not. There are stories. *Si dice in giro che...* Maybe they are only stories."

Irem walked with him to the spot that had been disturbed.

"See? Someone, he was digging here. He tried to cover the work."

"Who famous was buried here… buried in this field? Do you know?"

"Here?" He shrugged and grinned, displaying off-white teeth, perhaps he smoked. "My grandfather used to tell me about Joan of Arc. About her remains, stolen and recovered, then… ah… *determinate*… decide by someone they were not Joan's. That they were the bones of a house cat."

"Joan of Arc wouldn't have any remains," Irem said. "She was burned at the stake. Three times burned according to history, and the ashes tossed in the Seine." She thought of Levent's burned body.

"Some say the body of Matthew, Levi son of Alphaeus of Capernaum is buried in Salerno, Italy, the place where a cathedral was put up around the year one thousand." He paused. "But a few say he was buried in this very gravefield."

"Matthew? The apostle Matthew?"

"*Si*," Borghi said. "He would be a famous ancient person, *si*? But it is just a story my grandfather used to tell me." He paused and tipped his head back, looking skyward. "From time to time very old nuns come to this field. Maybe they heard the story also."

"Wow." But as interesting as this was, an unproven and likely preposterous story wasn't helping her ferret out why her brother was burned and what the two Sicilian scholars had been up to under Rome. Was it possible that those two men had disturbed this grave? She shivered again. Her imagination was taking her on a very wild ride.

"The sun is going down, Miss Chicago. I am going home."

And I am going to Sicily.

TWENTY-EIGHT

THE TRAIN WAS WHITE WITH blue trim, its nose tapered and sleek looking. Irem thought it futuristic, something she might see ferrying tourists between hotels at Disneyworld. Or maybe like that Japanese bullet train she'd read about. The ticket was ninety-three euros one-way; it would have cost a quarter of that if she'd booked it a few weeks in advance. Seven trains ran between Rome and Catania in the far south, four of them direct. She'd not arrived at the station in time to catch a direct route, and she wasn't going to wait for one.

The Donkor brothers worked at the university in Catania; shouldn't be hard to find them, right? Plenty of people in Italy spoke English; she'd get a taxi, go to the university, and find someone there who could direct her to the Donkors.

And then what?

She hadn't thought that through all the way. Confront them? Sure. Question them. About the apartment fire and the tunnel. About a lot of things. Get some answers. Find justice for Levent. Really, she should leave this for the police; that would be the sensible course. But the image of her brother in the hospital plagued her. At the university, in the daylight, she'd be safe. If she got some solid information tying the Donkors to the tragedies in Rome, she'd call the local police... and maybe Gregario—he'd told her he was investigating them. Someone had to answer for Levent and Lacy and Santiago. And she couldn't do *nothing* and wait for the authorities to put everything in order... because maybe they wouldn't. They had rules to follow, and she wasn't bound by those.

Irem could have purchased a round-trip airline ticket and saved time and money — an hour and a half from gate to gate. This ride would take a dozen hours, arriving around 10:00 A.M., and that was after the train would be ferried from the port in Reggio Calabria across the Strait of Messina. She'd packed a change of clothes and her pills in case she needed to stay a night or two. The pain medication coursed through her right now, the ache in her knee down to a dull throb. She'd overdone it with walking so much across uneven ground today.

This trip would give her time to rest, maybe. She'd not been sleeping well, nightmares about Lev and mysterious men trying to kill her. Mostly flashes of her brother heavily bandaged; she couldn't get that out of her head. She tried to picture the stunning impressionist painting he'd given her, thinking that might make her happy. It only made things worse... no right hand, likely diminished mobility on top of that; Levent would not be able to render anything so striking again.

"Expensive ticket." Gregario dropped into the seat across from her and placed a white paper bag and two bottles of sparkling water on the adjacent cushion.

She was too drained to show her surprise. "Are you following me?"

"*Si*," he admitted. "Does that bother you?"

Irem shrugged. But it did bother her.

"I am assigned to the fire, recall please," he said. "My investigation takes me where you are going, to Catania. I am tasked with you... and with investigating the Donkors at the university." He paused. "Not an unpleasant assignment, Miss Irem Madigan."

"Irem."

"An airplane would have been faster. And not as many euros, though my department will repay me for this."

She was a little relieved to have the policeman with her, someone fluent in Italian, and who'd certainly been to

Catania before and knew how to get around the city. "I like trains. I don't like to fly."

"You flew to Rome."

"Obviously. I couldn't take a train here." She sucked in her lower lip. *For my brother's wedding.* "Really, you're 'tasked' with me?"

"*Assigned* to you." He met her gaze levelly. "*Si.* They were going to task someone, as I said. What is the word? Bodyguard. I requested that be me. Fortunately, your destination matches where the inquiry would take me anyway. To investigate the Drs. Donkor. Convenient, *si?*"

"Inconvenient you had to rush to catch the train."

Gregario smiled. "It is not an inconvenient task, my watching out for you." He held up the paper sack he'd brought with him. "This train does not have meal service."

"I— I didn't think to get anything."

"Two apples and four cheese sandwiches," he said. "And bottles of water. Plenty enough for sharing. There was not much to choose from at the sandwich shop."

Bodyguard? Was he really here to protect her? Because people associated with Benito Abruzi were either dead or in the burn unit? A dozen or more people dead in the fire. A catacombs demolished. Or was Gregario here because she was suspected of something?

"You're supposed to follow me? Honestly?"

"*Si.* Yes, I said. Except for when I go to talk to the Drs. Donkor at the university. You will wait for me then."

"What about Shamoon, the vintner? What about him?"

"He is being investigated also, but not by me. I cannot be in two cities at the same time. There are other senior agents involved. Indeed, the other agents also look into the Drs. Donkor. But since you are going to the university—"

"—you are going there to talk to the professors."

"*Si.* Yes. In person."

"*I'm* going to talk to the Donkors, too. They've not been arrested. I checked the online news before I bought this ticket. Unless I didn't look in the right places for police reports. They're free, aren't they? The Donkors? And this is a free country, so I'm going to talk to them."

"Irem, we have photographs from your phone. We have suspicions. But we have no clear evidence... not against the Donkors or Mr. Shamoon. Suspicions. No hard evidence. So we investigate to prove or disprove any wrongdoing, to gain that needed evidence. And remember I am not the only one on this case. So far the Donkors are tied to nothing questionable or illegal. They have no criminal records, only university honors. They are clean, at least on the surface."

"I think they're involved. I know they are. The Donkors *and* the vintner. Call it a gut feeling." More than a gut feeling, the nun had told her to go home. "I think they caused the fire. And the explosion in the catacombs. I just don't know why. They're responsible for Levent."

Gregario folded his hands in his lap. "Perhaps I share the feeling in the gut."

"Are you going to arrest them?"

"As I said, I am going to *investigate* them further."

"You've been to Catania before," Irem said.

"No."

She raised an eyebrow.

"Have you been to Hell, Michigan, where your brother's doctor is from?"

"Point made."

"I know much about the city. I've been near it. To Palermo, Alcamo, Marsala, Milazzo, Trapani. Sicily is beautiful. I have just never been to Catania."

"Yeah, well, I've been to Detroit and the Henry Ford Museum — great museum by the way, but not to Hell. Same difference, I guess." Did Hell, Michigan, have a museum worth visiting?

Sleep wasn't going to happen right now. She pulled out her phone and started a Google search.

"Catania's patron saint is St. Agnes," she said. That popped up in tidbits about their destination. Irem wondered if Chicago had a patron saint. The Windy City could probably use one. "Sicily has more than one hundred wineries. Looks like Catania has eight. A lot of drinkers, I guess."

Catania's flag was red on the left side, blue on the right. Nothing else on it, just those two blocks of color. Easy to manufacture, maybe designed by a lazy man, she mused. She briefly thought about Googling it, what the flag signified. Chicago's flag was adopted during World War I; two blue stripes on a white field representing the lake and the river, with four red six-pointed stars stretched horizontally, each one signifying a major event... Fort Dearborn, The World's Columbian Exposition, Great Chicago Fire of 1871, Century of Progress Exposition, and each point meaning something as well. She missed Chicago; it was far more comfortable than this seat on the train. She closed her eyes and the red and blue blocks loomed. Didn't matter what Catania's flag symbolized.

"Nothing important to me," she decided. The flag had nothing to do with her injured brother or with the two men who might have set the apartment fire and who certainly had tried to kill her in the belly of Rome. The Donkors. The two men underground had to have been the Donkors. There was no other possibility in her mind, not after the nun's warning.

What had they wanted so close to Benito's dig? What had they discovered? *Who* had they discovered? It hadn't anything to do with Attila the Hun; the markings she'd seen on the walls in the mysterious stairwell bore that out. And the patron saint of Catania and the simple flag had nothing to do with any of this either — in spite of their now twirling in her head. And what about the other threads in the unrestored version of the tapestry? Did they really lead to places? Someone had disturbed the ground at the grave field outside of Rome. Threads had led her there.

"What is not important to you, Irem?"

"A lot of things," she opened her eyes and answered almost too quickly. "Too many things. Not enough things." She rubbed her temple as if there were dirt on it that she tried to wipe away. "Nothing. Just talking to myself."

"Talk to me instead."

She let out a hissing breath. "Says here that Catania is old. Really old. Some indigenous people called their village

221

Katane, which meant 'skinning place' or 'flaying knife.' Lovely image, don't you think? Another translation says 'uneven ground' or 'sharp stones.' Also lovely. Around 260 B.C. people called it *Catĭna* and *Catăna*, Greek, meaning something like a bowl or bay. Mostly it was a Greek colony. But some Arabs were there for a while. And a man named Calippus, who assassinated Dion of Syracuse, held the area. It was also under Roman rule for years, was sacked by German soldiers in 1194, and bombed by the Allies in World War II. It looks like Attila the Hun left the place alone." Would Benito resume his dig? Irem wondered. And would she go back down with him?

"I don't want to hear about Catania. I want to hear about you, Irem. I want to learn more about you."

"Because you're assigned to me?"

He looked disappointed. "Because you intrigue me. *Sei delizioso.*"

"You want to learn more about me." Irem's words were flat. "Well… how about learning that I wasn't wholly truthful with you?"

His face registered mild surprise.

"The night I was shot at, that I told you and Levent and the officers who came to my door that I took a wrong turn…. It wasn't wrong. I was following Benito. I saw the man give him a wad of money, heard them talk about the dig. Benito went one way, the man another. I followed the man. I don't know why, really. Curious. I'm always curious. Then he saw me, shot at me. I didn't tell anyone that Benito knew him, or at least knew who he was. I didn't tell anyone because Benito was going to be family. Is family. And because Benito gave me a key to Attila the Friggin' Hun. I didn't want to lose that opportunity. I didn't want to screw things up with Lev. I…. So you've learned something. You've learned that I'm awful and—"

"That you're human." Gregario tapped her knee. "But now maybe we can find that man. We will talk to Dr. Abruzi." He leaned back in the seat. "So tell me something about you. Who are you, Miss Irem Madigan?"

The sounds of the train and the conversations of other riders filled the space between her and Gregario. She listened to it for several minutes before answering his question.

"I'm an archivist," she replied, wondering if *delizioso* he had used meant "dizzy." "I love Chicago, but I dream of landing a gig at a big museum in New York. Maybe even with the Smithsonian in D.C., although I think I'd really have to get a Ph.D. for that, to get one of the awesome posts. I like baseball—the White Sox—and Mickey D's, Grant Park, my Field Museum, the planetarium, the Shedd Aquarium, walking along lakeshore path to see the boats in the harbor, going past Macy's at Christmastime, watching people play chess at the lake, flying kites there. I like crisp snow peas with water chestnut slices. I like the blues. I like going to Wisconsin with friends, sitting by the lake. I like seeing black and white movies from the thirties and forties at the Music Box Theatre in the near north; they run a lot of Laurel and Hardy, sometimes even the silent ones. I like the photography in the black and whites, the graininess. I like that there were no cell phones or personal computers back then, that people actually had to talk to each other and rely on their wits rather than electronics, digging the old-fashioned way, no Google. I like ancient documents. No, I *love* ancient documents, history. My future is hooked to the past, I guess. I like cats, and I think I should get one when I go back home. Or maybe I'll get a parrot. I need something in my apartment."

"Because you are lonely."

Irem shrugged. She was. She'd shrunken in on herself since her engagement dissolved, started shrinking in the months before that when the relationship had started to show strains. She had stopped going out, save for the occasional drinking night with Rowan when they would attempt to wash their troubles away at Scofflaw on the waves of craft cocktails, or by swilling beer at Vice District in the south Loop.

"I don't like flying. I don't know why, but I don't like it. I don't like liver and onions, bratwurst, okra, kale, turnips, unsalted butter, mayonnaise, or ginger ale. I don't like snowdrifts when they get black from all the car and bus exhaust, people who lay on their horns when traffic gets stuffed up, cab drivers who edge up over the curb, mothers who can't control their kids in museums, people who let their dogs poop on sidewalks and don't clean it up, weddings—I really don't like them, heavy metal music, *borseggiatores*, and I don't like cops who know that I like cheese sandwiches." She dropped her gaze to her phone and played with the keys.

"So you like cheese sandwiches?"

She gave a half smile, but kept looking at a picture of a Catania fountain on her cell phone. "Yeah, I like cheese sandwiches."

He passed her one, and she accepted it and quickly pulled off the wrapping.

"*Grazie*," Irem said. She thought it small, but it was thick with different cheeses.

"*Prego*," he returned. "I like old movies, too. I have a collection."

"Yeah? What's in it? Your collection." She took a big bite of the sandwich. Provolone, Pecorino, and Swiss, a nice combination, and probably a tad pricey. Good thing he bought two each; she was seriously hungry.

He chuckled. "Rather eclectic. *Gojira, Beast from 20,000 Fathoms, Island of Lost Souls, Murders in the Rue Morgue*—the Lugosi version--*White Zombie,* and *Them!*"

"*White Zombie.* Good movie. Them! That's the ant one, right?"

He nodded. "I have many more. Some night, while you are still in the city, you must come over and we will watch."

"That's all you're gonna tell me? You like old monster movies?"

"Comic books. I like comic books, historical fiction— Bernard Cornwell, eating out once in a while at good restaurants, and museums... any kind of museum. There is the Crime Museum at Via del Gonfalone I will take you to—wax models, crime scene photos, murder weapons."

"I like museums," she said softly.

"I like playing computer games one or two times a week when I'm off shift. Never more than two evenings, and not in a row, as I do not want to be addicted like a few of my friends are. I enjoy vineyard tours and rock concerts, though not often enough on either count. Perhaps I would like the blues. I like to fly, and so I travel once a year, to somewhere other than Italy."

"To see the world?"

"There is a lot of world to see. Earlier this year I went to the Canary Islands, next year Poland maybe. I am a budget traveler and sleep in hostels and cheap hotels. One spends so little time in a bed anyway when visiting another country."

She finished the sandwich and stopped herself from reaching for another. She'd save that for a little later. Their conversation lapsed for several minutes, and Irem focused on the rhythmic sound of the train and the occasional staccato *chunk!* when it went over an uneven rail. She saw Gregario take out his phone and search through it. A big man in ink-black pants and a long-sleeved white T-shirt walked down the aisle, pausing to glance at her, and then continued on and squeezed into the bathroom.

"Have you met Maritza Palma?" Gregario leaned forward and tapped her knee.

"No. I don't believe so. Is he important? Involved in all of this? Whatever 'this' is?"

"*She*," Gregario answered. "I am uncertain. She is a student at the university we travel to, and where the twin professors work. Perhaps they do not know each other, the men and the student. But perhaps they do. She was in the apartment building that burned, minor injuries, said she'd been visiting a friend on the fourth floor."

Gregario passed over an apple, and then he turned his phone so she could see a picture on it. "This is Maritza Palma. Seen her? Anywhere while you were in Rome?" It was only a headshot, and Irem could tell the woman was against a pillow. "I took this at the hospital when I interviewed her after the apartment fire."

That explained the pillow. The woman was young, no makeup, dark circles under brown eyes that had gold flecks, three silver ball studs in each ear. She had a nutmeg-hued complexion, deep russet hair shaved on the right side, short on the left, a long center hank with a pink streak in it that flopped over her forehead and covered her eyebrows. It was a modern cut that was similar to what Irem might see on the sidewalks of Chicago. She thought the girl would look prettier with a "normal" do.

"Never saw her before, Ari. I'd remember someone with a haircut like that." Irem registered the vibration of the train beneath her feet, felt it purring against her back, the sensations relaxing. Another *chunk!* Faintly, she heard the strains of Santana's *Maria*, a passenger sharing the music. "Did you ask her about the twins? The Donkors?"

Gregario frowned. "I met with her before I had the names and photographs of the brothers. When I returned to the hospital to ask, she was gone, had checked herself out. But I have her address in Catania. Very near the university."

"Then she's involved, too. Coincidence a Catania University student and two professors were in that apartment building? Nope. And those professors *were* in that building. I just know it. And I'd place a really big wager they were the two men underground who almost blew me up." She scrolled through her own phone, seeing an email from her mother asking how Levent was faring; maybe she'd reply later.

"So about the Donkors. What are they professors of?" *Explosives? Terrorism?* She'd been to the university website and poked around, but found no mention of them. She did, however, discover that it was a very large school and suspected its website did not cover everything and everyone.

"Rauf Donkor teaches Carpocratian Studies and Comparative Religions."

Irem bit into the apple. It was tart and crunchy, and the juice dribbled on her fingers. She ate it while Gregario continued.

"Uziah is a lecturer and a researcher in DNA sequencing. It appears he used to teach biology, but took a sabbatical and returned as a lecturer and graduate student mentor." He

226

put his phone away. "And so based on their backgrounds it makes no sense that they would burn an apartment building or blow up a tunnel underground."

He handed her a napkin. She wiped her hands, and when she finished the apple she rolled the core in the napkin. He started on his, removed the other two sandwiches, placed them on the seat, and used the empty paper bag for their garbage.

"A lot of things make no sense." She attempted a spelling of Carpocratian on her phone, she was pretty sure she'd read something about them before. "Gnostic sect founded by Carpocrates of Alexandria. They thought Jesus Christ culled much of his religion from Egypt's Temple of Isis, where they think he studied for some years. Sect members devised their own greetings, symbols, and words and persisted until sometime in the sixth century. Interesting."

She reached under the seat and retrieved her backpack, set it on the seat next to her. "I might stay tomorrow night, depending on what I do or do not find at the university, if I can talk to both of the Donkors. Maybe I'll be here two nights. I didn't know when I'd be done, so I didn't buy a return ticket."

"Neither did I."

"And you didn't bring an overnight bag."

"You did not give me time to pack one, Irem. I spent a good part of yesterday looking for you. Not at your physical therapy session, not at your apartment, and I missed you at the hospital when you visited your brother."

"I'd rented a scooter. Saw some of the countryside."

"That I discovered, but too late."

"Then I decided to go to Catania."

"And I barely got here in time to buy sandwiches and catch this train."

"Sorry I made it inconvenient. But I didn't know you needed to stalk me." She levered herself up and grabbed her cane, ambled down the aisle to the bathroom. Inside, she briefly glanced at herself in the small mirror, the bruises still ugly, but not as bad as yesterday, fading and yellowing. She might have used a little makeup if she'd known

227

Gregario was going to show up. Splashing water on her face and arms, she noticed a sign in multiple languages: *Do not drink the water.* She remembered reading something in a tourist brochure about never drinking the water on trains throughout Europe. Then she returned to her seat.

Irem curled across the seats and used her backpack as a pillow; only one change of clothes inside, it provided little padding. She angled her head so she could look out the window and watch the night pass by.

She woke sometime after midnight, her cell phone chiming mutely in her pocket. Sitting up and retrieving it, she saw that Gregario was sound asleep, head tipped onto his shoulder. She took a picture of him and then checked her messages.

Rowan had emailed her, an answer to the recording she'd sent.

> *Hey Irem:*
>
> *Sorry bout Lev. Pray he gets well. Good U R staying in Rome with him.*
>
> *What the hell did U get into? Odd language. Where was this recorded? Give! Some is easy, Latin, Italian, but that's not what U R interested in. U can probably translate that. I REALLY had to dig to get pieces of it. U owe me dinner. Some of it is a very old gnostic tongue, a patched together dialect stirred with some Aramaic, almost like a code. Basically your speakers say they have some god-touched bones. They say a bone of Cephas. I extrapolated from there. The apostle Peter, Petra in Latin, Petros in Greek, means stone or rock. His given name was Simon. Jesus was said to have renamed Peter to Cephas, which means 'stone' in Aramaic.*
>
> *That's all I got for U. Tell me where U got this, kiddo. I'd really like to hear some more of this language. And I'm thinking steak with the trimmings when U get back. We'll go to Scofflaw's after for cocktails... no umbrellas.*
>
> *Hugs and kisses, Row*

Was it possible the two men under Rome had recovered Saint Peter's bones? Or at least *thought* they did? Then destroyed the chamber and stairwell and tried to kill her, wanting it all to remain a secret? The man at the old cemetery yesterday... he'd said: "Some say the body of Matthew, Levi, son of Alphaeus of Capernaum is buried in Salerno, Italy, the place where a cathedral was put up around the year one thousand." He'd paused. "But a few say he was buried in this grave field."

Was it possible? And was Levent burned, Lacy and Santiago killed, to cover up a religious theft?

Irem saw that one sandwich remained, and she ate it. The ones she'd bought in the deli were larger, but she was grateful for this. Gregario had been considerate. She liked him. Maybe she would take him up on the offer of a black and white movie night.

Then she dozed on and off and stared out the window until morning came and Gregario woke and stretched and padded away down the aisle to the bathroom. The Catania skyline came into view. Postcard stunning, with a blue-tinged mountain behind it, the top shrouded in mist. She brought her phone up and took a picture.

Irem wished Levent could enjoy this view. What color number would he assign the sky?

TWENTY-NINE
OCTOBER 17

IREM STOOD IN FRONT OF a massive fountain, odd and interesting and definitely old, and nothing like the ones she'd seen in Rome. It consisted of a ten-foot tall boxy white marble pedestal crowned by a black elephant with curving white tusks. Rising from its back was an ivory obelisk. Irem and Gregario had been on their way through Piazza Duomo to the bus that would take them to the university when she saw the elephant and felt compelled to stop.

"Before all of this awful stuff happened, I was supposed to be back to work tomorrow; my vacation would have officially ended today." She took a close up of the elephant's head. "I have some photos to actually show friends back home that there was vacation involved. Sort of. Traveling involved anyway. Wait until Rowan hears that they put a train on the ferry to get us to Sicily."

"Your workplace, it is good to you," Gregario said. "You do not have to be back for a long while. Months. They are understanding."

She picked another angle and took more pictures, catching Gregario in a few. Nearby, tourists held phones and cameras, capturing everything.

"Do you know what it symbolizes?" she asked Gregario. "I mean, it's strange, an African elephant in the center of a Sicilian city."

A weathered-faced man answered, one of a handful also taking pictures. He spoke with a German accent.

"It is called *U liotru,* according to this guidebook." He started reading. "The Catania elephant, carved from lava rock, is the city's official symbol. Ha! African elephant in Italy. You are correct, it is strange. There is a deep connection, this literature says. Likely built during the Byzantine or Carthaginian period. Legend says Eliodoro was a Catanian aristocrat who wanted to be an archbishop. Instead, he was disfavored and accused of being a sorcerer and sent to the stake. Eliodoro created the *liotru* to escape and used it to ride back and forth between Catania and Carthage. Others say this statue was built to honor those who died in the war between the Carthaginians and the Libyans, or that it is a magical idol that protected Catania from Etna eruptions."

"Thank you," Irem said.

"*Bitte.*"

She took pictures of the square and its baroque architecture, another of Gregario against the fountain, and then they headed to the bus stop with as much speed as her awkward gait allowed. She paused when Gregario put a hand on her elbow and pointed to a café.

"Several minutes we should spare," he suggested. "I, too, want to be about my investigation. But my stomach has other ideas right now."

"I am hungry," she admitted. "*Really* hungry." The cheese sandwiches seemed a distant memory. "I could spare a half hour or so."

Trattoria Catania Ruffiana had an elephant on a counter inside, as if the exquisite carving guarded an array of wine bottles. There weren't many tables, and most of them were occupied, but she and Gregario found a small one in the corner under a hanging light made from a section of tree bark.

Irem stared at the menu; it was written in Italian, and while she recognized *primo* and *secondo,* most of the other words were lost on her, the passes through *Italian for Dummies* and the guidebook not sufficient. *Antipasto, primo, secondo, bevanda, dolce della casa e coperto,* all for one price... whatever all of that included. Maybe she could just ask for spaghetti and hoped the waiter understood. Wait! Levent

232

had told her spaghetti wasn't Italian and difficult to find in most restaurants, at least not under that name.

"I see what the other customers are served here. This will be a lot of food, split it? One order to share? My work, I will expense this. And then we will go somewhere very nice for dinner tonight."

Irem nodded. She pointed to the menu, eyebrows arched.

Apparently Gregario sensed her lack of understanding. "*Antipasto*... this means 'before the meal,' appetizer."

"Yeah, I figured that word out. It's all the words below it."

"How about the *bruschetta*, toasted bread with toppings for the appetizer?"

"Sounds good," Irem said.

"*Primo*, first dish, gives us a choice of pasta, soup, or *risotto*... creamy rice."

"The rice." Irem was only a little adventurous today. Certainly not adventurous enough for soup... all manner of things could get tossed into soup. "*Risotto*."

"Good selection. *Secondo*, the main dish. Here we can have *bistecca*, steak; *pollo*, chicken; *agnello*, lamb; *gamberi*, shrimp; *frittata*, an omelet; *salmone* —"

"Salmon. Got that."

"Okay, we will select salmon."

"No, I just meant I understood that word. *Pollo*, too. Are you up for *frittata*? I haven't had eggs in days."

"I love omelets, and this one says four eggs. Big. With cheese? It comes with little potatoes and a fruit muffin, too."

"Dear God, I love cheese." She thought that should have been evident with her penchant for cheese sandwiches.

He grinned. "*Bevanda* refers to wine. If you want water here, we will have to order a bottle of it."

"Wine. Your choice."

"Dessert is included. I recommend sigarette, which in English is cigarette but does not mean the same thing. Famous in Sicily, sigarette is thin, rolled pastries filled with amazing chocolate or fresh ricotta."

"With amazing chocolate."

"*Certo*," he beamed.

He ordered the Etna Rosato, the waiter calling it a *passito* wine made from sun-dried grapes. Irem thought it delicious with the omelet. During the hurried lunch, she told him about Rowan's translation.

"Gnostic, Aramaic, like a secret code. Irem, you should have showed me this email right away." He quickly forwarded it to someone at his department in Rome.

"Sorry."

"You did not know to do so."

"What I do know is that the Donkors are responsible for all the bad things, and that the girl with the pink devilock—"

"What?"

"The girl with the weird hair is involved."

"She is," Gregario agreed. "The wine, I think, brought it together, her involvement. In the hospital she told me that she was on her way out of the apartment to buy wine, a Barbera Bianca or a Syrah. It struck me as odd that someone young, who looked as she did—yes, judgmental of me— would be so specific about wine. Then later, at the winery, the nun knowing the Donkors. The vintner Shamoon knowing them. The wine ties it all together, makes them related. *In vino veritas,* I suppose you could say."

"Were you married?" Maybe the wine helped the question escape.

Gregario grimaced and touched his ring finger. "So you notice things."

"I— I didn't mean to pry. Just curious. I am terribly curious. About everything."

"Eight years," he answered. "Married at twenty, the both of us, still at the university. I got on with the state police right after graduation. Seven of our years were good. But my Angela, she didn't like some of my long hours and met someone else, and after a time decided she loved him more. Divorced two years now. I took the ring off last Christmas, and after these months still I have a mark on my finger. Maybe in another year there will be no sign and the skin will look all the same."

So Gregario was thirty. If this was Chicago, if he was in Chicago, Irem might consider the notion of looking for more than lunch and chatter about old movies. She thought it awful she'd even entertained that idea... she should only be thinking about Levent and getting to the bottom of all of this.

"I really shouldn't have asked," she said. "My nose trouble causes trouble."

"*Nessun problema.* No trouble. And your nose, it is cute."

"I was dumped, too." Wine! It must be the wine that was making her babble to him. She was sharing secrets she wouldn't have otherwise. "I was engaged, we were living together, and he found someone else." *Younger. No doubt pretty. Gorgeous. And stupid with a capital S-T-U-P-I-D. The girl is stupid because she fell for him and they'll get engaged and she'll get dumped for the next one.* "I probably wouldn't've come to Rome if Ronnie and I were still together."

"Perhaps finding someone else is not a bad thing, eh?" He caught her gaze.

They finished the meal and on the way to the bus stop passed more buildings she took pictures of, hoping the images did not turn out blurry because of her haste... Gothic, Roman. She'd read a little about Sicily in one of her wakeful bouts on the train. The largest island in the Mediterranean, it was sought after throughout history and occupied by various peoples who left their mark in the architecture: Punic, Greek, Roman, German, French, Muslims, one after another wanting the land. It had an active volcano, Etna, which she could see between gaps in the buildings. It had last erupted in 2002. Wars, volcanic eruptions, earthquakes... all of them had scarred the place; yet, it persisted and thrived.

The bus drove past ornately decorated churches in the downtown area, the side streets narrow cobblestone, much like she'd noticed in Rome. Sidewalk vendors sold ceramics and jewelry, the artisans crafting things while tourists stopped to watch. Small shops offered gelato and blood oranges. She held her phone to the window and took pictures. Away from the center, modern apartments and hotels rose, seeming at odds with the old section of the city. In the green patches she saw palm trees and fruit gardens.

"Were the circumstances different, I could enjoy this city," Irem said as they got off the bus and started toward Maritza Palma's apartment. The university loomed across the street. "Actually, I would have enjoyed Rome more, too. I only had a few days to be all touristy and to go under the city with Benito. Lev and I, we just had a single day for sightseeing, tagged with the promise for more. He gave me this painting he'd hung in an art gallery. It's amazing. Maybe you'll come look at it. I have it on the wall in my micro apartment."

She brought her cell phone up and took pictures of some of the campus buildings and of a haunted looking tree, half-dead; the top part of it blackened branches stark against the bright blue sky. Then she took a picture of Maritza's apartment building, stone, four levels, with someone's laundry hanging from clotheslines near the edge of the roof. Flower boxes beneath every window dripped with color.

"I would very much like to see the painting your brother gave to you." Gregario plucked her cell phone and took a picture of her against the apartment front and a window box spray of pink and red oleanders. He handed the phone back. "It is good that we are here now, this time of year. Sicily is fine in October, but summer... July, August, an oven it can be. Only once did I come to this island in the middle of summer. Not again."

"You don't have to shovel hot," Irem returned.

"Shovel hot? I don't understand."

"Ari, Chicago can have brutal winters, lots of snow. Crews are always shoveling the sidewalks."

"Ah, I understand. Clever. You don't have to shovel hot. More than thirty-eight degrees all the time in the summer here, I think. Sicily. No snow to ever shovel. Don't have to shovel hot. I like that."

Irem tried to mentally convert thirty-eight Celsius to Fahrenheit, and decided the translation amounted to sweltering.

"I won't have to worry about being in Sicily in the summer. I have up to a six-month leave of absence. That'll take me through April if I stay that long. If. Depends on how Lev is doing."

"*La neve.* Snow is rare in Rome. In 2012 I took pictures of snow on the Spanish Steps. It did not stay long, more slush than anything. So I would say there is no snow to shovel in Rome, either. But perhaps you will see a little this winter. It can be briefly pretty."

"I don't know how long I'm staying."

"Hopefully all the six months your employer allows," Gregario said. "You can't spend all of it at your brother's bedside or chasing after people."

"I can't chase anybody right now," she answered. "I'm way the hell too slow with this gimpy knee."

And because of the gimpy knee, Irem waited in a comfortable chair in a lobby that smelled of baked bread, while Gregario went up the four flights to Maritza Palma's apartment. She figured she'd save her stamina for any stairs that needed climbing to reach the Donkors.

He came down a half hour later, shaking his head.

"Not here," he said. "Most people are not here right now. A few neighbors on her floor I found said she is at class all afternoon and works until the early evening. A neighbor on the floor below said the same... and that she is quiet, no loud music or dancing to make his ceiling jiggle."

"Does she work on campus?"

Gregario shrugged. "The few I talked to, even the one next door, they do not know much about her. They say she is a private person, keeps to school and work. They don't know what she studies or what she does to earn money. The landlord's wife, she says Maritza Palma is a good tenant and pays with cash. She thought perhaps Martiza works for a professor, something the girl once said to her."

"Did you look inside Martiza's apartment? Get the landlord to let you in?"

Gregario shook his head. "I had no legal cause to do that. Not *in questo circostanza.*"

Irem scowled. "I should have gone upstairs with you. I would have found a *circostanza* that let me snoop inside. I would have found a damn big *circostanza.*"

THIRTY

GREGARIO FOUND A HELPFUL CLERK in a campus administration building. She said Dr. Nazih Rauf Donkor was teaching a class, but it was nearly over. Donkor had posted hours and would be in his office in twenty minutes — the clerk provided a map with directions. However, his brother, Dr. Uziah Donkor, was not scheduled to be on campus until an evening lecture tomorrow. The clerk said it was against policy to release a residential address for either of them. It didn't matter on that count; Gregario told Irem he had their address.

Several minutes later, Gregario rested his hands on Irem's shoulders as they stood outside one of the older campus buildings. "Please wait here."

"No," she said. "This trip... this was my idea. I want to talk to him, confront him in his office. I need to know —"

"You need to know that I am a trained police officer, and that I know how to do my job. I can do that better if you are here and I speak with him alone. You are a distraction, Miss Irem Madigan —"

"And you can't risk that I'm going to pop off and say something that —"

"*Si.*"

Irem inwardly fumed. This truly had been her idea, coming here, meeting with the Donkors, whom she'd saddled with all her suspicions. Free country, Italy, she could do as she wanted, and he could not prevent her. But —

"Fine." She hoped he could tell by her expression that she wasn't happy with the plan.

"I will have my phone record our conversation," he said. "And I will play it for you when I am done."

"Fine." It really wasn't fine, not wholly, although she knew he was probably right. A senior policeman, he certainly could handle an interview. But if she wasn't satisfied after listening to his recording, she would go talk to Donkor on her own… unless he was in jail. "Are you going to arrest him?"

"Perhaps. If I can gain evidence, if he admits to wrongdoing."

"Do you have handcuffs and—"

"*Si*. I have handcuffs."

"A gun?"

"*Si*. I have a gun."

Irem's eyes widened. She didn't see a gun on him. Her gaze dropped. Maybe he wore one near his ankle, like some of the cops did in the police shows she watched.

"You will wait, *si*?"

"*Si. Si. Si.*" Irem spotted a trio of benches on the sidewalk. One was empty. "*Si. Si. Si.* I *capiche.*"

"That is slang, and slang is fine. But *capisco* means 'I understand.'"

"Fine. *Capisco.* I could rest my knee anyway." She ambled to a bench, looked over her shoulder. "But I get to hear the recording."

"Of course."

"And there's the other Donkor. I might want to talk—"

He was inside the building before she could finish her comment.

Irem sent a text:

Mom:
Lev is still critical in the burn unit. In a coma. Doc might wake him in two or three days. Right hand and part of his arm amputated. BTW, I was in the hospital too, knee surgery. In Sicily now.
Irem.

There was a lot more she could have added; that maybe she should be with Levent right now. That instead she was determined to discover why he was burned, Lacy and Santiago and others killed — who did it; who was buried in the catacombs — and then buried again with the explosives; and how a vintner, two university professors, a student, and perhaps a nun figured into the mix.

Why someone had tried to kill her.

And the tapestry... what did it have to do with all of this? Irem also could have texted that her mother should be in Italy, too, at Levent's side, meeting Levent's new husband, or at least sending flowers, showing some tiny measure of real concern. Maybe the brevity of her text would let her mother know just how pissed she was. Maybe she was glad her parents were apparently staying in Chicago.

Irem's mind whirled. She panned through the pictures she'd taken on her phone, lingering on one of Levent outside the art gallery. He was so beautiful and happy in that moment. She selected a few shots to email Rowan, including the one of Gregario at the elephant fountain. *I like him*, she wrote with the photo. She looked at the time; the policeman had been gone nearly thirty minutes.

Gregario would be in Rauf Donkor's office, interrogating him. Oh, to be that fly on the wall... or oh, to have argued with Gregario and tagged along. He probably would have caved if she'd kept pushing the issue. Irem glanced up from the phone and stared across this section of the commons.

Groups of students walked together, chattering, laughing; a few rode bicycles; two young women spread a small blanket and sat, and by their bobbing heads Irem guessed they were listening to music; an occasional professorial-type strolled along at a purposeful pace; a few loners stood in the shade, eyes glued to their cell phones. All the conversations the breeze carried were in Italian; she recognized some scattered profanities. The air smelled good, of old buildings and flowers, and a hint of the sea. She missed Chicago, but she'd be wearing a heavy jacket there and smelling bus exhaust on her way to and from work.

Irem didn't notice a scrap of litter, everything clean and the grounds well-tended. She took a few more pictures, and then went to thumb off the cell phone to conserve its charge when she noticed that one of those lone students who was engrossed in texting had a complexion the shade of nutmeg, shaved hair on one side, short on the other, and a long center hank with a thick hot-pink streak dangling across her forehead.

Said student was roughly fifty feet away.

Maritza Palma; the hairdo was likely too unique to be sported by multiple girls. Had to be Maritza Palma. The girl glanced from her phone to the building Gregario had entered. It seemed like she was staring at a third- or fourth-floor window. Dr. Rauf Donkor's office? Not a coincidence in Irem's mind that the girl Gregario had met in the hospital was outside this building. It was related, the student was involved.

· Irem texted Gregario.

Martiza Palma is here.

She waited a beat; no reply. She called him; he didn't pick up. Of course, he didn't… he'd said he was going to record his conversation with Dr. Rauf Donkor on the phone. The policeman certainly wouldn't take an interruption from Irem while he was working.

She sent another text:

Am real sure Maritza Palma is fifty feet away. Am going to chat with her.

She watched Maritza stare at the window several minutes, gaze dropping to her phone, then back up to the window. Probably texting… or maybe getting a text from someone in the building.

No coincidence.

Maritza had been in the burning apartment building in Rome. That evidence still clung to her. She had a bandage wrapped around her left arm and another around her left calf. There was a gauze pad affixed with surgical tape on her neck — smaller than what had been in the picture from the hospital that Gregario had shown Irem.

242

What the hell did a pink-haired student from Sicily have to do with the fire?

Could she have set it?

Finally Maritza turned away, still engrossed in her phone, walking slowly as her fingers played on the keys. Slow meant Irem could keep up with her. Irem's knee ached, and she was overdue for her medication. But she'd had wine at lunch and so had decided to skip the pills. Maybe the pain would keep her alert.

Irem guessed Maritza to be in her early to mid-twenties; the age fit with the student descriptor and with the hair and clothes. She wore cutoff, frayed white jean shorts and over that an ombre-dyed blue tank, flowy, a small canvas backpack slung over her right shoulder, leather walking shoes. Gregario had said shoes were often a way to tell the locals from the tourists in Sicily, as locals tended to only wear tennis shoes when they were at the gym. Irem shouldered her own backpack and leaned on the beautiful cane.

Irem briefly wondered if following Maritza was a bad idea. Sicily was so far from Chicago. Catania was an unknown; she wasn't a native speaker and knew so little Italian that any real effort to converse was close to worthless. But she was bolstered by her black belt and the notion that Gregario wasn't all that far away. She let her inquisitiveness tug her.

And so she trailed after Maritza, unconcerned about whether the student noticed her. She and Irem had never met, and so Maritza would have no reason to be suspicious. Not once did the girl glance behind her, and she looked up only when she came to sidewalk intersections. Irem wished Maritza would stop so she could stop, too. Her knee throbbed now.

Irem almost tried to call Gregario again, but the girl had put her phone away and was moving faster. Irem clamped down on her lower lip and pushed herself to keep up.

Finally the girl stopped in front of a lamppost festooned with colorful paper. Maritza reached around to her canvas backpack, pulled out a flyer and tape, and added to the collection.

"Mari!" A young man several yards away called and waved his hand. Maritza returned the wave and walked toward him. A few more students joined them. A gaggle of students brushed past Irem and nearly knocked her over.

"*Scusami,*" one of them offered.

Irem went to the lamppost, angling so she could read the flyer and keep an eye on Maritza. Two young women joined her, one of them taking a picture of a flyer that appeared to advertise a play. All the posts were in Italian, the only words she recognized on Maritza's flyer were Carpocratian and *Professore* Donkor. Irem took a picture of it with her phone.

"*Stai andando?*" Another student came up behind her and tapped her shoulder.

Irem turned; he was thin, wearing blue jeans and a plain brown T-shirt, backpack over one shoulder, glasses slid halfway down his nose. He had a mass of curly black hair, a horseshoe mustache, and a dusting of pimples. Geek, she thought.

"My Italian is not too good," Irem admitted. "I'm just visiting here."

He grinned and she saw that a front tooth was badly chipped. "I know English. You sound American. I asked if you were going to that lecture."

"Lecture?"

"This one says the Carpocratian lecture is tomorrow night, off campus."

"Oh."

He stared at her, and finally said: "Did someone beat you up?"

"No. I was— I was in an accident." A pause: "Do you know anything about this Carpocratian thing? This lecture? I guess I'm interested."

He shrugged. "Sure. A little. I used to be a theology major, comparative religions. The more I studied, the more it all seemed fiction. Atheism agrees with me. I switched schools. I'm getting my masters in Global Policies and Euro-Mediterranean Relations."

Irem regretted starting the conversation. "Good for you."

The young man kept going. "But my roommate is into it, religion and all that bullshit. They are all *pazzo, strano*. Especially the campus Carpocratian study group. Crapocratians, I call them."

"Why is that?"

"They want to scientifically prove that Jesus Christ was divine. I guess they look to quantify God. Most of them are scientists, not theologists... uhm theologians. *Strano*, eh?"

"Yeah, odd." Irem glanced over to make sure Maritza was still there. "Is it a big group? A lot of students?"

He shrugged again. "Big enough to post these notices almost every week. If you don't speak Italian well, I'd take a pass. They recruit sometimes. My roommate, he goes all the time, sometimes works for that one." He bumped his knuckle against Donkor's name on the flyer. "Said they needed a bigger meeting place, more than a hundred go now, usually. He tried to get me interested. But I told him I was done with religion, fiction, you know. A new major. I can help change the world with politics, not divine science." He ground the ball of his foot against the sidewalk and laughed. "God? I'm not interested. I think—"

"*Scusami*," Irem said. She'd remembered the Italian word for "excuse me." Maritza Palma was moving, and Irem hurried as much as she could to keep her in sight.

Maritza left the campus grounds and crossed the street. Irem figured Martiza was headed to her apartment. She would holler and get her to stop, talk to her without attempting the four flights up. But the girl passed that building and kept going. It was a struggle now, keeping pace. Fortunately there were others out on this section of the walk, and Martiza had to slow to weave in and out of them—mostly locals judging by the shoes.

It was good that the university was large and some of the buildings massive; Irem could see them over her shoulder and so didn't worry about getting lost.

Where the hell is she going?

Irem entertained the notion of calling out to the girl, to have a conversation right here, but Maritza jaywalked across another street and headed toward a small shopping mall.

Crappity crap crap. The noise level increased — cars, music spilling from upper floor apartments, a siren in the distance, people on the sidewalk chatting, two of them in a heated argument. *Tu bastardo...* she recognized that. The girl went into the mall, and Irem forced herself to move faster still. If she didn't hurry, she could well lose her.

She called Gregario again and left another message. "I'm at a shopping mall. It's called *Piazza Mercata*. I'm following Maritza. I'll meet up later on the campus."

The air was different inside the mall; it had that circulated tang mixed with a variety of cooking odors — she picked out the scent of fried fish and garlic. Ahead and to her right, a narrow-fronted seafood restaurant, and a few yards beyond that was what amounted to a food court, where some shoppers sat with drinks. Above their heads dangled inverted tricorne lights on chains a dozen or more feet long. Fortunately the mall was relatively small — two levels, and no big, honking anchor store emerged — and not crowded, making it relatively easy to follow Maritza.

Where to confront her?

If she stopped at the food court, that could be perfect. Maritza was headed in that direction.

Irem glanced at a couple of empty storefronts farther inside. This place reminded her of some of the shopping malls around Chicago, which were having a difficult time hanging onto the big brick-and-mortar businesses in the face of online shopping. There weren't all that many shoppers going in and out of the open stores.

In fact, there had been more people out on the sidewalk than in the mall; it was not difficult to keep watch on Maritza and to catch up to her. The girl stood with her nose pressed against a window, studying something, raising her hand to the glass. Maritza's fingernails were long and expertly manicured, mostly red, with a sliver of gold at the tips, the ring fingernail white with red stripes. Irem limped closer, noting that the girl peered into a jewelry store, one that sold kitschy pieces — odd-looking gaudy fobs on thick chains, bracelets and cuffs made of garishly colored plastics, earrings so large and heavy appearing she imagined they would stretch the wearer's earlobes. The shop next to it was a consignment clothing store, and Irem pretended to look in the widow of it as she mulled over what to say to Maritza.

Do it now; get it over with. Irem turned. "Excuse me, Miss —"

Maritza glanced away from the widow, giving Irem an up and down. "*Cosa vuoi da me?*"

"I was wondering —"

"*Scusa?*"

"*Che orario fate?*" Irem remembered a phrase from her Dummies book. She tapped the store window. "English?"

"*Si, parlo inglese.*" Maritza smiled. "The mall is open to six, maybe seven. I am not wholly certain. I pay no attention to the hours." Her phone chirped and she spun away from Irem to take the call. "*Mi arriverà presto. Ho appena finito con classi.*"

Something about "arriving soon" and "finished" with a class. Irem couldn't overhear more than that because the strains of Cielito Lindo poured from speakers in the adjacent food court atrium. A half dozen couples in Spanish-style dresses moved into the open space and started dancing. A man hopped up on a bench and gave instructions. Irem picked out a few of his words:

Saluto... greet

Musica... music

Castilian waltz

Maritza was moving again. Past the dancers, around the corner, still on her phone. Irem hurried to catch up, whirled around the corner and —

Lost sight of her.

Crappity crap crap.

Irem hobbled quickly, glancing in the nearest store window. "Why the hell didn't I just talk to her on the street?" The shop was some sort of artists' mart. Frames, mats, easels, paint. A place Levent would frequent. Didn't

247

look like a single customer was inside. She moved to the next, a store that sold baby clothes. It looked as if a lot of the pieces were hand-knitted, business cards next them perhaps with the names of the crafters. Irem had thought she and Ronnie would have a child or two. Would she be eternally single? She certainly wasn't going to look for another man... though she was adamant about looking for Maritza Palma.

Another closed business, a watch repair shop. She scanned up. There were groupings of skylights, obviously going straight through the second floor and looking like chimneys. She spotted a post in the center of this aisle; it had a lot of colorful pamphlets tacked to it. One carried the face of a sheepdog. Someone's lost pet?

She made her way through the lone clump of shoppers and to the next business—a dentist's office with two men sitting in the waiting area, then on to what looked to be either an accountant's or lawyer's office, where she could only see the receptionist. Maybe Martiza was inside, in one of the offices.

Apparently the mall was a mix of shops and small businesses. Across the aisle she saw two more closed storefronts; one had plywood stretched across the front, and it had been painted shades of blue, triangles, misshapen squares, broad strokes of yellow and white interrupting it. She wondered what Levent would think; maybe he'd find it artistic. She thought it amateurish and garish. Next was a cell phone retailer and a trendy beauty salon, maybe where Maritza got her hair and nails done. Irem darted toward it and crossed her fingers. There were four stations, two empty, two with older women in the chairs, one getting a haircut, the other having her stark-white hair curled with a brush and blow dryer. Another woman sat waiting for her turn, thumbing through a fashion magazine. No sign of Maritza.

Christ on a tricycle.

There! At the end of the wide aisle that ran between stores, Irem saw a flash of pink hair and white jean shorts. Maritza was entering what served as the endcap of this section of the mall. The sign above the door was small and printed in a thin font. As Irem got closer she could read it: *Scelta Ebrioni.* She figured the *embrioni* was close to "embryo," and so this was either a fertility clinic or a gynecologist's office. Irem could wait until Maritza came out, but there wasn't a single bench in sight in this part of the mall, and the storefronts on either side were closed. She texted the name of the place to Gregario.

Should she wait out here?

Or she could go in and sit, give her knee some relief.

She sucked in a breath, opened the door, and saw Maritza march past the reception desk and through a door at the back.

Bingo!

The reception area was bland, boring and relaxing, all pale creams with beige accents. The scent of lavender hung thick. Pictures were grouped on the walls, to her right babies of various hues, to her left, young mothers beaming, toddlers in their arms. The area was empty, except for the receptionist. Irem set her backpack on a chair and came forward.

The woman at the desk looked too thin, like her skin was stretched over her bones, her wrists knobby and cheeks overly pronounced. Her dark hair was pulled back from her head in a bun, so tight it looked painful. But her smile was friendly, her lips glossy peach, and her eyes wide and with a generous amount of mascara.

"*Buon Pomeriggio. Posso aiutarti?*" she asked.

One of the problems with trying to learn Italian by the *Dummies* book is that it covered written words, not how they sounded spoken. Irem thought "help" was somewhere in there. If she was going to stay in Rome a few months because of Levent, maybe she could take a language class.

"English?" Irem crossed her fingers. "Do you speak—"

"*Si.* I speak English. Good afternoon. How may I help you?"

"That young woman." Irem gestured the way Maritza had gone. "Does she work here?" This might be the after-class job one of the tenants had mentioned to Gregario.

The receptionist's eyebrows arched high.

"I'd like to talk to her. I—" *Shit!* She'd had a few opportunities before now. She should have taken them. Irem had chatted with her at the store window, shouldn't have let her walk away then. "I— I want to ask her a few things. She was in a fire, with my brother. Does she work here? Should I come back? When is she on break? Can you—"

The receptionist held up a bony finger, touched an earbud phone, and spoke Italian so softly and quickly that Irem caught none of it. Irem almost turned around, intending to hobble back to the university and meet Gregario.

"*Si.* Miss Palma works here, for Dr. Donkor."

Irem's skin tingled. She hadn't seen any doctor's name on the door or window, anywhere. Dr. Donkor... Gregario was talking to him. Dr. *Rauf* Donkor, she thought.

"Dr. Donkor?"

A nod. "A researcher here. *Si.*" The woman spoke more fast Italian into the phone. "You can go back. The last door straight ahead. Miss Palma has time to speak with you."

"I—" Irem glanced down the corridor. Was it odd that the receptionist did not ask her name? Two doors on the right, two on the left, one at the end of the hallway. "Thank you," she said, as she headed to the far door. Maybe she should wait for Gregario. He spoke the language, and he had a gun. The doors to the right and left had signage: *clinica* 1, 2, 3, 4. The one at the end: *ufficio.* Office. One more glance behind her, a straight shot to the front door. The receptionist was there, turning the sign to "*chiuso*," and leaving, locking up.

Hairs stood up on her arm. Maybe she should leave, too. But there was Lev hovering in her mind. She tried Gregario again, but the reception was poor, no bars. Wait or.... Irem decided to forge ahead.

"For Lev," she whispered. "Show no fear."

Irem walked to the office, raised her free hand to knock, but the door opened.

"Please come in." The tingling intensified. Dr. Uziah Donkor reached toward her. "I insist."

THIRTY-ONE

GREGARIO FELT BAD ABOUT LEAVING Irem sitting on the bench. She was passionate in her pursuit of information... about the fire, why someone had tried to bury her under Rome. Driven and curious and lovely. Without fear, too, it appeared. He remembered the day he met her in the alley after she'd taken down the pickpocket. It was unfortunate the circumstances that were keeping her in Italy, but in a way he was glad she'd be here a while. He felt drawn to her.

He waited outside Donkor's office, trying not to think about Irem, and so instead listening to the conversation that seeped out under the closed door.

"*Ho provato con forza.*" That was a young man's voice.

I tried hard. Tried hard at what? Gregario wondered. The conversation continued. The student claimed he put his best effort in a report. Apparently Dr. Donkor disagreed and went on at considerable length about missed points and ill-made conclusions.

"*Non ha senso. Sconnesso,*" Donkor shot back. "*Errori nella logica. Errori ortografici!*"

"*Dammi un'altra possibilità,*" the student implored.

Donkor relented. "*Ti do una settimana.*"

It is good to be given a second chance, Gregario thought. But if the Drs. Donkor were involved in the apartment fire, as Irem was so convinced, the student would have to turn in his new paper elsewhere because his professor would be incarcerated.

The student, red-faced and gaze cast down at the floor, shuffled out of the office. The door hung open in his wake. Gregario was fast inside.

251

"*Buon pomeriggio, Professore* Donkor." Gregario stepped up to the desk and took immediate inventory of the surroundings. He thought the room large for an office, a dozen feet square. Bookshelves lined the walls except for the interruption of another doorway, which led to a private bathroom ... and indicated to Gregario that the man had some status to rate this corner place. The desk was large and walnut, solid so he couldn't see the man's legs. Two chairs were opposite it, high-backed ones with red leather cushions. He picked the closest one and sat, feeling the warmth the student had left behind.

Donkor's chair seemed throne-like, and the broad-shouldered man filled it. Gregario guessed he was between forty-five and fifty, no older. His face was round and friendly, lined at the corners of the eyes and across the forehead, the complexion the shade of whole wheat bread, hair short and black, with a hint of white along the temples. Behind him rose more books, and Gregario noted some of the titles. They mostly appeared to be about religious studies: *The Lost Books of the Bible, The Simonians, Montanists and the New Prophecy, Marcion of Pontus,* and a variety with Carpocratian something-or-other on the spines. The titles were in Italian, German, and English.

"*Tu chi se?*" Donkor didn't hide his surprise at the unannounced appointment. He'd been texting on his cell phone when Gregario came in. He continued to text, eyes drifting from the screen to meet Gregario's stare.

"I am *Agente Sceito* Ricci of the Polizia di Stato." He reached in his pocket, turned his cell phone to record, and placed it on the desk so Donkor could see. Everything proper. "English please."

"I speak *Inglese.*" Donkor's eyebrows arched in curiosity.

Gregario had promised Irem she could listen to the recording, so he wanted it in English to make that easy for her. If his superiors in the department questioned the *Inglese* interview, he would explain that the professor seemed to be proficient in many languages, and he was testing that.

"I investigate an apartment building fire in Rome," Gregario began.

252

"You investigate in the wrong city, *Agente Sceito* Ricci. Rome is far from here."

Gregario noticed that the desk was mostly empty, the top polished. There were two small picture frames, but they faced toward Donkor, a leather-bound notebook was open, an expensive-looking pen resting across it. "Witnesses put you at the scene of that fire, professor."

Donkor growled softly, then put on a stunned expression. "Not possible." But Gregario knew how to read people, and believed the surprise was feigned. "When was this fire? Recent? I have been here. At the campus. I am full-time faculty."

"Airline records put you in Rome at the time of the fire, and leaving the day after."

"I was in Rome some days back," Donkor admitted. "I travel to the city for festivals and to visit friends, and to conduct research. Mostly to conduct research."

"Were you also there to visit Mr. Hamadi Shamoon? The vintner?"

Donkor shook his head. "Who?"

"I understand that you are friends with him."

Donkor's cheeks twitched. "Ah, yes, the vintner. I remember. I do know of Mr. Shamoon, although we are not so close I could call him friend. I appreciate his wine. I might have met him at the vineyard on this or the previous trip. I have been on a few vineyard tours. Mostly I go to Rome to gain insights into my passion and profession—religious studies. On this latest trip I reviewed manuscripts about Marcion of Pontus to gain lecture material."

"And this Mr. Pontus—"

"Is long, long dead. The Marcionites, an old Christian sect, were followers of Marcion of Pontus. An influential Christian and a ship owner, history claims he was expelled from the church because he seduced a virgin. Mere propaganda by his enemies, I contend. In any event, Marcion went to Rome, teaching his version of the doctrine, drawing a large following, and threatening the survival of the Roman Church, which was in its early stages."

"Interesting." But Gregario really didn't care about whether Marcion of Pontus seduced a virgin. That Donkor chattered was intriguing. The guilty liked to talk, maybe because they were nervous.

"I understand you have been teaching religious studies here for nearly a decade."

"Historical religions, actually, with an emphasis on early Christianity and its sects."

"Carpocratian?" Gregario remembered Irem talking about that.

"That is my specialty."

"I think I read somewhere that the Carpocratians were a gnostic group trying to prove or disprove the divinity of Christ through the apostles." Gregario had done a lot of Googling when Irem slept. That was one tidbit he remembered.

"You use *were*, agent Ricci. Carpocratians continue today."

"Witnesses put you at the apartment building," Gregario repeated, throwing the conversation back to the crucial matter. "The one that burned last week in Rome."

"I had no cause to visit any apartments when I was in Rome," Donkor cut back. He quickly texted something then put his phone aside. "Who are these witnesses? Whoever they are ... they are wrong. No video exists of me at any apartment building. Otherwise you would have announced that. No video exists because I was not at an apartment building in Rome." His eyes drifted left, the tell of a lie, Gregario decided.

Donkor was correct about no video because there were no surveillance cameras in the old apartment building or the businesses near it. Cameras a few blocks away in either direction had yielded nothing, nor had video segments taken from police and firemen's body cams. The tourist sections of the city had more cameras, but older neighborhoods such as the one the apartments nested in, lacked surveillance. The people in those neighborhoods appreciated not being spied on. Gregario suspected Donkor knew this.

"What about your brother? He, too, was in Rome, though he flew out a day after you."

"You would have to speak with him." Donkor shrugged. "My brother's schedule is not mine. He is in a different area of the university. He is not an instructor; he is a researcher and mentor. He lectures. My brother comes and goes as he pleases. But neither was he in an apartment building."

"I will talk to your brother, when I am finished here." Although Gregario would have to locate Uziah Donkor first, or go to their home in the evening and hope to find the other twin there. "You share a residence with him."

Donkor stiffened. "Sharing a residence does not make me his keeper. He has his pastimes, and on our latest Rome trip our paths happened to cross. We attended an exhibit at the Conservatori. And there was a Carpocratian ... I struggle for the *Inglese* word ... convocation."

Gregario doubted he struggled for anything, the language seeming effortless to him.

"We attended that, the convocation, then we separated, he to a concert, I believe. Myself, I went to the libraries to gain material for lectures."

"And you studied multiple religious sects in the Roman libraries on this trip? Or just the Carpocratians?"

Donkor spoke like a teacher now. "It is all so interesting, Agent Ricci, the early threads of divinity. And to lecture fresh I must ever learn. This trip, I studied sex, a topic that draws my students' attention. The Marcionites practiced celibacy, almost to the extreme. The Carpocrates were the opposite. The Carpocratians are among the most fascinating of the sects. They believed in reincarnation. They were encouraged to experience everything life offered so they would not have to be reincarnated and be made to go through all the things they'd missed the first few times around. The sect prided itself as being above the laws of man and above morality; they had transcended that."

"Go on." Gregario acted curious. He'd noted a change in Donkor. He spoke with more passion now, and his dark eyes glistened.

"The Carpocratians enjoyed a little rebirth in the twentieth century when the Secret Gospel of Mark was discovered. Perhaps you read about that?"

Gregario shook his head.

"It was a spiritual telling of the Gospel of Mark canon. The secret gospel detailed a scene in which Jesus, naked, is teaching another naked man. Some considered this a homosexual encounter. It seems the Carpocratians used this passage to justify gay lifestyles at a time when society did not tolerate such. The Carpocratians were more liberal, open-minded, had few inhibitions. That mindset of the sect continues today."

"Are you a Carpocratian, professor?"

There was a slight pause. "If one must have a label, I suppose I would be considered that."

"And there are others like you, certainly. You mentioned the Carpocratian gathering in Rome." Gregario was uncertain just where this interview was leading. It needed to wind back to the apartment fire. But he would give this notion a little more leash. "You hold meetings regularly, *si*? The Carpocratians? Here? And in Rome?"

Donkor gave a quick nod and looked at his watch. "I would not say regularly. Or often. Occasionally."

"Your twin brother, is he a—"

"If one must have a label. But he is not a religious scholar. His pursuits are scientific."

"You can be both. My father was a mason, *and* a chemist."

"But not you."

"No. No on either count." Gregario shifted in the seat. "Did your research in Rome take you under the streets, to the crypts and vaults?"

A facial twitch. "To the libraries, Agent Ricci. And what business is it of yours where I research?"

"Just curious. You teach many courses on religion and its history, some on numerology according to the university catalog. Numbers intrigue me, but I never considered them tied to religion."

"Numbers intrigue me as well. The Marcosians held a deep fascination with the theory of numbers, numerology, especially what was derived from the Pythagoreans. They believed it was significant that words had numerical equivalents. In Greek, for example, each letter has a number value. Jesus, in Greek, is spelled I E S O U S and has a number equivalent of eight-eight-eight. Ancient people thought that number sacred, perhaps magical. When you add up all twenty-four Greek letters, the numerical value equals eight-eight-eight."

"Now that *is* very interesting. That apartment building that burned, where so many people died, it had twenty-four units. Eight and eight and eight."

Donkor reached for his phone. "The spiritual significance of certain numbers has nothing to do with apartment fires in Rome. My classes—"

"If I lived in this area, I would take one of your courses." Gregario nodded toward a small bust on the closest bookcase. "Is that Marcion?"

"Hardly. That is Valentinus, a gift from my department head. Valentinus was almost elected the Bishop of Rome in his day. Now the position is called Pope. Valentinus believed in a Primal Being, the male aspect of it called Depth, the female Silence. And from this being, fifteen pairs—the Aeons—were formed. The last Aeon—Sophia—"

"I met a nun in Rome named Sophia," Gregario put in.

Donkor's cheeks twitched. "The Aeon Sophia was said to have fallen into ignorance, and from that material creation and all its flaws and evils resulted."

"Do you know Sister Sophia in Rome? A pleasant woman, really. Not at all ignorant. I met her at Mr. Shamoon's vineyard. You've been to the vineyard, correct? I believe you mentioned taking a tour there."

"I've been to Rome many times, Agent Ricci, as I told you. Been to many places in the city. I believe I once toured his winery, I told you. Too, have I toured wineries in Catania."

"And now Mr. Shamoon is in your city. Curious. Is he touring the university? Was Mr. Shamoon one of the Carpocratians at the gathering in Rome?"

"How would I know the religious leanings of a vintner in Rome? Perhaps he is agnostic or Catholic. Baptist. A

Sethian? I also lecture about the Sethians, the revered of Seth, whom religious history counts as the third son of Adam and Eve. And I teach the New Prophecy of Montanus, who birthed what is considered the ancient forerunner of Pentecostalism. Montanus, once a pagan, allowed women to hold prominent positions in his sect. They could be deacons and bishops."

"Women. I met a young woman who survived the apartment fire. She's from Catania. Studies at the university here. Maritza Palma. Is she one of your students?" Gregario saw tiny beads of sweat on Donkor's forehead.

"I have many, many students."

"I'd think you'd remember her. She has a striking appearance, a clump of pink hair. Or maybe she studies with your brother. I have to talk to him."

"What does this have to do with an apartment fire? Any of this? You waste my time. You insult me. My hours are valuable, Agent Ricci. You should be conducting this investigation in Rome."

"Witnesses place you at the fire," Gregario stated again.

"You have no video. I contend I was not there." Donkor paused. "And you have overstayed your welcome, Agent Ricci. *Addio.*"

THIRTY-TWO

DR. UZIAH DONKOR'S GRIP WAS firm. His fingers wrapped around her wrist, and he yanked her inside, slamming the door behind her. Irem could have screamed, but who would have heard? The office was closed — and so were the businesses on either side of this place. And screaming wasn't in her nature. She could have kicked him with her good leg — black belt in hapkido and all, used that beautiful walnut cane. Maybe she would.

But first she'd let him draw her farther inside, more her curiosity doing the tugging than his strength.

"American."

"Yeah, I'm American. We've seen each other before, but weren't really introduced. You were at the Conservatori, ogling the bone shroud. You were under Rome, trying to kill me. You were in the apartment building that burned. You were —"

"Shut up." He released his grip and gestured for her to walk ahead of him. "*Cazzo Americano.*"

Although the door had read "office," it really wasn't one. The room was roughly twenty feet across and a little longer than that, filled with sparse equipment, tables, shelves, a couple of laptops with big screens, one showing a turning DNA helix. There was a double-wide freezer with glass doors. Maritza Palma was in a chair, blood pressure cuff around her arm, a man in a gray lab coat hovering. The place smelled of antiseptic... stronger than the hospital had.

"What the hell is all this?" Irem walked with an exaggerated limp. Her knee really did hurt, but not to the extent she let on.

Look fragile, she decided. *Let him think I am no threat.* Because maybe she wasn't; Uziah Donkor was a solid man. Irem tried to take in the surroundings. It looked like they were boxing everything up. There was a back door, propped open, and a man in a white lab coat was carrying out a big plastic bin. More bins were on the floor and were being filled by a third man, also in white. Five people present that she could see — the three in lab coats, plus Dr. Donkor, and Maritza Palma. Maybe there were more outside, but this had the feel of a small operation. They were definitely packing this place up.

"Who else is here with you, Miss Madigan?"

It gave her a jolt that he knew her name.

"No one. I came alone. Just like I was alone under the city. I like being alone."

"You lie. You are with a man from the *polizia di stato*. A nosesome *agente* who bothers my brother."

"No," Irem's voice was steady. "I came here alone."

"Coincidence the *polizia di stato* man talks to my brother while you follow Miss Palma? No happenstance. That you were under Rome rather than at your brother's wedding? No happenstance."

I did attend the wedding, Irem thought. *And you just admitted you were under Rome.*

"No happenstance," he repeated.

"You like that word, eh?"

"Tell me who you are with. CIA? Interpol? Injured, why didn't they replace you with another agent?"

Irem feigned faltering, and Donkor propped her up.

"CIA? I'm a museum archivist," she said.

"So my patron tells me," Donkor returned. "But that is a cover, *si*? Who are you —"

Irem took a step away and gestured with her head. "I *really* am an archivist. But I am curious. What the hell is all this?" Irem swayed and steadied herself on the cane. *Look weak.*

"A research laboratory," Donkor said. He let out an angry hiss. "We also function as a fertility clinic, for income and to give us a visible place to do our real work, disguised in plain sight. We edit human embryos with cell and gene therapy."

"Designer babies?"

Donkor frowned. "Molecular cutting, shear away unwanted parts of an embryo's genome, and replace it with improved sections of DNA. Therapeutic, preventing spiritual and physical diseases. We are ahead of the United States and China in this research. Many of our blessed children are four, five years old."

"It doesn't sound legal. Or ethical."

"You are not my judge."

"And you're telling me this because—"

"Because I guess it does not matter who you work for, Miss Madigan. This time I will not trust explosives and a cave-in to tie this dangling thread."

Irem's heart pounded and her hand drifted into her pocket. She turned on her cell phone, hitting "record" and fumbling for the numbers, pressing 1-1-2 and hoping there was a signal and that Rome's equivalent of 9-1-1 worked all the way south in Catania. She spoke loudly to keep his attention on her face so he might not notice what she was doing with her concealed phone.

"So this is a 'before I kill you Mr. Bond' moment, right?" Irem asked. She limped forward and leaned into him and sneered, then teetered to keep up her frail act. "This is where you spill all your plans because you have to gloat. This is where you tell me what you were doing under the city, stealing something, covering your tracks with explosives. Before I kill you, Mr. Bond. Right?"

Donkor cocked his head as if he didn't understand the movie reference.

"At least tell me what you were doing under Rome... when you tried to kill me. Give me that much. What you took."

"It is of no concern to you. It does not matter to you. And now you do not matter to me."

"What about the apartment fire? You were there. You *caused* it, didn't you?"

His eyes narrowed, and she noticed a small crescent-shaped scar on his face.

The lab tech that had been hovering over Maritza took off the blood pressure cuff and spun to face them. He was blond, pale-skinned, and had a spray of freckles across his face. Maybe a college student. He grinned.

"Professor, Mari's fine. The fetal heartbeat is excellent. She's good to fly."

"Thank you. Help with the packing, David, and take all the computers. Make sure the therapeutic embryos remain frozen. Get them to the airport quickly." Donkor grabbed Irem's wrist again. "*Veloce*, David. *Veloce*. I have hired cleaners. They are on their way here."

"*Therapeutic* embryos. DNA. What the hell are you doing here?"

"I saw her following me, Professor." Maritza stood and massaged her arm where the cuff had been. "Isn't she the one that was supposed to be dead from the cave-in?"

Obviously Maritza had not been paying attention to the exchange between her boss and Irem. "I *was* buried," Irem said. "But it didn't last. The apartment building fire. You were there, Maritza. You were burned."

Maritza shrugged and looked to Donkor. "Do I have time to pack a suitcase? There are a few things I want to keep."

"*Veloce*. Hurry," Donkor said. "Pack your few things, your laptop, anything with identification, any papers. Hurry. David, go with her. Move. Move."

"My apartment? Are the cleaners going there—"

"*Veloce*, Maritza. I will have the building burned."

Maritza left through the back door, squeezing by two men in white lab coats who were coming in to pick up another load. The tech named David carried a bin behind Maritza. Irem had been distracted watching them and did not notice that Donkor had pulled a gun.

He retrieved a silencer out of his pocket, and she reacted. Three men in the room, Donkor the nearest, the two in lab coats loading things into bins. She used an elbow strike, a close-in technique Ronnie taught her early on. It was a self-defense move, devastating if done well, which she did, landing it against Donkor's sternum. Keeping hold of the cane, she used her other elbow, spinning, striking in the same spot.

Donkor, taken by surprise, doubled over, and the silencer dropped. The gun fell when she followed with a ridge hand strike against his gun arm. Lightning fast, she turned the maneuver into a grab, catching his wrist, pulling him into her and down while he was off-balance, then raising her good knee and striking his chin. Irem was swift, using her knee twice more. Donkor didn't struggle; she'd incapacitated him.

The two lab techs shouted.

She twisted just as they reached her. In classes she'd once been paired against four attackers, and she won. She had to win here, too.

Irem forced herself to stay calm as she raised her cane and drove it like a sword into the closer man's stomach, pushing him back so she could use a knee strike against the other one, catching him in the groin.

Her injured knee hollered in protest, but she managed a roundhouse kick on the same man, and then she dropped the cane and pressed forward with a series of hammer fist blows on his face and throat. A sweeping side kick to the other man, then she put herself between the staggered duo and followed up with more elbow strikes until they were down.

Now Irem was truly limping. She retrieved her cane and surveyed the aftermath. One of the lab techs stirred, and she clocked him on the back of the head. Donkor worried her, and she shuffled toward him and rolled him over... still out. She retrieved his gun, made sure the safety was off, and stood so she could see both doorways. There was one more man in the gray lab coat—the one Donkor had called David, and Maritza Palma, but neither appeared. She felt the phone in her pocket buzzing, meaning there was indeed a signal in this room. But she ignored it, cane in one hand, gun in the other... Irem wasn't about to drop either to see if it was Gregario calling. Faintly, she heard a siren. Had her 1-1-2 worked?

"What the hell should I do with you?" Irem kept watch on the men and limped to the chair Maritza had been in, pulled it closer, and sat. "Oh God, that feels almost insignificantly better." She swore someone was stabbing her injured knee with an icepick. Leaning the cane against the chair, she finally reached for her phone and pushed Gregario's number.

Through the open back door, she heard an engine start. Probably the third guy, maybe Maritza with him. No way in hell she could stop them. Tires squealed, and whatever vehicle was out there sped away.

She put the phone to her face. "Gregario?"

She listened to his rapid-fire speech, half of it in Italian. She caught a few words.

"Yeah, I'm all right. Mostly all right. I lost track of Maritza Palma, but I found Uziah Donkor. You can come arrest him. He tried to kill me again. Attempted murder, at least that charge will stick. But that's just the beginning. You need to lock this *fottoto bastardo* up forever."

THIRTY-THREE
OCTOBER 18

SOPHIA HAD TWO LARGE SUITCASES. Everything she owned was in them.

She watched as men carried four heavy trunks down the stairs and out the front doors—their second trip. Her uncle had more clothes and personal items in all those trunks than she would ever accumulate. And it was only part of his possessions. She knew he had ordered only the most precious of his things packed, as they were in a hurry.

Hopefully matters would settle and they could return to the vineyard in time for the next harvest, or the one after that. She loved this land.

"Sister Sophia, will we be gone long?" James clutched her hand.

"I do not know," she answered truthfully. She knew Hamadi was confident the Donkors would not mention his involvement in the Carpocratian endeavor. Yet she was worried the police might nevertheless poke around. And perhaps the archaeologist would talk. "I hope we are not gone for a long while."

"Where are we going?"

"To Egypt, James. At least for several months."

"Egypt." The boy drew his features together in thought. "Genesis fifteen-eighteen, Sister Sophia. 'In the same day the Lord made a covenant with Abram, saying, unto thy seed have I given this land, from the river of Egypt unto the great river, the river Euphrates.' Will we see the Euphrates?"

"Perhaps," Sophia answered. "Would you like to?"

"I think so, Sister Sophia. Revelation says... I don't remember the chapter, but it says: 'And the sixth angel poured out his vial upon the great river Euphrates; and the water thereof was dried up, that the way of the kings of the east might be prepared.' Papa is like a king, isn't he Sister Sophia?"

She didn't answer.

"Papa says I can't take my croquet set. But I am taking some of my books." He pointed to a green leather chest inside the front door. Sophia had helped him pack it. "Egypt might be too hot to play croquet. But I saw in a book about Egypt, pictures of beautiful buildings. Will you take me to see the buildings?"

"Of course, James."

"And can my brother, John, come, too?"

"He is just a baby and would not appreciate such things."

James stuck out his lower lip. "I think I will like having a brother. Good that Papa brought him home last night. Did you hear Papa say I will get another brother in the summer, or perhaps next fall? And that we will name him Matthew?"

"I did." Sister Sophia smiled, remembering the grave field she had traipsed upon a few weeks ago, and the bone she retrieved from the earth, knowing it would be used to create an embryo that could help prove a link to the divine. "Then there will be three of you."

Three in this family. There were more James and Johns in other cities in Italy, two in Austria, another two in Greece, all carefully placed with Carpocratian families. Soon there would be Matthews and Peters, too, as the materials from the lab had been saved and whisked to safety. All commonplace names, nothing to draw attention.

"I will like John," James said. "I just know I will. And I will be the big brother."

"Always, James. Always the older brother."

Hamadi stood in the doorway. "The plane is ready, Sister."

Sophia gently tugged on James's hand and led him out. There was a hint of light on the horizon, dawn crawling up into the sky.

THIRTY-FOUR
OCTOBER 20

IREM WATCHED LEVENT SLEEP. They'd eased him out of the coma yesterday, and the doctors were pleased with his progress. Irem was happy he was alive, but she remained devastated by his condition. A right-handed artist without a right hand, mobility issues... what life would he have?

He was still wrapped in bandages like a mummy, but he was propped up and breathing on his own. They continued to make people wear scrubs and masks... one visitor at a time, with instructions not to agitate him. A bag of *something* dripped down a tube and into his arm.

Irem cried.

Her brother had been so beautiful. He still was, she told herself. The inside is what mattered, the heart and soul and spirit. She would take every day of that six-month leave the Field had offered. She would visit every day... here at the hospital, later at the rehabilitation center... likely emotionally beating herself up with each trip. She could not escape the notion that if she'd attended the festivities, danced with him, he might not have been in that apartment building when it burned.

Why had the Donkors destroyed the place? Or maybe Maritza Palma had. Maybe they'd worked together. Why couldn't Uziah Donkor have told her something... *something*... anything? Why couldn't someone have admitted to the fire so her heart wouldn't hurt so much? Her mind spun. What had been down in the catacombs? What were they doing with the lab? What did Benito Abruzi have to do with this?

She had macabre suspicions, the stuff of nightmares.

Irem wheeled herself out of Levent's room. Benito was outside, waiting to trade places with her, take his vigil at Levent's side.

"Talk to me," she insisted. "Before you go back in there. Talk to me or so help me I'll—"

"Sure." Benito looked old and exhausted, and the skin on his face sagged like he'd lost weight. Probably wasn't eating much, or sleeping well. The circles under his eyes were dark. A part of her was happy he couldn't sleep. "Sure, Irem. Here?"

"There." She nodded toward a lounge near the nurse's station. She didn't argue when he got behind her wheelchair and pushed.

Irem had been brought to the hospital two days ago, flying back from Catania with Gregario, who said he did not have time to waste on a train ride. She'd managed to tear her ACL during the fight in the lab; an injury like a football player got, and ended up in surgery yesterday.

"What do you want to talk about, Irem?"

She leveled a stern gaze, not a trace of sympathy on her face. "About the tapestry, Benito. About every *futtuto* thread that was removed. About the vintner who has left the city, about two Egyptian professors who had a lab in Catania... and who tried to kill me... who probably caused the fire that burned Lev and—"

"—killed Lacy and Santiago."

"And a lot of other people, too."

He turned her to face a chair that he eased himself into. They were the only people in the lounge. A nurse pushing a medicine cart rolled past. Faintly, something beeped from another room.

"What first? What do you want to know?"

She dug her fingernails into her palms and took a deep breath. "The threads in the tapestry. The tapestry started all of this, right? It started every damned awful thing that happened. Threads were removed." She took another deep breath and made a mental leap. "You're the one who wanted the threads removed, right? Ordered it. It wasn't an accident. *You had it done.* And you needed a different restorer to do the work. The woman at the Conservatori, the one who died, she wouldn't have done it. Too many principles to alter the fabric."

"Correct. She would not. She said it was not acceptable to change the weave so."

"So she had to die."

Benito's hands trembled. "I wanted her to retire. I offered her that, Irem. She would have been given money to walk away and to stay quiet."

"But she wouldn't walk away."

"No."

"And she would have talked."

"Yes."

"You had her killed."

"That one wasn't *my* direction. I had looked for another *alternativa*. My patron did not want to wait."

"So he did it, Hamadi Shamoon." Irem spat the last word out like a piece of bitter lemon.

"He directed it, yes."

"And you let him. You didn't prevent it from happening." Irem swore she could hear her heart beating. "You wanted her dealt with and ordered the threads removed. *You* did. You might as well have killed her yourself."

Benito closed his eyes, nodded, and opened them. He looked wholly resigned. "The tapestry needed to be restored, preserved, and I hadn't those skills. I had the links to graves removed after we recorded them, documented everything, took pictures. Those threads and symbols. Yes."

"Because—"

"It was as I mentioned before, I did not want others reading it like a map, leading to the graves of the famous dead." He paused. "And the divine dead. Some of the divine anyway. Those apostles that the old scholar—the one buried in the tapestry—had tracked. It's mostly the way I first told you, Irem. I discovered the burial shroud, the bone tapestry as you call it, and realized its importance, spent time researching… both the weave and the scholar who made it."

"Who was—"

"A Carpocratian professor who marked the entombments — or supposed burial places — of the apostles and other men of biblical and more recent times. He was a cartographer of the dead. Texts helped me decipher the shroud, passages and the threads indicating the tombs. Beyond the apostles there were also graves marked for Attila, Ovid, Alaric, a few others. Attila and Alaric most interested me because of the financial gain. Archaeology by itself is not terribly lucrative. I needed a sponsor for the digs, and so I turned to Hamadi Shamoon. I knew him from an organization I belong to, modern Carpocratians who meet in Rome from time to time."

"Why him?"

"I knew he would be interested because of the tapestry's origins and its biblical links. I proposed that I show him the tapestry and the text, share my findings."

"In exchange he agreed to fund your digs."

Benito rocked back and forth and stared at his hands. "Yes. He has a great deal of money. I would pursue Attila and Alaric, and perhaps Ovid someday, others. To him, I would leave the apostles. There had to be a tradeoff for his sponsorship. To be blunt, there would be treasures with the burials I was interested in. Gold, silver, artifacts."

"You sell some on the side, artifacts."

Benito's shrug served as a "yes" to Irem. "Apostles would not have been buried with material wealth. Hamadi did not need any more wealth."

Irem shuddered.

"I had not considered it a bad arrangement, you understand. And it was furthering our sect's goals, proving the divine. There was no wrong way to go with it. A win-win, the American phrase is. But there is no win for me now. Levent... I've lost everything that truly mattered. When I confess to him—" Benito let his thought hang.

"Did Shamoon have the restorer's husband killed, too?"

Benito sat back, his gaze fixed on something far beyond Irem.

"And the assistant? For you? So the shroud could be altered by a man of his choosing? Or your choosing? Which one of you selected the restorer willing to pull the threads? Who really brought in Gustavo?"

No answer.

She tried something different: "What did Shamoon want with the apostles? Their DNA, right?"

Benito rubbed at his lower lip. "He wanted to find a way to reach into the past. Perhaps he was trying to touch God. He thought his work could bring God to Earth now, creating new apostles to lead people to salvation. The world is a mess, Irem, and we all could use some divine influence, eh? He believed some spark of the original holy men would continue into the new bloodlines. Give society a new hope."

She dropped her gaze to her lap and moved her fingers as if she knitted something.

"You did nothing. You said nothing. You didn't contact the police when Shamoon had the restorer killed. Her husband, assistant killed."

"I did not want Hamadi's plans, and my dig, jeopardized."

Irem raised her head and glared.

"I told you archaeology is cutthroat, difficult. I wanted Attila very much."

"More than you wanted Lev?" She heard him sob; she'd thrust the dagger and turned it. "More than you wanted your assistants, Lacy and Santiago? Yes, you told me archaeology is cutthroat. You just never mentioned you were the one doing the cutting."

He reached for her hands, and she pulled them back. "You don't understand, Irem. Lacy and Santiago, they sent some emails, they talked about the tapestry, didn't stay focused on our prize. They dreamed of Alaric and riches and caught the wrong attention. I'd begged them to keep everything secret. But those emails to California—"

"So they were killed to keep things quiet. Did you tell Shamoon to have me killed, too?"

Benito shook his head. "No. I said nothing about you to the vintner."

"And what about Lev... what the hell did he do wrong?"

"It was not supposed to happen that day, the apartment fire," Benito said. "Not on the wedding day. Not until a night

271

or two after that, Hamadi had said. It was not supposed to happen when Lev was there."

"You *knew* they would destroy the building, kill all those people just to get Lacy and Santiago." Irem fought the tears. "That divine influence you mentioned... you'll never find it. I hope you burn for eternity for this." She wheeled away and went back to her room.

Gregario was waiting for her. He was wearing his uniform, looking all business and polished. Yesterday he'd been in plain clothes and had played her the recording of his interview with Dr. Rauf Donkor, as he'd promised.

She brushed at her face, realizing she probably appeared awful. Had she ever looked nice in front of this man?

"I get out tomorrow sometime," she said. "I promise not to skip any physical therapy sessions this time."

He smiled warmly. "That is good news, Miss Irem Madigan."

"Listen, Ari, I—"

"I said I would keep you apprised."

"You have something? Know something about the lab and—" Irem leaned forward in her chair.

He took a deep breath. "Something. I know something. Not everything, but we fill in the gaps with guesses. The laboratory that *you* shut down before police arrived—" He winked at her. "—most of the equipment was gone, but enough remained that we learned Uziah Donkor was involved with DNA cloning, molecular cloning. I am not a scientist, but it is something about..." Gregario took out his phone and scrolled. "...recombinant DNA, creating gene fragments for reproductive cloning and therapeutic cloning."

"I heard Donkor mention therapeutic cloning."

"Before you clobbered him? Knocked him into next Christmas?"

"I hit him hard. I didn't want him getting back up."

"When he eventually did get up, we got nothing out of him when we interrogated him in Catania. More, we got from his assistants. One of them, you broke six of that man's ribs. He said the cloning was an involved process, more complex than Dolly the sheep. Apparently they had women who were donor mothers for these embryos when they reached a suitable stage. Fragments of research we recovered from a laptop suggest that they were using very old bones to extract DNA. The lab technicians said they did not know where the bones came from. But they knew what they were doing wasn't legal."

"Ancient bones under Rome," she said softly. "And probably from elsewhere. I think they were trying to clone the apostles." Then she thought about the disturbed grave field she'd visited outside the city. Matthew might have been buried there.

"That is the stuff of fiction, *si*?"

"Maybe." Irem wasn't sure it was fiction. Nightmares? Yes, it was the stuff of that.

"Dr. Uziah Donkor *still* refuses to speak. He's been brought here, has *avvocati*... solicitors —"

"Attorneys?"

"*Si*. Yes. He is being stubborn," Gregario said. "But our detectives are persistent, and the court will threaten. So at the moment there is no link yet to the vintner Hamadi —"

"Shamoon." Irem pictured the nun who advised her to leave. "There *is* a link. Benito knows it. Benito's in thick with him. They're Carpocratians. Benito will talk to you." Softer: "I'll make him. Benito will serve up all the links you need." She gripped the arms of her wheelchair. "Benito is involved with all of it, going back to the Conservatori's restorer who died... was *murdered*. He knew the apartment building was going to be destroyed, and Lacy and Santiago... and a lot of other people killed. He didn't light a match, but he's deeply connected. He might have even ordered the fire. He and Shamoon, doing the devil's work to get close to God."

Gregario rubbed his thumb across the back of Irem's hand. "He is in Egypt, Hamadi Shamoon, supposedly visiting with relatives... where, we have not found him. Proof against him will be the difficult thing, but I am obstinate, and I will pursue this. And perhaps with information from Benito Abruzi we can build a case."

"A case against both of them. All of them."

"My fellows search for Dr. Rauf Donkor. Maritza Palma and another student, David Harchis, were stopped at the Catania airport. They are being questioned, too. And they are also being difficult. But Dr. Rauf Donkor... we will find him, I am—"

Irem's eyes widened. "How could he have vanished? You talked to him. You played the recording for me—"

"Sometime between when my fellows arrested Uziah and then went to the university looking for his brother—"

"—he disappeared."

Gregario nodded. "But the world is not so large anymore, Miss Irem Madigan. We will find him. He will not stay disappeared long. The Donkors... and perhaps Benito Abruzi... they will answer for the apartment fire, for trying to kill you, and for much more." He paused. "And we will find Hamadi Shamoon, too."

"This isn't how I thought my Italian vacation would turn out."

Gregario grinned. "And when you are well, will you be trying to find Attila the Hun?"

She shrugged. "My brother-in-law, the archaeologist at the heart of the Attila hunt, should be in prison. *Will* be in prison. He's broken. He confessed it all to me. He'll confess it to you. Broken. I don't think there will be any digging for—"

"I know people in the city," Gregario interrupted. "I know how to get you permission to dig the catacombs."

Irem sucked in a breath. "I'm so mad. Benito, because he wanted to eliminate his archaeology students, wanted Lacy and Santiago to burn, Levent got burned. Despite all of the bad things, I would lie if I said I don't care about Attila. The Hun is history. I'm not a trained archaeologist. But I breathe history. Still, Levent comes first and—"

"Dr. Abruzi was really close, wasn't he? To finding Attila the Hun?"

"I think so. Days away from a discovery. And I'm scared that I won't be able to get that dig out of my head. It wouldn't take long, days. A few days. Maybe a few weeks. I think—"

" —that you should look for Attila when you are well. Attila would be a good hobby, *si*? I will get the permissions. I'm not an archaeologist either. But I know how to use a shovel. And I suspect you know at least *something* about archaeology."

"Some scattered classes. I went on a couple of digs in college. I watched Lacy and Santiago."

"So Attila and your brother should keep you in Rome, Miss Irem Madigan. Your brother will need you."

"I—"

"Truly, I can gain your permissions for working under the city. I've already started on that. Besides, we have old movies to watch, museums to visit. McDonald's to dine at."

Finally, Irem smiled. She really did like the handsome policeman.

"Yeah, and if I go after Attila, what will I do next? That won't take long. Benito was so very, very, very close. What will I do after that?"

"After that? Here's an idea for you." He placed a printout on her bed. "I will stop by later, when I am done work for the day." Gregario leaned down and kissed her, his lips warm and lingering. "And I will bring a cheese sandwich."

She stared at the printout after he left. The Vallicelliana Library in Rome, in operation since 1565 and filled with documents dating to medieval times, had posted a job opening for an archivist.

ACKNOWLEDGEMENTS

SPECIAL THANKS TO PETER CHIAPPORI for making sure I got the words corretta; Bill Gilsdorf for keeping my policeman precise; Carol Clarkson for treating my injured characters; S.H. Roddey for her publishing expertise; Mindy Mymudes for publicity; and my readers Donald J. Bingle, Vicki Johnson-Steger, and Malima Wolf for their eagle eyes.

ABOUT THE AUTHOR

I WRITE...A LOT. Currently mysteries.

And I write with dogs wrapped around my feet. I get to wear sandals or bedroom slippers to work, and old, comfortable clothes. When the weather is fine I get to write on my back porch. I love summer.

I started getting published when I was twelve, studied journalism at Northern Illinois University, and then went to work as a news reporter...eventually for Scripps Howard, where I managed their Western Kentucky Bureau. Getting itchy feet, I moved to Wisconsin and went to work for TSR, Inc., the then-producers of the Dungeons & Dragons game. I wrote Dragonlance novels for several years. I've been on the USA Today bestseller list, wrote a book about spousal homicide with F. Lee Bailey, picked up three Silver Falchion literary awards, and won a chili cook-off.

I've written forty novels, most of them fantasy and science fiction, more short stories than I care to count, and I've edited a lot of magazines and anthologies.

But now it's all about mysteries...thrillers, suspense, and uncozy-cozies. I had to change genres because my feet were itching again and I needed to do something different with my writing life.

I am a geek, a gamer, and a glass-fuser. I love dogs and museums and books, and I write about those things in my monthly newsletter.

Readers can sign up for the newsletter on my website: jeanrabe.com. I have an active Facebook page, where I probably post too many pictures of my dogs.

"Mystery just got a little less cozy..." — *New York Times* and *USA Today* bestselling author Steven Savile

"Jean Rabe always manages to surprise and never fails to deliver the goods! *The Dead of Night* has plenty of twists and turns. Highly recommended!" Jonathan Maberry, *New York Times* bestselling author

Published by Imajin Books
Available from
Imajinbooks.com
Amazon
Barnes & Noble

THE FINEST TRILOGY

Enjoyably entertaining…it is as if C.S. Lewis had decided to write Black Beauty as a fantasy. Mel Odom, Alex Award-winning author

The fairy tale landscape, driven by the eternal mortal struggle between good and evil, evokes a darker Narnia… J.K. Rowling and Garth Nix fans should find this trilogy exciting and memorable. Publishers Weekly

Available in ebook and print
Amazon and Barnes & Noble

Boone Street Press